Twelve Wicked Nights

Twelve Wicked

Nights

Nadia Aidan

HEAT

HEAT

Published by New American Library, a division of
Penguin Group (USA) Inc., 375 Hudson Street,
New York, New York 10014, USA
Penguin Group (Canada), 90 Eglinton Avenue East, Suite 700, Toronto,
Ontario M4P 2Y3, Canada (a division of Pearson Penguin Canada Inc.)
Penguin Books Ltd., 80 Strand, London WC2R 0RL, England
Penguin Ireland, 25 St. Stephen's Green, Dublin 2,
Ireland (a division of Penguin Books Ltd.)
Penguin Group (Australia), 250 Camberwell Road, Camberwell, Victoria 3124,
Australia (a division of Pearson Australia Group Pty. Ltd.)
Penguin Books India Pvt. Ltd., 11 Community Centre,
Panchsheel Park, New Delhi - 110 017, India
Penguin Group (NZ), 67 Apollo Drive, Rosedale, North Shore 0632,
New Zealand (a division of Pearson New Zealand Ltd.)
Penguin Books (South Africa) (Pty.) Ltd., 24 Sturdee Avenue,
Rosebank, Johannesburg 2196, South Africa

Penguin Books Ltd., Registered Offices:
80 Strand, London WC2R 0RL, England

First published by Heat, an imprint of New American Library,
a division of Penguin Group (USA) Inc.

First Printing, November 2010
10 9 8 7 6 5 4 3 2 1

Copyright © Tiffiany Howard, 2010
All rights reserved

HEAT is a trademark of Penguin Group (USA) Inc.

LIBRARY OF CONGRESS CATALOGING-IN-PUBLICATION DATA:
Aidan, Nadia.
Twelve wicked nights/Nadia Aidan.
p.   cm.
ISBN 978-0-451-23131-4
1. United States. Navy. SEALs—Fiction.   2. Women lawyers—Fiction.
3. Virginia—Fiction.   4. Blizzards—Fiction.   I. Title.
PS3601.I325T94 2010
813'.6—dc22   2010029341

Set in Arno Pro
Designed by Alissa Amell

Printed in the United States of America

To my mother, Ora Simmons

ACKNOWLEDGMENTS

My mother was always a source of constant support, love, and strength. In her absence, my family and closest friends have stepped in to fill her role. To my aunts, Jewel Simmons, Margean Franks, Dee Graves, and Jetta Simmons, I thank them for being a source of comfort throughout this process. I also thank April Franks, Nagoster Franks, Roxanne Galloway, Rosita Galloway, Rodney Graves, Tyrone Graves, Rhonda Miller, Debra Johnson, and the many other family members who have provided love and encouragement as well. To Bina Pittman, Kia Haselrig, and Alonda Thomas, the lifelong friends who have been a source of steady strength, unwavering love, and enduring support. And finally, I owe a special debt of gratitude to Betty Pendergast, Melanye Price, Brighid Dwyer, Menna Demessie, Tosin Alao, Kristina Richardson, Melissa Rice, Gwen Tucker, Laura Morgan, Bryr Aiken, Michelle Kuenzi, and Rebecca Wood.

I also thank my agent, Vivian Chum, for believing in my work, and my editor, Talia Platz, who helped me fulfill the dream of publishing this book and has guided me through the entire process. Last, I thank all the members of my local RWA chapter who have taught me so much over the past years. I could not have done this without you!

Twelve Wicked Nights

Prologue

sabella's eyes fluttered open, and she let out a long, satiated yawn, a contented smile spreading across her face. Trading in the string of DC holiday parties for some time back in her quiet hometown might not have been such a bad move after all. She and Justin had been in bed all night, making love off and on as the snow continued to fall outside.

She reached for him, but stilled when she realized she couldn't. Her arms were tied at the wrists and secured to the headboard above her. She jerked against the ropes, her body writhing against the bed as she struggled to loosen her bindings.

"Relax, Isabella. Before you hurt yourself."

She froze, and her gaze slid around the room, for the first time noticing the transformation of Justin's master bedroom. A dozen candles lined its edges, their tiny flames flickering, casting eerie shadows along the walls.

"Justin?" Her voice was foreign to her ears, tentative, uncertain.

He stepped from the shadows, the hard, tanned length of his naked body a beautiful bronze in the candlelight—but there was something different about him, something dangerous. She'd been so busy struggling with her bindings that she'd failed to notice the changes in Justin's demeanor. His expression was gentle, but his emerald eyes were possessive, the rigid set of his jaw unyielding. She bit back a gasp as heat fluttered in her belly, her body shivering under the weight of his intense gaze.

"I would never hurt you, Isabella," he whispered, and she stilled when her gaze dipped to his hand, where his thumb absently stroked the hilt of a braided whip.

"Um, yeah. So, the whip? That's just for show, then?"

He grinned. "Not quite." His eyes darkened, and before she could take her next breath, she felt the sting of the hot leather against her breasts, the pleasure of the strike forcing her to cry out even as her skin throbbed from the sharp bite of the whip.

Holy shit! What the hell had she gotten herself into? The first of their twelve nights had begun, and this holiday, she could forget all about the partridge in the pear tree.

This was the season of giving, and from the look in Justin's eyes, his gift promised to be more naughty than nice.

Chapter One

sabella was in mourning—that deep, soulful kind where people fall to the ground wailing as if they are possessed. Her fiancé of two years had just broken up with her over the phone, the same phone that had died right after her sleek silver Aston Martin Vanquish had gone kaput on the side of the road.

Yes, she was in mourning—mostly for her shoes. Where was she ever going to find another pair of white kid-leather knee-high boots that fit her legs perfectly? Her favorite Jimmy Choos would be ruined if they got any wetter, and she'd worn them only twice.

Maybe if she sent up a prayer, God would save her boots right after he saved her from the worst blizzard to hit her small hometown of Jacksonville, Virginia, in more than ten years. She mumbled something that was as close to a prayer as a wicked Catholic girl was ever going to get, and trudged ahead. Her plea certainly couldn't hurt, although it was going to take a miracle right now, because she hadn't seen one car come down this road since she'd started her snowy hike fifteen minutes ago.

The faint sound of tires crunching against ice and snow made her halt. She glanced down the two-lane highway, squinting to see through the whiteout conditions as wind whipped across her face, the biting air stinging her cheeks and flinging hair in her eyes. She tucked her hair back with her gloved hand, straining to see the two bright white orbs in the distance.

Headlights.

If ever she needed proof that there was a God, she had it now. He had just saved her *and* her Jimmy Choos.

Justin Rourke was on a well-earned and much-needed vacation—thirty days' leave, to be exact. No Navy SEALs for thirty days, no dodging enemy fire, and no monotonous, mind-numbing training exercises. For the first time in years he was home for the holidays. So the last place Justin wanted to be was in his black SUV in the middle of a snowstorm, collecting Isabella Andreu's shapely but very annoying butt off the side of the road—and yet that's exactly what he was doing.

Everyone had told her to stay put, but as usual, she hadn't listened. She just *had* to get back to her life in DC and her glamorous and exciting friends—*her* words, not his. She'd claimed she was just going home for the weekend to get a few things from the office, and then she'd be back, but he wondered whether her urgent need to leave *that* night had less to do with work and more to do with that idiotic fiancé of hers, Harry.

As far as Justin was concerned, Harry was a selfish, manipulative prick, and for the life of him, Justin couldn't figure out why Isabella was still with him. She was beautiful and independent, a fiery, hot-blooded Italian. Harry was as cold and dull as a fish. He'd seemed bored at the funeral, as if it was a monumental struggle to console Isabella, whose grandfather had just died. And as soon as it was polite to do so, he'd hightailed it back to DC.

Justin slowed down his SUV as he rolled up beside Isabella. She was a pain in his ass. He should have been home in his warm bed, but Maggie had called him, frantic when Isabella hadn't picked up. And Isabella *always* picked up when her mother called, because there would be hell to pay if she didn't. The same was true for Justin. His parents and Isabella's had been close friends for many years, so Maggie was like a mother to him, and when Isabella needed saving, who did she call? None other than the sucker Justin.

He rolled down the passenger-side window and leaned forward. "Get in, Izzie."

She stood there, her stance wide, her arms folded across her chest as she glowered at him with those dark, sultry hazel eyes that reminded him of a fading sunset.

"How many times do I have to tell you not to call me that? It's *Isabella. Iz-uh-bella.*"

He was incredulous. He couldn't believe she was giving him attitude right now. He'd gotten out of bed to come find her at no small peril to himself, and she had the gall to argue with him.

"Dammit, *Isabella.* Every minute you stand there, the storm gets worse, so get in the car."

"You're a pain in the ass; you know that?" she snapped, but she still slid into the SUV beside him and slammed the door.

"Yeah, well, the feeling's mutual, *Izzie*," he quipped, his eyes twinkling as he flashed her a cocky grin.

"If I weren't a lady I would smack that grin off your face with the palm of my hand."

He snorted. Yeah, right. Isabella hadn't been able to beat him up since he'd seemingly grown ten inches overnight the summer before freshman year.

"I take it my mom sent you."

"Why else would I brave the worst snowstorm in a decade to get your spoiled butt?"

She glanced sideways and said sweetly, "Because you don't want to see me die from hypothermia?"

"As hard as it would be, I'm sure I would somehow find the strength to get through my guilt and grief over losing you," he muttered dryly.

"Ohhh, but I would haunt you, Justin."

He glanced at her, his lips thinning into a tight line at the teasing glint in her eyes.

"I'm sure you would." He looked away and flipped the defogger on, because he didn't want her to see how much her words rankled him. Ever since she'd returned to Jacksonville for her grandfather's funeral with that simpering fiancé of hers in tow, she'd haunted him more than he cared to admit. It was one thing when he'd never met Harry, but to finally encounter the man Isabella planned to marry and then to know he was all wrong for her was another.

And it wasn't because he envied Harry. He'd known Isabella all his life—long enough to recognize she wasn't his type. She was beautiful as sin, but she was a bit high maintenance, and certainly a handful. Yet of late he couldn't seem to get her sultry image out of his head.

"What's wrong with you? Mom's house isn't this way. Where are you going?"

"Back to my place. Most of the roads are closed, Izzie."

"Well, how come yours isn't blocked?"

"I live right off the highway, which is thankfully still open, or else we would both be stuck out here." He glanced at her, meeting her irritated gaze with his own. "I guess you didn't think about that when you decided to flee home to be by Harry's side in your useless luxury car."

He expected her to lay into him with a snappy comeback. Something bitchy, along the lines of "You're just jealous" or "You wouldn't know a luxury car if it rolled up your ass." So he nearly swerved off the road when she said *nothing*. That was so unlike her—Isabella *always* had something to say, and he almost swallowed his tongue when her fathomless hazel eyes clouded with pain just before she turned her head away.

He crinkled his brow as he frowned, studying her for another moment before returning his attention to the road.

Something—or, more likely, *someone*—had hurt her. It wasn't often that anything got past Isabella's steely armor, but he'd seen that look before, on the night she'd been jilted by her date to her junior prom and he'd been coerced into taking her. After all, he didn't have *anything* better to do while he was home from college for the summer.

He glanced at her again, his frown growing deeper. *Goddammit, Izzie.* Who the hell was he going to have to beat up for her now? He shouldn't have felt responsible for her, but he did. For some reason, he always took it as a personal insult when someone made Isabella cry.

"So, how long do you think we'll be snowed in?"

Justin stood in the kitchen preparing sandwiches, but stopped to glance at her from across the room. "I would have said just one night, but with the snow still falling like this, maybe two, even three." He shot her a smug grin. "Why? You have a hot date with Harry the wimp?"

Isabella scowled. "No."

She wasn't quite ready to tell Justin she'd just been dumped. He'd warned her about Harry. Told her the things she'd already known—that Harry was a selfish, manipulative jerk. But it was hard to disentangle herself from Harry when his father was managing partner and his grandfather had been named partner at her firm. Harry had been practically breast-fed on the firm's culture. He'd never given her crap about the late nights, and he'd made it a point to attend the annual holiday party.

Dating Harry had felt like an extension of her job—a job she was good at, but of late was starting to feel more like a necessary routine. No, Harry hadn't been perfect, but their relationship had been comfortable. Justin wouldn't understand that. She already knew what Justin's reaction would be when she told him about the breakup, and she just didn't want to hear him say "I told you so."

"If you don't want to talk about whatever's bothering you, then fine, but just know I'm here if you change your mind," he said, setting the sandwiches down in front of them on the coffee table.

Ooooh, he thought he was so clever. He'd been an attorney in the Navy for years, until he'd grown restless and decided to transfer out of JAG to become a SEAL. She knew what he was doing: lulling her with his gentle words to a place where she felt comfortable so that she would let her guard down with him—and that's when he would strike. What type of fool did he think she was?

"Yeah, whatever."

He sighed. "I'm serious, Izzie. You drive me crazy, and you get on my last nerve, but you know you can always talk to me."

She did. No matter what, she'd always been able to count on Justin. Her heart skipped a beat at the intensity that burned in his emerald green gaze, and for just a moment she was plunged back to a time when she'd adored Justin. Just two years older than she, Isabella had followed him everywhere, worshipping him, even as she tried to best him at every turn. Whatever he did, she just had to give it a try—but she was never satisfied until she was better than he was.

She furrowed her brow and frowned, and a tiny sigh escaped her. She hated that she would have to listen to him gloat, but she knew she wouldn't be able to keep the news from him for long. "I know I must seem a bit off-kilter, but it's been a rough couple of weeks, and when you mentioned Harry, you just struck a nerve. That's all."

She peered at him, hoping he would accept her explanation at that, but he didn't.

"I'm listening."

She dragged in a long breath. She really should just tell him the truth.

She dreaded it, because she knew Justin was going to have a field day with this.

"Promise me you won't gloat."

"I can't promise you that, Izzie. But I can promise you I won't rub it in too much."

She glared at him, her lips furling at the teasing laughter in his eyes. He was so immature. And for the life of her, she had no idea why she felt the need to share this with him. It was probably out of habit. Good or bad, Justin already knew so much about her. After all, they'd been *forced* to grow up together because their parents had been neighbors and best friends, which meant she and Justin did practically *everything* together as kids. Besides, even if she didn't tell him, he would hear it from her mother soon enough.

She sighed again and stared at her clasped hands, unable to look at him when she finally found the nerve to speak. "If you must know, Harry broke up with me." She snorted. "He said I wasn't refined enough for him, and then he dumped me."

Justin clenched his jaw tight, biting back the angry curse that hovered on his lips. He couldn't wait to get his hands on that asshole. The man was weak and pathetic, and had projected his own insecurities onto Isabella.

"Why would I gloat about something like that? It doesn't make me happy to see you upset; although I'm not going to lie and say that I'm sad to see him go. Izzie, you're fine the way you are, and if Harry can't appreciate that, then you're better off without him."

"Oh, I know that," she said quickly, and a small grin tugged at the corners of her mouth. That was more like the Isabella he knew, and not the cheerless woman he'd glimpsed in the car earlier.

"I certainly don't want anyone who doesn't want me, but maybe Harry has a point. I would be so much more agreeable if I didn't curse so much— if I wasn't quite so brazen and loud. Men want *nice, sweet* girls." She chuckled dryly, but her smile didn't quite reach her eyes.

A frown spread across his face.

"So you're not known for being nice and sweet. Nice and sweet are overrated—and trust me, I have a fairly good idea of what men want."

Nothing. Not even the hint of a smile or a snappish retort. Damn, that jerk had really gotten to her.

He blew out a long deep breath. "Izzie, you are who you are. You can't really change that, and you certainly shouldn't alter yourself because of a guy like Harry."

She cocked her head to the side, the waves of her dark, unbound hair cascading over her shoulder. He found himself momentarily mesmerized by her midnight locks, wondering if they were as soft as they looked. He shook himself. Where the hell had that come from? Izzie had always been like a sister to him—an annoying, aggravating sister. It was weird to imagine running his hands through her hair. But ever since she'd returned to town last week, he'd been having the oddest thoughts about her at the most inappropriate moments.

"I would never change for a man; but be honest, Justin. Would you ever be interested in a woman like me?"

He froze, every muscle in his body cording with tension. He felt like a deer caught in the headlights. There was nothing searching or hopeful about her gaze. Nothing about her expression said that she had some deep-seated longing to hear him profess his undying infatuation with her. She just wanted to know straight up—did a woman like her interest him?

How did he even begin to answer that question without winding up in a mucked-up mess? If he said no, then it would make Isabella believe there was something wrong with her, that she somehow needed to reinvent herself when she didn't. But then if he said yes, he would be admitting something he'd never admitted to anyone before—that he'd noticed her, that at times she did get under his skin. As hard as he fought against it, there were moments when he looked at her and saw a beautiful, voluptuous, intelligent woman, with enough fire to light up the sky.

He didn't want to answer her, but she'd pinned him into a corner, forcing him to tell her the truth. Damn, he hated when women pulled this sort of thing. There was no way a man could ever win.

He shifted in his chair as he searched his brain for a sufficient reply. "Ummmm..."

Yeah—that's brilliant, jackass.

Trying again, he pinned her with his gaze, his eyes not once leaving her. He'd never lied to her, and he wasn't about to start now, even though he knew this was a mistake.

"You're a smart, attractive woman, loyal to a fault, who's not afraid of anything. If the circumstances were different, I would definitely be interested in y—" He cleared his throat. *Pull it together, man.* "What I meant was, I'd be interested in a woman *like* you."

Whew. He'd barely just dodged that bullet.

Blood rushed to her ears, so she was sure she hadn't heard him correctly. Justin thought she was smart? Attractive? That was news to her. She'd been so sure he'd say no that she'd gotten her rebuttal all set and ready on the tip of her tongue. She sat in stunned silence, several seconds ticking by before she found her voice.

"You would?"

He nodded. "I would."

"Me?"

He gathered his plate as he stood. "Well, I said a woman *like* you.

Dating you would be weird. It would be like dating my little sister or something."

"You don't have a little sister."

"You know what I mean."

She frowned at him as he crossed the room to dump his empty plate into the sink. No, she didn't know what he meant. Yes, they'd grown up together, but she *wasn't* his little sister.

"But I'm *not* your little sister, Justin." He looked up from washing the dishes, his entire body rigid, and his eyes darkened to a forest green. The temperature in the room seemed to plunge, and goose bumps scattered across her skin in the wake of a slight chill. She realized immediately the error of her words. Why had she said that? She sounded as if she were coming on to him, but she wasn't. She was simply pointing out the obvious. She *wasn't* his sister, and she wished he'd stop thinking of her as if she were.

So little could embarrass her, but she was mortified by the expression on his face, as if he didn't need any reminders that she was no kin to him.

"I know *who* you are Izzie, and I know *what* you are to me."

She wanted to ask "What is that?" but she didn't dare. His eyes were dark and hooded, his expression closed off from her. Whatever she was to him, he didn't intend to tell her because he didn't want her to know— which was probably for the best.

Harry had already delivered one crushing blow to her ego. She didn't need another one from Justin by being reminded that after all these years he still saw her as the girl who'd grown up next door to him, and probably always would see her that way.

Chapter Two

Justin slammed his shovel into the ground, casting the snow to the side in order to clear a pathway to his SUV. All this effort was probably futile, as flakes of snow continued to fall, seemingly covering the walkway as soon as he cleared it. But he didn't care. He needed to be outside, away from her. He needed the distraction, because her words from the night before still dogged his every move.

I'm not your little sister, Justin.

Yeah, well, he didn't need Izzie to tell him that, he thought grumpily as he plunged his shovel into the snow again. She was *like* a little sister, or at least that's what he kept telling himself, but there was nothing remotely *brotherly* about how he was starting to see her—or think of her.

He searched his brain, struggling to figure out when Izzie had begun to look, well, just different. For as long as he could remember, she'd been there, dragging behind him—a loudmouthed tomboy, with the prettiest hazel eyes he'd ever seen. She aggravated him to no end, always needing to compete with him, one-up him at everything he did, until eventually she'd grown out of that.

With time, she'd shed her grimy jeans for designer duds, and transformed herself into *Isabella*—the beautiful, hotshot attorney. While everyone in their small town of Jacksonville treated Isabella as if she was the second coming of the messiah, the hometown girl who'd gone on to big things, he still saw her as just Izzie. Or at least he had until last week at the funeral. All of a sudden he'd started to notice things about her that he never had before.

He wasn't quite sure how or when it happened, but Izzie had changed. At the funeral, her entire family had been falling apart around her. But instead of joining the fray with her usual attention-seeking antics, she'd stepped into the shadows, becoming a steadfast anchor for her mother. She'd even raised some eyebrows when she offered to stay for a month to help her mother run their family bakery. Izzie was far too busy to be working by remote access for a month, even during the slower holiday season. No doubt her clients weren't thrilled, and her bustling K Street life was sure to be far more exciting than backward Jacksonville—or at least that's what she always claimed. And yet, she hadn't hesitated to offer.

He dug his shovel into the snow, harder than necessary, as he grew more agitated. He was attracted to Izzie. It was an alien thought to him, but it was the truth. Long after she'd gone to bed last night, he'd lain awake thinking. The moment she'd arrived with Harry, he'd started to see her differently—as a woman, and not just Izzie. And now he couldn't seem to stop. It was as if he saw *everything*—her fathomless eyes, the way she crooked her full lips into a small smile when she was teasing him, the rosy blush that stained her cheeks whenever she laughed hard.

He saw it all now, but he didn't want to. Not when he was snowed in with her for what would likely be at least the next couple of days.

He heard the creaking of the door behind him, but didn't stop his task of shoveling the snow until Isabella spoke.

"What are you doing? Digging for gold?"

He glanced down, letting out a small groan at his handiwork. He'd been so worked up that at some point he'd stopped trying to clear a pathway for his SUV and just started digging a hole in one spot.

He turned his irritated gaze on her. "Go back inside, Iz—"

His next words died on his lips, and he had to bite back a grin when he saw her. She wore a pair of his jeans, along with his flannel coat and snow boots. Her statuesque frame looked petite in his clothing, as if she were a kid playing dress-up in her father's clothes. She looked—*adorable.* A word he hadn't used to describe Izzie since she was—well, *never.*

"I came out here to help," she explained, apparently glimpsing the look of surprise on his face.

"You want to help?" He swept his gaze over her. "In that?"

"What's wrong with what I'm wearing?"

He grinned. "Can you even walk?"

His grin grew wider at the challenge in her eyes, but as soon as she stepped down off the porch, her earlier bravado disappeared, and he laughed when she struggled just to keep her footing.

"Oh, shut up," she snapped.

"Here, let me help you before you break something."

"No, I'm fine," she argued, her arms flailing as she fought to keep her balance. He ignored her protests and reached for her, his arm encircling her waist. She leaned into him, her body molding perfectly to his as he set her down on the ground, her booted feet sinking deep into the snow.

"I told you I was fine," she whispered, her voice soft, almost breathless.

She stood before him, her body steady, but he still held her, his gaze roaming over her face until it settled on her pretty bow-shaped mouth. She licked her lips, and he found himself tracing the slow slide of her tongue across them. Out of nowhere the image of him kissing those full lips materialized in his head. And the bolt of desire that shot through him was so sharp and unexpected that he hissed before he could stop himself, drawing her curious gaze to his face.

He immediately released her and spun around, nearly stumbling himself before he quickly regained his balance. Picking up his shovel, he resumed his task.

He felt her staring at him, and imagined her pretty face twisted into a scowl, silently wondering what was wrong with him—why he was acting so weird. He heard the questions so loudly, like a ringing in his ears, but she didn't voice any of them when she finally spoke.

"We'll probably be snowed in for another night," she remarked.

"I know," he grumbled, his back still to her while he continued working. He felt her eyes on him, tracing his every move, but he didn't stop, nor did he turn to face her. He struggled to gather himself. This was *Izzie* he was thinking about. It was one thing to see her in a different light, quite another to imagine kissing her.

Splat!

Justin stilled when something exploded against his back.

Splat!

He twisted around. "What the—"

Splat!

Icy fingers seemingly closed around his face as the bitter cold of wet snow chilled his skin. He'd barely recovered from the attack when another one came, but this time he saw the snowball hurling toward him, and he ducked out of the way just before it could smash into his face again.

"Izzie, what are you doing? Stop it."

Soft feminine laughter, rich and warm, swirled around him as her eyes twinkled with mischief.

"I have work to do, Izzie," he shouted, but she only laughed harder as she playfully dodged him, ducking his advance when he tried to lunge for her.

More snowballs came whirling toward him like missiles, and he realized she'd been putting together an entire arsenal of powdery puff ammunition while he'd been shoveling.

"Izzie—"

Splat.

Another snowball hit him in the forehead, which was luckily covered by his hat. That was it. He was done being nice. He planted his shovel in the snow and reached down, gathering a large pile of snow into a ball. He ducked to avoid two more of her speeding snowballs before sending back one of his own. And just like that, the war was over. What he lacked in quantity and speed, he made up for with sheer size and accuracy. His huge snowball hit her square in the chest, sending her tumbling backward, flat on her back into the snow.

He called her name as he trudged toward her, concern filling him when she didn't move. Finally she sat up, and another bubble of laughter floated from her lips.

"You're a brat; you know that?" He shook his head when she flashed a wide smile, and as much as he didn't want to, he couldn't stop the grin from spreading across his face as he bent to scoop her up, holding her against him as he stomped toward the house.

I'll make some coffee while you change," he said, setting the kettle on the stove.

Izzie nodded and headed toward the guest bedroom down the hall. She was halfway there when the phone rang. Justin reached for his cordless, frowning when he caught a glimpse of his caller ID. He stifled a groan at the thought of Izzie's best friend. He was sure the world could barely handle Izzie, so he was shocked that God had made two. The notion that opposites attract certainly wasn't the case here. Celeste was even more outrageous than Izzie, if that was possible.

"Hey, Izzie; don't go anywhere. It's for you."

He dragged in a deep breath as he held the phone against his ear and answered it.

"Hello, Celeste," he said dryly.

"Captain Save-a-Ho," she purred in her sultry, silky voice.

He glared at the phone. "What do you want, Cruella?"

"I'm just checking to make sure you haven't buried my best friend in your backyard."

Izzie rounded the corner, her eyes questioning.

"No, your friend is still alive, but if you would like to take a little trip down to Jacksonville, I'm sure I could dig a perfect spot to bury *you*—"

Izzie glanced sideways at him as she grabbed the phone.

His lips widened in a smug grin. "I'm going to go change. Make sure you don't burn the water."

She scowled at him, her palm over the receiver as she whispered, "Go away."

"Don't worry. I'm already gone. The last thing I want is to listen to you two gossip," he said with a smile as he shuffled down the hallway toward his bedroom.

"I 'm sorry about Justin."

Celeste chuckled. "Don't be sorry for Justin. Justin is sorry enough on his own."

"Celeste," Isabella said in warning as she frowned. If people thought she and Justin were bad, they should see him with Celeste. It was a constant battle between them. Her mother once said that they fought for their place in her life. But if that was true, Isabella saw no reason for them to compete over *her*. Justin had been there throughout her childhood, and she'd met Celeste her freshman year in college. They both were equally important in her life, and that would never change.

"I'm sorry. I know how much you hate it when we argue, but I can't help it. Captain Save-a-Ho—"

"I really wish you wouldn't call him that."

"Well, that's what he is. He saves every damsel in distress, including you."

"Did you just call me a ho?"

"Sort of. But if it makes you feel any better, I don't really think you're a ho," Celeste said sweetly, and Isabella couldn't help but smile.

"I appreciate that. I would hate it if my best friend thought so little of me."

"Never," Celeste said with a mock gasp, and Isabella could picture her with her hand clutched to her chest. "But all this talk of damsels and hoes . . . I digress. Honey, I just called to see how you were doing."

Isabella smiled. "Aww, thanks Celeste, but I'm fine. Justin found me on the side of the road—"

"The side of the road! I'm going to fucking kill Harry—"

"Harry?"

"I heard you broke up. Never heard anything about you being left on the side of the road, though. When I get my hands—"

Oh, that. She was ashamed to admit it, but she hadn't thought of Harry—not even once—since she'd woken up that morning. *Of course* Celeste was calling her about Harry. It had been only a day, but news like that traveled fast.

"Slow down there, Annie Oakley. I can see you already have your pistol in your purse—"

"Damn right I do."

"Yes, but before you land yourself on death row, Harry didn't leave me on the side of the road. He broke up with me over the phone, and then my car died."

"Ummm, so *why* don't I get to shoot him? Breaking up with you over the phone after two years of dating deserves one bullet—"

"No."

"In the leg?"

"*No.*"

"All right, the foot?"

"*Celeste.*"

"*Okay.* I won't shoot him, but I just don't think he deserves to get away with this."

"You act like he got away with committing murder. What do you want me to do to him?"

"I already told you what to do."

"I'm sorry, Celeste, but I just don't think shooting people is the way to go on this one."

"*Shooting people?*" Justin's voice interrupted their conversation, and Isabella glanced up as Justin sauntered into the room in a fresh pair of gray sweats and a white shirt.

"I told you Cruella was a bad influence. Izzie, hang up right now so I can call the police."

Isabella hung her head as she sighed. That was her cue to wrap up the conversation—she knew she couldn't handle the two of them at once. "I better get going."

"All right. I'll let you go, but are you sure you're okay?" Celeste asked softly, her voice full of concern.

Isabella moved to reassure her best friend. "Really, Celeste; I'm fine. I promise," she said.

The phone crackled as Celeste sighed against the receiver. "Well, if you're sure you're all right . . . But if you start to feel down, just call me, and I'll take off and head down there."

"Don't you dare come here—you're swamped at work. Besides, I really am okay—"

"But—"

"Good-bye, Celeste." Her voice was firmer this time.

Celeste sighed again. "All right, I'm going. Call me if you need anything."

Isabella promised she would, although she knew she wouldn't. No doubt they would talk again soon; they talked every day, but she was determined not to discuss Harry. One sign of distress, and Celeste would burn up the highway to Jacksonville, and Isabella refused to do that to her friend. Celeste was a workaholic like her—she had enough on her plate right now. Isabella would sort through this mess on her own. She disconnected the call and set the phone back in its charger. She glanced at Justin, who'd just finished turning off the kettle and pouring two cups of coffee. He leaned against one of the counters, his arms folded across his chest and wearing a frown on his handsome face.

"Cruella cannot come stay here."

"Justin—"

"I'm sure the homeless shelter has space."

"Hopefully it won't come to that," she said with a long-suffering sigh as she walked out of the kitchen. "If she does come, I'll likely be back at Mom's house by then, so she can stay with me—"

"Or whatever man she gets her tentacles into."

She shook her head as she marched toward the guest room once again. The insults that flowed between Celeste and Justin never ceased to amaze her.

"Where are you off to?"

"I need to change," she shouted back as she walked down the hall. "Try not to miss me too much, but if you get bored you can always call Celeste back."

Isabella smiled at the sound of Justin's strangled groan.

———

I sabella was just walking back into the kitchen when Justin's phone rang again, but the puzzled frown on Justin's face told her the call was for him this time.

"Yes, ma'am," Justin said into the receiver.

Isabella almost snapped to attention, his voice was so crisp and precise. His cool authority washed over her. She knew it was the military, and from the deference in his voice, she suspected it was his commanding officer on the other end. She rarely saw this side of Justin, and whenever she did it was always a bit jarring. It was easy to forget how dangerous Justin's life could be.

She pretended not to listen as she busied herself by fixing a quick breakfast of fruit and cold cereal.

"So soon?" He released a weary sigh, his hand massaging the back of his neck. "Yes, ma'am."

Isabella didn't miss the resignation in his voice. He wasn't happy with whatever news his commander had just delivered.

"Yes, ma'am. Thank you. You have a nice holiday, too." He disconnected the call, slamming the phone into its charger harder than necessary.

"Is everything okay?" She promised herself she wouldn't pry, but she just couldn't help it. His handsome features were twisted in agitation, and it was impossible to ignore the tension that had settled over the room.

He blew out a long, ragged breath. "Yeah. Everything's fine. That was just my vice admiral. It seems I'm going to ship out earlier than expected."

"Why? Or will you have to kill me if you tell me?"

"And risk Cruella's wrath?" He shook his head, and the hard planes of his face softened just a bit with his slight smile. "It's my next assignment. This one is in South America. Colombia, to be exact. Apparently the situation between the government and the drug cartels has continued to deteriorate faster than we all expected. So my unit needs to get over there sooner than we'd planned."

"How soon?"

"I leave in fourteen days."

"Wow. That is soon. I'm so sorry, Justin. I know you were looking forward to enjoying your time off over the holiday."

He shrugged. "Just part of the job," he said with a small smile. His expression was nonchalant, but his eyes gave him away. She knew that look; she'd seen it five years ago, just before he'd made the decision to leave JAG, a decision that had come on the heels of his parents' sudden death. She knew it was still hard for him with his parents gone and his two older brothers scattered across the country, spending the holidays with their own families.

He never talked about it, but she knew one of the reasons he'd become a SEAL was to keep his mind off the family he'd lost and the brothers he rarely saw anymore. Until this very moment she would have said Justin loved his job and the peace it gave him. But in his eyes she glimpsed a man who was weary and restless. She sensed he was growing tired of the endless travel into dangerous situations; the uncertainty of when he might be able to return home.

"Have you ever thought about quitting?"

Deep grooves formed in his brow when he frowned. "Some days I do, but then I wonder what the hell I would do if I weren't a SEAL. Right now I haven't been able to figure out what I love doing more than this."

"You could always go back to law." She spoke quietly, knowing she was rocking the boat on this one. She couldn't even look at him when she said it.

"You know how I feel about that."

His voice was stern, but she finally mustered up the courage to meet his brooding gaze. "You were—*are* a good attorney, Justin."

"But I hate it."

Liar. That single word was only in her head, but she might as well have screamed it from the rooftops, it echoed so loudly in the silent room.

"You didn't always hate it—"

"Izzie—"

She recognized the warning in his voice for what it was. On many things she pushed and prodded him until he reacted to her, but on this issue she would not tread any further.

"I just want you to do what you love most. What makes you happiest." She felt like such a fraud telling Justin he should do what made him happiest when even she didn't have the guts to do that. Her dream had always been to open her own practice, but here she was still slugging to make partner at a corporate law firm.

He snorted. "What would make me happiest is you with a muzzle."

She looked up at him. He was making jokes, using humor to back out of a sticky conversation. He always resorted to his veiled barbs when she got too close to a truth he wasn't ready to reveal.

"A muzzle?" She would leave the subject of his career change alone because that's what she knew he wanted. But she planned to have this conversation with him again at some point before he shipped out. "Did you just call me a dog?"

"I'm sorry." He didn't look sorry at all.

"And you wonder why you're single?" Oh, that got his attention. His hand froze in midair, just before he could shove another spoonful of Cheerios into his mouth.

"I don't wonder about that—and who says I'm single?"

"When's the last time you were even on a date?"

She curled her lips into a Cheshire grin when he glared at her.

"You're getting on my nerves."

She shrugged. "I have to entertain myself somehow."

"Read a book. Turn on the TV. Go to sleep."

"But that isn't as much fun as driving you insane."

"Maybe you can play solitaire. I think I have some cards around here."

She wrinkled her nose. "I don't want to play a game by myself."

He sighed. "Scrabble?"

She instantly perked up. Scrabble in itself would bore her to tears, but maybe she could convince him to make it more interesting.

Justin stood to cross the room, and she studied him in silence, her eyes tracing every single detail of him as he began searching for the game on one of his bookshelves. Isabella was transfixed by his broad back, the corded muscles bulging beneath his shirt with the slightest movement. His sleeves were rolled up to reveal perfectly defined forearms that were covered in a soft smattering of dark hair, and when he stooped down on his haunches to slide his fingers along the panel, she followed his every move.

She grinned when she thought of the perfect way to make Scrabble exciting—something to spice things up. Strip Scrabble. Now, what a game that would be! Justin peeling off his clothes, garment by garment. She took a deep breath to suppress the shudder that raced through her at the image of a tanned and naked Justin before her. Justin naked—things didn't get more exciting than that. She wondered what he would say to the idea. She imagined he would balk at first, but she knew how to ruffle him, get under his skin, bait him until he was forced to give in.

Her eyes twinkled with mischief. He was normally so composed, so in command of everything—his emotions especially. But she liked it when Justin was flustered and out of his element.

"I've seen that look before. It means you're up to no good," he quipped as he set down the game on the coffee table.

She slid off the barstool and joined him in the living room. "I was simply thinking of a way to make this game more interesting."

"Scrabble's been around for years. I don't think it needs your help."

"But perhaps we can modify it a teensy tiny bit?"

He wasn't fooled by her syrupy sweet voice as he stared at her, his eyes full of skepticism.

"I know I'm going to regret this, but what's this modification?"

"Strip Scrabble."

His eyebrows shot up. "No."

"How about X-rated-word Scrabble, then?"

"Oh, this keeps getting better and better. Do you have any more?"

She shrugged as she shook her head. "Nope."

"Why don't we just play regular Scrabble—"

"Or why don't we talk about why you're still not married? I hear the military's 'don't ask, don't tell' policy is less strict these days."

"Why do I feel as if I'm being blackmailed?"

"Because you are. Come on. Let's play strip Scrabble. This will be fun. Player with the lowest score at the end of the round loses a piece of clothing." She didn't know why, but she was nearly bouncing on the couch with excitement. Justin always ran from her at the slightest mention of sex—it was probably that little sister thing. So the fact that he looked as if he was caving in was exciting in itself. Hell—no matter what he said, they both knew it sure beat the original version.

"Let's flip on it."

That wasn't exactly a victory, but she also didn't expect Justin to simply say yes with no qualms. If he wanted to flip a coin, then at least she had a fifty-fifty chance of winning. And if she lost, she would just force herself to suffer through at least *one* game.

"Okay, we'll flip on it. If you win, we'll play plain old, boring, vanilla Scrabble. But if I win, it's going to be strip Scrabble."

She knew he was fighting the urge to protest when his jaw clenched tight, but he didn't put up a fight and finally nodded his head. He fished in his pockets for a quarter and flipped the coin high into the air. She felt as if she were a contestant on *Let's Make a Deal* the way her heart slammed in her chest.

"Heads," he called out.

They both followed the shiny silver piece as it rotated in the air, their eyes glued to it until it landed on Justin's carpeted floor.

She smiled when she saw the side facing up. *Tails.*

"Get ready to strip, baby."

Chapter Three

zzie didn't realize how close her little moth wings were batting to his flame, thought Justin. He'd already imagined kissing her once today. He wasn't sure he could stop himself from doing it if they somehow ended up naked in his living room.

"Izzie. I don't think this is a good idea."

She glanced up. "Are you going back on our deal? Because if so, then that would make you a punk."

"Izzie—"

Her eyes flashed at him as she pulled out the game board and arranged it on the coffee table. "And I can just imagine all the guys in your unit would love to hear what a wimp you are—so afraid of one little woman that you couldn't even sit down and play a game of strip Scrabble. I can just see it now." She cast her arms wide with dramatic flair. "*You*, the butt of endless jokes when you receive a care package, full of nice little pink frou-frou stuff, like a frilly little tutu, some pretty bows, and, of course, a cute note from me."

He cringed at the picture she painted. He had no doubt Izzie would send him a nice little care package, full of girlie shit to embarrass him, along with a card detailing his emasculation in vivid detail. After all, she'd pulled a similar stunt before when he'd refused to go skinny-dipping with her and some friends the summer he'd returned from his first year of law school.

"You really are the devil's daughter; you know that?"

She shrugged.

He settled on the floor across from her, grudgingly picking up his seven wooden tiles.

"I'll play one game with you, Izzie, but that's it."

"Nope. We play 'til we're naked. Bare, buck, birthday suit naked."

"Let's compromise on that—"

"No."

"But I don't want to see you naked, Izzie." He regretted the words as soon as they were out and saw the light dim in her eyes. That's not what he meant at all. Izzie had to know she was beautiful, from the inside out. It was just that if they went all the way with this game, he didn't know whether he would be able to keep himself from touching her. He was already on the edge. Yet before he could get an apology out, her eyes twinkled again, and just like that she was back in the game.

"Why don't you want to see me naked? Are you afraid you won't be able to help yourself—afraid you'll lose control and have your wicked way with me?"

He bit back a strangled moan as he fought to keep the shock from showing on his face. Izzie was wading out into some deep water. He knew she was only baiting him. But if she had any idea how close her words were to the truth, she would have backed off.

"You can take your clothes off all you want, but I'm not going any further than my boxers."

She arched a single eyebrow above a wide hazel eye. "Just know this, Justin. If I win, those boxers are coming off, even if I have to pry them off you with my bare hands." She smiled mischievously, arranging her letters on the rack.

"That's assault." He frowned. "I don't feel safe anymore. I think we shouldn't play."

She rolled her eyes as she picked up her last piece. "Don't be such a baby," she said.

"We're playing this game." She placed her first word down on the board. "Starting *now*."

W as it just her, or was the thermostat set on *hell*? She was half naked, but she was still burning up.

Her throat was parched, and she desperately wanted to retreat to the kitchen for a drink, and shove her head in the freezer while she was there. Justin was teasing her—flashing that stupid, charming, crooked grin of his every time he made a move, forcing her attention to the muscles that flexed in his chest. Okay, maybe he wasn't doing it on purpose, but that still didn't stop her from feeling as if she was being taunted every time he took his turn and put a piece down on the board.

"Izzie, it's your turn." He stared at her as if he worried for her sanity. He should be worried, because he was driving her crazy, and not for the usual reasons.

She put down three letters to form her word.

He frowned at her. "Are you even trying to win this game?"

She was all distracted and flustered, barely hanging in the game with her bra, tank top, and a pair of boy shorts. She'd thought she was over this silly crush. Had told herself many times, over many years, that she was not attracted to Justin Rourke—but maybe she'd lied.

She couldn't keep her eyes off him, the muscled planes of his chest and arms that rippled beneath his bronzed skin. He was a handsome man—she couldn't deny that. Still, she probably would have been able to keep her head on straight if it was just her own simmering lusts that she had to battle, but she swore that every time Justin looked at her, a fire leapt in his emerald eyes before they became dark and shadowed.

She knew Justin didn't want her—that she wasn't his type. But she was convinced that she didn't just imagine his gaze sliding down the length of her legs. And she swore just now, when she'd leaned forward to place her pieces, that his eyes had followed her, dipping to the deep V of her cleavage, where they'd remained for several seconds.

"I thought this was strip Scrabble, not dirty word Scrabble."

"Huh?"

Justin pointed to her words scattered across the board. "Everything you've spelled is something related to sex or a body part."

Orifice, tongue, cream, mouth, breast, sexual. Her cheeks heated as she felt herself blush. No wonder she couldn't focus on winning; she was too distracted by all her gutter thoughts.

"'Cream' isn't a dirty word."

His eyebrows shot up as if to say that of course it was. "'Cream' as in 'whipped cream,' and then there's 'cream' as in—um"—he cleared his throat—"the *other* cream."

Their gazes locked, and the air around them shifted, making her lungs ache as she tried to drag in her next breath.

"Yeah. *That* cream. I got it," she managed to croak out. Damn. Had she just creamed her panties? She couldn't take them off *now.*

"We can end the game now if you can't handle it," Justin taunted, and she probably would have thrown in her tiles had it not been for that smug grin of his. He seemed completely unfazed by any of this, and she knew he was just trying to prove a point—that he'd been right. That playing strip Scrabble was a bad idea.

"I'm fine, but if you're having trouble, then I understand," she shot back.

He shrugged, his eyes still glowing with amusement. "No. I'm good." He leaned forward and put down his tiles to spell another word.

Jezebel.

"That's a proper name. You can't use proper names in Scrabble."

"It's also a noun used to describe a shameless woman. You of all people should be familiar with the word."

She glared at his grinning face as she reached for the dictionary. "Make jokes all you want. You still can't use proper names."

He arched one brow. "You want to challenge me? You'll lose a turn, because I'm right. Trust me."

She snorted. Trust him, her ass. She picked up the dictionary.

Damn. He *was* right. She cast the dictionary aside and met his gaze.

He nodded as if to say "Told you so, and now your shirt." She was supposed to be a brilliant attorney. Why couldn't she come up with clever words like "jezebel"?

"Take off your shirt, Izzie," he said in a soft, coaxing voice. His expression was open as he simply watched her to see what she would do next.

That's when she realized this was truly a game to him, a battle of wills. He kept goading her so that she would cave, but she had no intention of ending this game until he threw in the towel first.

She glanced at him, and he mistook her hesitation. The arrogant grin on his face told her that he thought he'd already won, that he'd succeeded in making her nervous, had already forced her out of her element. Well, he was wrong. She returned his smile with one of her own and was delighted when his cocky grin faltered.

She might lose this game, but there was no way she was going to let him win this battle of wills between them.

She shrugged off her tank top and tossed it toward him. She smiled when it landed atop his head.

Justin might not have known it yet, but the gloves were coming off.

———

He was in big trouble.

He knew it the moment her shirt landed on his head. He sensed a change in her, just before he glimpsed a wicked glimmer in her eyes. It was as if she'd switched strategies and now had her game face on.

He pulled her shirt from his head and threw it aside. He slid his gaze over her, trying to remind himself that this was Izzie he was ogling—even as his eyes dipped to the swells of her breasts, which spilled over the tops of her pale pink bra. He was a bit surprised to see the soft lacy cups with a tiny pink bow in the center. He'd never figured Izzie would be one for dainty underthings.

"Nice," he said. "Although I would have thought you were a red satin or black lace kind of girl."

He smiled when she followed his direct gaze, and crimson splotches stained her smooth cheeks.

Isabella cleared her throat loudly. "It's your turn."

Fortunately for her, his next word was only seven points, forcing him to abandon his sweats, which only made it harder to hide the evidence of his arousal, which pressed against his boxers.

He had to get her out of this game, and *soon*, before he embarrassed himself. He was convinced that no matter what Izzie said, there was no way she was going to strip naked before him. All he had to do was win the next round, and she would throw in the towel.

They went round after round until he finally got her.

Quiff.

"What the fuck? Where do you come up with this crap?"

"It means a promiscuous woman."

She gave him a scathing look. "I know what it means. I'm just trying to figure out how you've been coming up with this stuff. If you weren't half naked, I'd say you had some tiles up your sleeves."

His lips twitched as he fought to hold back a grin. She hated to lose almost as much as he did. "I'm trying to figure out which one I want first. That girlie bra or those boy shorts."

Still seated on the sofa, she settled back against the cushions with her legs crossed and her arms folded across her breasts.

"It's your call, Justin. Pick your poison."

He dug his hands into the carpet, fighting the heat that roared through him. She was calling his bluff—or at least she was pretending to. He wondered how far she would go before she gave up this charade. Well, there was only one way to find out.

"Your boy shorts are cute. I think I want to see you in them a little bit longer, so that bra has to go."

She lifted one brow. "Are you sure?"

Hell no. "Positive."

She held his gaze as she reached behind her back, and he almost choked on his next breath as it lodged deep in his chest.

"I need your help. I can't get it."

He grinned. She was chickening out. "I understand, Izzie. It's okay. You can keep your bra on." He stood and turned toward the kitchen. As expected, she'd caved. He'd won. The game was over.

"No, I'm serious. It's stuck."

He turned around to face her. "Give it up, Izzie. I know you're chickening out. Game over."

Her expression was incredulous, as if that was the last thing she would do, which made him nervous all over again. If she wasn't giving up, then her bra really was stuck.

"This game is *not* over. We agreed to play until one of us was butt naked, and I intend to finish, but if you can't handle it I completely understand."

Was that a smirk on her face? It was. She really thought he couldn't see right through her. It was so obvious that she was bluffing.

"Stand up." He marched toward her. "Turn around," he said when she stood before him.

He grasped the bra clasp in his hand, his fingers brushing against her smooth skin as he studied it.

"The clasp looks fine to me."

"Well, then, take it off."

He couldn't see her face because she didn't turn all the way around, her head tilted just slightly to the side, while her silky hair brushed against his fingertips.

Her sultry laugh whispered across his skin like soft satin, and he knew then that he'd been baited. Her bra had never been stuck; it was just a ploy to get him over there, a dare to see how far he would go.

Well, if she was prepared to go all the way, then so was he.

Three hooks. He undid each one slowly. His heart pumped faster, and if she had dared to look over her shoulder she would have seen the effect she was having on him, tenting against his boxers.

"Last chance, Izzie," he said in a hoarse voice that was foreign to his own ears.

"I don't know what you're waiting for."

There was not the slightest hesitation in her voice. Was he really going to do this? Was she really going to let him?

He released the last hook, and her bra instantly snapped apart.

He stood there frozen in a trance, his gaze gliding over the smooth, creamy flesh of her back.

He didn't realize he was touching her until he heard her soft gasp. He ran his fingers across her bare skin, the rough pads of his fingertips gently caressing her back.

She turned then, still clutching her bra to her chest. He let his hand fall back to his side as he met her gaze. What he saw in her eyes made him shudder as heat crawled inside his gut, inflaming his skin before dipping dangerously lower to harden his cock. Her hazel-hued eyes were wide, brimming with desire, and he found himself unable to tear his gaze away.

It wasn't until she shifted before him that he finally let his gaze travel down. She still held her bra against her, but he'd barely formed that thought in his head when she relaxed her arms and let it drop.

Chapter Four

She didn't know who moved first.

"Isabella."

He called her name in a tortured whisper, and it struck a chord deep within her, fanning the flames of desire that burned inside her, with just that single breathless word. It was a warning, a last attempt to stop the inevitable, and she ignored it, heedless of the consequences. She knew how stupid this was. She realized they'd both allowed their game to get out of hand, but if Justin wasn't going to stop, then neither was she.

She reached for him, one hand cupping the back of his head as the other snaked behind his neck, tugging him toward her.

She closed her eyes at the first touch of his lips against hers, savoring the taste of him as he slid his tongue against the seam of her lips before gently coaxing her mouth to part, sweeping inside.

She moaned against his lips, her tongue twining with his as he deepened the kiss, his mouth insistent and demanding. The steel-hard length of his erection dug into her belly, and she rocked against him, wanting more.

Her body trembled in his arms, his hands slowly sliding down the length of her before settling on her hips. Clutching her flesh, his palms gliding across her bare skin, he ground himself harder against her, sending shocks of pleasure skating across her flesh. She gasped at her insistent need for him, feeling light-headed and breathless.

She moved her hands from around his neck and flattened her palms against his taut chest, her fingers sliding across his muscled flesh. He jerked beneath her, the muscles in his torso bunching tight as she let her hands graze his skin.

"Isabella, if you want to stop, you better say something now," he groaned against her lips.

She didn't take his words lightly, and she leaned back to meet his searching gaze, breaking their kiss. She read on his face what she was sure was written across her own. If they did this, there was no turning back, and they both knew it. But it was too late now. The moment their lips had touched, their relationship had changed. She could see Justin had a harder fight than she did. She'd harbored feelings for him for many years, labeling them as a silly crush, while Justin had only just begun to notice her.

"I don't want to stop, Justin."

She waited, watching him for any sign that he'd changed his mind. She wanted to give him one last chance to pull away, as he'd just given her, so that there would be no regrets in the morning.

"Touch me," he said softly, his eyes darkening with passion. She gave a soft sigh, a mixture of relief and pleasure, as she did just that and stroked her hands across his skin, as she slid her palms down the planes of his torso, feathering through the dark sprinkling of hair below his navel. He sucked in a breath when she reached the waistband of his boxers.

He seized her lips again, the kiss more insistent this time as his tongue probed deeper and harder while her fingers dipped under the waistband of his boxers to stroke his skin there, but traveled no farther.

She tore her lips from his, and he called her name in a broken whisper, his face drawn and taut with need. She teased him, her fingers sliding through the coarse nest of hair that surrounded his manhood before inching her hand beneath his jutting cock to cup the heavy sac nestled there. He hissed, drawing her attention to his face. His eyes were closed, his head thrown back as he panted through slightly parted lips.

His surrender to her touch made her dizzy as blood rushed to her head. Every single inch of her flesh was aflame, sweat beading along her skin as her internal temperature climbed and climbed.

Her nipples tightened and the folds of her sex grew heavy, the juices of her arousal pooling between her thighs.

She curled her fingers around him, his thick hot length jerking in her hand. He groaned her name as she lightly pumped his shaft, his rigid flesh swelling in her palm as it grew even harder.

She quickened her strokes, tightening her hand just a fraction, dragging a hoarse moan from his lips. She swiped her thumb across the broad head of his shaft, wiping away the tiny droplet of precum that gathered there.

She gingerly pulled her hand from his hardened length to suck his essence off her thumb, and that was his undoing. He backed her toward the couch, taking control once again.

He crushed his mouth against hers, his hands everywhere, and she shuddered against him.

He scooped her up into his arms and carried her the last few feet to the couch, kissing her the entire way, finally setting her atop the cushions, his body coming down to cover her.

He plundered her mouth again, his tongue sweeping inside, making her melt right there in his arms. She ran her hands along the length of his back, tracing his corded muscles beneath the fine sheen of sweat that glistened on his skin.

He tore his lips from hers, then, dragging a soft whimper from her mouth. He chuckled softly at her needy response as he kissed a trail of kisses from her lips, along the column of her slender throat, to the swells of her breasts. He kissed between the valley of her breasts as he cupped the full globes in his hands, tugging on her coral-tipped nipples, sending bolts of heat straight to the center of her body.

She writhed beneath him, her breath coming out as choppy pants. When he closed his mouth around one nipple, she swore she stopped breathing. The hot, wet cavern of his mouth was like warm honey on her aching flesh. He sucked gently, pulling her hardened bud deeper into his mouth as he swirled his tongue around it, flicking it until it grew impossibly harder, and then he nipped it with his teeth, forcing a sharp hiss from her lips.

"Justin." She didn't recognize that tortured, needy voice as hers as she clasped the back of his head, holding him against her breasts.

Her body was on fire, blazing out of control, but Justin didn't show her any mercy as he released one nipple, with a slight popping sound, only to capture the other. He lavished that one with the same attention as the first, until she was mindless with pleasure, completely boneless beneath him.

She tightened her arms around him as if she were flailing in a raging storm and he was her anchor. The sticky wetness of her arousal trickled from her body, pooling at the center of her core. Pleasure consumed her, and she was light-headed and dazed from his foreplay, but she needed more.

"Justin." She called his name again as he moved down the length of her body, blazing a wet trail of kisses along her belly until he reached the gate to her womanhood.

He grasped her thighs, roughly parting them with his splayed palms as he settled between them, opening her completely. He spread the lips of her swollen pussy with his fingers and then leaned forward, his warm breath fanning across her sensitive skin just as he slid his tongue deep inside her, curling against her hot tunnel to graze her G-spot.

Tremors rolled through her as she dug her nails into his scalp, her eyes clenched shut. All she could do was feel. Her thighs trembled around him as he closed his mouth around the tiny nub of her clit, tugging it gently between his lips.

A soft gasp fell from her as more wet heat gushed from her body. She arched into him as she felt herself cresting, the velvety slide of his tongue into her pussy dragging her to the edge.

She was poised there, her breath shallow and uneven, as he devoured her cunt with his mouth. When he encircled her clit with his lips, the long slow slide of his finger replacing his tongue inside her, she shattered, her body completely breaking apart around him.

She came on a soul-stirring moan, the liquid heat of her passion trickling from her body. He eagerly lapped it up. She stroked her hands through his hair, down his back, along his shoulders, and lay there satiated.

He moved up her body, and she clasped her legs around him, holding him tightly imprisoned between her thighs. Their eyes met just before he dipped his head to kiss her, and she shuddered with the spicy taste of her essence on his lips. She deepened the kiss, her palms flattening against his cheeks, as she drew her knees higher, wrapping her body around him like a cocoon.

He shifted against her, and the tip of his cock pressed against her wet opening. He ripped his mouth from hers just as he jerked back.

"Shit." His expression was tight. "We need a condom," he forced out between stilted breaths, struggling to maintain control.

"It's okay. I'm on the Pill." She was almost afraid to let him go, afraid that if she did he would find every excuse not to make love to her, that he would talk himself out of it, remember that because she was *Izzie* she was somehow untouchable.

Relief eased across his face. Still he hesitated, as if giving her one last opportunity to change her mind, but she wasn't about to. She tightened the muscles in her thighs around his hips and thrust her own hips upward, taking the head of his cock inside her, engulfing him in her wet flesh.

That was his undoing, the absolute moment where his control snapped. Sheer agony twisted his features as he closed his eyes, calling her name on a jagged breath as he pressed her down into the couch and thrust his hips forward to bury his hard length deep inside her warmth.

He grazed her G-spot as he entered, setting off another maelstrom of pleasure inside her, and before she could catch her breath she erupted again.

Isabella shattered around him, her wet, tight pussy clamping around his cock like a steel vise. Her orgasm exploded through her, and he gritted his teeth, fighting back his own climax as she broke apart in his arms.

As the aftershocks of her orgasm quieted, he moved again, but knew he would not last for long. Isabella felt so good in his arms as he buried his length deep inside her body. He gripped her thighs tighter, his fingers digging into her flesh as he rode her, splaying her thighs wider, to rock deeper inside her heat.

Soft sighs of pleasure wafted around him, but he kept his eyes clenched shut. He didn't dare open them, knowing that if he glimpsed her face glowing red with arousal, or her full breasts bobbing beneath him, wearing the scarlet marks of his lips, he would shatter, that the last vestiges of his control would finally snap. His other senses were alive with her, and it was already a monumental struggle to stem his nearing climax.

Sweat dripped from his body, making every single movement a slippery slide. Her low, sensual moans mingled with the sounds of sweat-drenched skin slapping together as the perfumed scent of her climax tickled his nose. He inhaled, filling his burning lungs with her.

He felt his balls draw up and tighten against him, and he plunged into her harder, faster, his thick shaft tunneling deeper into her with each thrust.

"Justin." She called his name as he fucked her harder, the breathy whisper like a sensual symphony to his ears, urging him to find release inside her body.

Isabella screamed his name again, and his eyes flew open as he stilled, wondering if he'd hurt her.

"Don't stop. Please don't stop," she cried out, and it was as if his body had a mind of its own. He plowed inside her, stroking through the slick folds of her sex, to brush against the back of her sheath. She was just so tight around him, her wet tunnel like liquid fire seeping inside him until he was powerless to stop the volcano that erupted within him.

He shouted her name and slammed into her body on three final, hard thrusts, before stiffening against her, his cock buried deep. He collapsed, his face nestled in the crook of her neck as he emptied his seed into her tight channel that spasmed around him, milking his engorged flesh. She'd come again with a tiny tremor of pleasure, not as explosive as her last two orgasms, but the vibrations that rocked her body made her clench even tighter around him, and he released a feral growl against her neck as he poured his essence inside her until he was completely spent.

They lay there, twisted in each other's arms, their breathing choppy and labored. He rolled off her, to gather her within his embrace and hold her draped across his body.

He shoved his hand in her wild mane and nudged her head down as he lifted slightly, kissing her gently. He explored her mouth slowly, a sensual, languorous kiss, before falling back again, ending his lazy perusal of her soft lips.

He met her heavy, hooded gaze, but neither of them said a word, too afraid to break the spell. He expected that he would feel awkward, but he didn't. It almost seemed ridiculous now that he'd fought so hard to keep this from happening, given how perfectly they fit together.

She laid her head on his chest, and he closed his eyes, listening to the rhythm of her breathing until it grew even. When he was sure she was asleep, he closed his eyes and allowed himself to drift off. For the first time in what seemed like forever, the restlessness inside him had quieted.

I sabella awoke with a yawn, naked in Justin's bed, and realized he must have carried her into his bedroom while she'd slept. She stretched lazily, a small smile stealing across her face at why she'd needed to rest in the middle of the day. *Justin.*

He'd been so tender with her after they'd made love, so gentle. She'd half expected Justin would do something stupid, like apologize for letting their game get out of hand, but he hadn't. Instead, he'd seemed almost content as she'd drifted off to sleep in his arms.

She rolled her eyes at her ridiculous thoughts—thoughts that were so unlike her when it came to men and sex.

Yes, sex with Justin had been fun, but that's all it was. Justin could never be content with her—nor she with him, for that matter. And while Justin had seemed at ease as he'd held her earlier—what about now? If he was still as content as her wild imagination had made him out to be, then why wasn't he curled up beside her, still asleep?

Wrapping a soft quilt around herself, she slid out of the bed to search for Justin, but stopped when she heard the hushed staccato of rushing water. He was in the shower.

She walked around his room as she waited for him to come out, busying herself as she absently fingered his things.

His four-poster king-sized bed dominated the large space, along with the wide-screen plasma TV that hung on the wall. The boxers he'd worn earlier lay on the floor by the door leading into his bathroom, and she noticed a few of his toiletries scattered across his dresser. His room was pretty much barren, a glaring testament to a man who rarely lived there.

She crossed the room to where his boxers were on the floor and bent to scoop them up. She figured she would neatly fold up his boxers and then put them aside, but while she was down there something caught her eye, something that made her completely forget all about his underwear.

She crawled on all fours toward his bed, her gaze fixed on the shiny silver object that was tucked beneath it. She stuck out her hand, her fingers closing around the cool metal. She leaned back on her haunches, her eyes wide as she studied the object in her hand.

Handcuffs? Justin owned handcuffs?

It would have made sense if she'd found them somewhere near his uniform. Then she could have even rationalized it to herself. But in his bedroom and under his bed? Uh-uh.

She set them aside as she leaned back down, her hand taking yet another foray beneath his bed. Again it struck gold, and she nearly fainted when she pulled out a long object, the taut leather jagged and uneven beneath her fingertips.

A whip? *Ohmigod*. What type of kinky shit was Justin into?

She placed the whip aside, where it joined the handcuffs, and once again she went on a hunting expedition.

It was her curiosity that made her careless—that made her forget all about the fact that Justin was still in the shower.

She never heard the water shut off, or the door creak open. So when Justin walked into his room, he found her with her ass high in the air, still searching beneath his bed for more kinky treasures.

J ustin left Isabella asleep in his bed and headed straight to his shower. He turned on the water and stepped into the tub, immediately jerking as the freezing droplets pelted his skin. He did that every morning. The initial cold blast jolted him awake before growing warmer. Today he was wide-awake, but he kept the knob turned only a little so the water was cold, and he welcomed the beads of ice water to cool his heated flesh.

He closed his eyes and leaned his forehead against the slippery tiles, wondering how the hell a simple game of Scrabble had forced him to seek refuge in his shower. He didn't have to wonder for very long. It was Isabella. This was all her fault—well, mostly; okay, hardly. But it was tempting to place the blame with her.

Isabella might have started them on the path, but he'd been just as content to follow. A game of Scrabble should not have led to them falling into bed together. He'd slept with Izzie, the girl he'd known all his life. He should have exercised some common sense and self-control. He should have stopped the game when they'd both been down to their underwear, but his pride wouldn't let him back down. Well, to hell with his pride now. He was stuck in a freezing shower, struggling to get the tempting images of Isabella out of his mind as he fought to ease the powerful hard-on he still sported. Yeah, so much for pride.

He turned off the water and stepped out, the cool air chilling his flesh as goose bumps broke out all over his body. He reached for a towel, hurriedly drying himself off before wrapping it around his waist.

He hesitated before walking into his bedroom to stare at his reflection in the mirror. What would he say to Isabella when they came face to face again? Would he apologize, or would he tell her the truth? He gripped the sink tighter as he struggled with that. He wanted Isabella—had for some time—and now he wanted her all over again if his raging hard-on was any evidence. He didn't want to, knew it was wrong, but he couldn't help it. This was Izzie—the girl he'd known since he was two. He wanted to pretend that things hadn't changed between them, that they could somehow go back to the way they were before, but he knew they couldn't.

The moment he started to see *Isabella*, not Izzie, was when he should have realized nothing would ever be the same between them. Now he just had to figure out what the hell he was going to do next. He had two choices. He could bury his longings, pretend that they hadn't made love, and then *try* to go back to being normal again, or he could do what he longed to do and slip right back into bed with her and enjoy the rest of his Christmas vacation.

He knew what he *wanted* to do, but every sane and rational thought in his head fought against it. He still wasn't sure what his next step would be as he started toward his bathroom door. But as soon as he opened the door he realized the choice had already been made for him—his handcuffs and flogger were lying on the floor beside Isabella, who was frantically searching under his bed with her lush, curvy backside high in the air, pointed straight at him.

"Let me guess. You dropped an earring—"

The deep timbre of Justin's voice startled her, and she let out a string of curses when she bumped her head.

She struggled to scramble from under Justin's bed, wondering how the hell she hadn't heard him *before* he'd come out. *Because you were too busy ogling cock rings and butt beads.*

She crawled out from under his bed and turned to face him, balancing herself on her knees. She knew she looked guilty as hell, but Justin didn't seem the slightest bit bothered by the fact that she'd just been caught rummaging through his stuff.

"You want to tell me what you're planning to do with my handcuffs and flogger?"

Was he serious? He looked at her with that cocky grin as if she was the one who was into some wild bondage shit, when in fact *he* was the sexual deviant.

"What *I* plan to do? They're yours. You want to tell me what *you* plan to do with them?"

He crossed the room and bent down to pick up the aforementioned items, tossing them onto his bed.

"What do you think I do with them, Isabella?"

His voice was soft, dangerously so, and she stared at him as if she'd never seen him before. Was this Justin? The same Justin who'd refused to skinny-dip with her years ago, who'd just balked at playing strip Scrabble? He was obviously into some kinky stuff, but he blanched every time she mentioned the word "sex."

"I don't know, Justin. As long as I've known you, you've always run from me at the first mention of sex."

His brows lifted. "Just because I refuse to talk to *you* about it doesn't mean I don't have it."

She stood to her feet. "Uh-uh. There's sex, and then there's whatever freaky shit you do in this room."

She was incredulous when instead of taking offense, he smiled. "Have you ever experienced any of this so-called 'freaky shit' you seem to so disdain?"

She gasped when his hand lifted and he teased his fingers across her parted lips, stroking them softly.

"Have you ever once felt the sting of leather against your skin, or the cool impressions of metal against your bound wrists?"

Her eyes grew wide when he leaned closer to her, his lips hovering above hers—so close, but just far enough out of reach to tempt her.

All of a sudden she felt feverish, and she shivered. Again, she wondered whether this was the same Justin she'd known all her life. Normally, it was she who tempted Justin with provocative words, and ruffled his composure. But in this room, on his territory, surrounded by *his* things, she was out of her element. She was the one who was now ruffled and flustered, mesmerized by Justin's seductive voice.

"I asked you a question, Isabella."

Dominance and possessiveness flashed across his face. Never once had she seen those emotions blazing so intensely in his eyes.

"No."

"Then how do you know what you would like or dislike?"

She didn't know, and in many ways that scared her, because until that moment she'd thought she'd seen and done it all.

"I don't."

"That's right, Isabella. You don't," he whispered as he dipped his head to the crook of her neck, his warm breath feathering across her skin.

"You have no idea the pleasures to be had, but I can tell you're curious."

She was. A strange mix of excitement and nervousness filled her. She'd thought she was open and adventurous, but this new version of Justin was prepared to teach her even more.

He lifted his head, and she met his gaze, wondering what would happen next. A teasing glint blazed in his green eyes, but it was barely visible as desire swirled in their depths.

"I can see the anticipation in your eyes, but you're not ready," he finally said.

She was a bit offended. What did he mean she wasn't ready? Of course she was ready.

She parted her lips to point out just how wrong he was, but he didn't give her an opportunity to protest when he lowered his head to capture her lips with his. She was powerless against the onslaught of sensations that weaved their way through her body as Justin branded her with the intensity of his kiss.

Sex with Justin? She really hadn't known what to expect. That it would be good—well, she'd figured it would be. But she'd never expected him to make love to her with such an overwhelming, all-consuming passion, where everything else around them ceased to matter, where her senses were full of him and only him.

He backed her to the bed, his hands easily peeling away the quilt that was barely wrapped around her curves. Her back connected with the mattress, and he came down atop her, his lips still fused with hers. Her nipples tightened as heat furled in her belly, and she wrapped her legs around his waist as her arms twisted behind his neck.

He entered her body on one smooth thrust, a groan ripping through him as he tore his lips from hers. Her hips surged off the bed, meeting his driving thrusts as he buried himself deep within her. She clung to him, his naked wet flesh slipping against hers, his muscles clenching and unclenching beneath her fingertips.

He pumped inside her harder and faster, and she gasped when he brushed against her G-spot, her head falling back and her eyes clenching shut when he did it again, and then again. She erupted like a wildfire in the middle of summer, her voice hoarse as she screamed out his name.

His hands settled beneath her ass, lifting her onto his cock as he pumped and thrust into her with deep strokes until he shattered inside her, calling her name on a tortured moan as his warm seed exploded inside her.

They both were breathless as he collapsed against her before rolling to her side to nestle her atop his chest. Her lids were suddenly heavy, and she wondered what it was about Justin's lovemaking that left her feeling so satiated, and so sleepy, as if she had no energy to do anything but snuggle in his arms. Which was exactly what she did as she once again drifted off to sleep.

Chapter Five

Justin awoke to the pleasure of a soft palm stroking his chest, and the last question he'd ever expected to hear.

"So, when are you going to tie me up and spank me?"

He groaned. Trust Isabella to ruin postcoital cuddling bliss.

"You're not ready," he said, planting a quick kiss against her lips before rolling out of bed.

She sat up, the sheet clutched to her chest. He grinned. They'd made love well into the morning. He'd seen every inch of her. And that sheet sure wasn't doing anything to stifle the vivid memories in his mind.

"*Sooo* is there something I need to do to get ready?"

"I told you, Izzie. I'll know when you're ready."

"I don't believe you. I don't think you have any intention of showing me this other side of you." She frowned. "And I think it's because you're scared."

He stilled. "Scared? Of you?" He snorted.

"No, not of me. I think you're afraid to explore your darker nature with me—I think you're afraid it would be like opening up Pandora's box."

That was because it would be, he thought. Making love to Isabella was one thing—but introducing her to his darker nature, as she called it, was quite another.

"You leave for base in thirteen days," she hedged. "That's just twelve nights together—twelve nights for you to do every sinfully erotic thing I want. It's really quite fitting, considering Christmas is right around the corner."

"You don't know what you're asking, Izzie," he said in a low growl. Not only did she have no idea what she was asking; she had no idea what kind of effect her darkly provocative words were having on his senses—his body. The image of Isabella bound before him, completely helpless and at the mercy of his desires, had the blood in his veins roaring through him, hardening his flesh.

"It's only twelve nights, Justin. That's all," she whispered.

He forced himself not to shudder with need. Damn it, she had no idea how badly he wanted to take hold of her, master her. But no matter what she said, he knew Isabella wouldn't take very well to exploring his fantasies. Isabella didn't have a submissive bone in her body. But then, that's also what intrigued him—what set fire to his senses. What would it be like to command her in their bed—to control her, to watch as she struggled giving her power over to him, until she could do nothing else but surrender. He suspected Isabella would never yield. She could never truly submit to him, but he ached to push her boundaries, to see just how far she would let him go.

He leaned across the bed, his lips inches from hers as he teased her with the promise of a kiss. "Twelve nights—exploring our fantasies—having my wicked way with you. Sounds tempting . . ."

She panted with anticipation, already thinking he'd given in. Oh—if they did this, then she certainly had much to learn about submission, about patience, about who was *really* in charge. He bounced off the bed. "I'll think about it," he said with a teasing chuckle, eliciting a sharp curse from Isabella and a sour frown.

He laughed harder when he was forced to duck inside his bathroom just before one of his fluffy pillows knocked him square in the face.

Yes, she had a *lot* to learn—but maybe he was just the man to teach her.

I sabella rolled out of bed and shuffled across the room to snatch one of Justin's shirts off his chair. She buttoned it up as she made her way into the kitchen to fix herself breakfast.

Sitting down at the breakfast bar to eat, she glanced out the window. Slivers of sunlight peeked through the curtains, and she noticed the snow had finally stopped. That was a good sign. If they were lucky they might actually be able to get out by the afternoon.

As much fun as she was having with Justin, she really needed to remember why she was still in Jacksonville. With Christmas season orders pouring in to Angelo's, the family bakery, her mother was in dire need of help. The snow had slowed things down a bit, but now that it was letting up, it was time to get to work.

She was just finishing her breakfast when Justin sauntered into the kitchen. For the briefest moment, a wave of tenderness washed over her, and she found herself hiding her smile behind the coffee cup at her lips. The sunlight danced off his tanned skin, highlighting every sinew of muscle in his bare chest.

"If you keep staring at me like that, I might think you like me."

She snorted as she bit back a grin. "I told you your eyesight was failing you. You really need to get that checked. With your advancing age these things become more important."

He frowned down at her, but she didn't miss the slight flash of laughter in his eyes. The morning after could always turn out strange, but she was happy to see there was no awkwardness between them. Their interaction was just as effortless—and, well, *contentious*—as it had always been.

"I glanced outside earlier. The sun is out, and the snow has stopped. Do you think we might be able to get out of here sometime today?"

He shrugged. "Depends on the plow and salt trucks. I can clear a path out of my driveway, but with all the snow that's fallen, the street I came in on off the highway is now blocked. If they don't get up here today, then we'll be stuck at least until tomorrow, but not much longer. They usually clear the streets closest to the highway first."

She sighed as she shoved a hand through her tousled hair. "I imagine Mom's neighborhood is in the same boat. I just hope we aren't stuck any later than tomorrow. With all the orders we have to fill for Christmas, we really can't afford to fall behind another day."

He took a sip of coffee. "Yeah, about that—I was surprised when you offered to stay and help."

"How could I not? Mom would be the only one working, and there's no way she can handle Angelo's all by herself."

He arched a single brow. He made her nervous when he took another sip of coffee but didn't say another word.

"What?" she snapped, unable to take the silence any longer.

He quirked his mouth into a half smile. "Don't you think maybe you should have hired someone?"

"For Angelo's? Why would we hire someone when I've offered to help out?"

His half smile turned into a full grin. "Because you can't cook worth shit."

She glowered at him. "I can cook."

His expression was incredulous, which really pissed her off. She *could* cook.

"What?" he asked, the challenge ringing clear in his voice.

She pursed her lips into a frown as she searched her brain. She really *could* cook. Not well, but certainly there was something she could call her specialty.

"Well, I can make eggs, and toast—oh—" She perked up. "And oatmeal."

He rolled his eyes. "My point exactly."

What was that supposed to mean? Those were dishes. "I may not be able to make a whole bunch of stuff, but I can handle a bakery. It's all about following recipes. Besides, I've done it before."

As soon as the words were out, she wanted to snatch them back. Damn it. Why had she brought that up? Justin didn't need any more ammunition.

"Yeah, I remember the last time you ran your family's bakery back in high school. Actually, I believe everyone in Jacksonville does, too." He started to laugh, and if he noticed her hard glare, he didn't let it stop him. "It was only two days, but you nearly burned the entire town down."

She cringed as the image of the fire she'd started flashed in her mind. Luckily the fire department had quickly put out the flames before they could cause any damage, but that was the last time she'd been left in the bakery alone. Let's hope she didn't have a repeat performance of one of her most humiliating moments.

"That was years ago, and I was just a kid. I'll have no trouble handling everything now."

She could tell he was doubtful by the expression on his face. Well, she would show him. She could run a bakery. After all, how hard could it be?

By late afternoon, Isabella realized that it was a lot harder than she'd thought. She was sprawled out on the floor of the bakery, covered in what was left of the five-pound bag of flour that must have knocked her out. What had possessed her to try to pull four five-pound bags of flour from the top shelf without a ladder—and all at once? Luckily the other three hadn't exploded across her forehead, or she probably would have had a concussion. With a low groan, she clutched her throbbing head and stumbled to her feet just as the doorbell to the bakery chimed.

"Dammit," she muttered. She *would* have a customer at a time like this. She ran her palms down the length of her body in a futile attempt to remove the white residue that clung to her designer jeans and cashmere sweater.

Much to her surprise, soon after she and Justin had finished breakfast the plow trucks had rolled through, clearing a path to the highway. Justin had dropped her off at her mother's home so she could change and head straight to the bakery.

Her mother had wanted to come in, but Isabella insisted she stay home and rest for one more day. Well, this was what she got for thinking she could run a bakery when she could barely manage to make a stack of pancakes. Allegedly she was a brilliant attorney, so why couldn't she seem to bake a damn apple pie?

"I need a drink." She stepped over a sack of flour and headed out of the storage room to greet her customer. Yes, a stiff martini would be nice; the only thing better would be a one-way ticket back to DC, where there were plenty of bakeries that made pastries she could *buy*.

"Hi, can I help y—" Her next words died in her throat as soon as she saw who stood on the other side of the counter. "What are you doing here?"

Justin ambled toward her with a smirk on his face. Damn it. She didn't need this right now. There was no way he was going to let this one go.

"I take it the flour won."

She glared at him. "We're closed. Go home."

He was delighting in her fall from grace—or better yet, her graceless fall.

"The sign outside says you're open for fifteen more minutes." His lips twitched, and she knew he was fighting back his urge to explode with laughter.

"Don't start with me, Justin. I've had a long day, and I'm tired."

His eyes softened. He smiled, and, despite her irritation, Isabella felt a small tingle of warmth spread through her belly as she met his gaze.

"All right. I'll leave you alone—for now."

"What are you doing here?" she asked again, with less bite in her voice this time.

"I just wanted to stop by to see how you were doing in here." He swept his gaze over her, and she knew a smart-ass retort was on the tip of his tongue. She braced herself, ready to fire back with one of her own, so she was surprised when he simply said, "And from the looks of it, not so good. Would you like some help?"

She appreciated his offer, especially since he was a far better cook than she was, but she'd had enough of pastries and pie fillings for the day.

"Thanks, but I was just about to close anyway. All I want to do is go home and get some sleep."

His eyebrow arched over those wicked green eyes of his, and she knew he was up to something.

"Are you sure about that?"

His voice was low and husky as he moved around the counter and walked toward her. He backed her against the long shelf and braced his hands on either side of her, effectively trapping her body with his.

She smiled up at him. "Now, did you come in here for a booty call?"

"Truthfully, I came in here to see how you were doing, but I have to tell you that you're turning me on. *White* is definitely your color."

Her eyes flashed. "Keep it up, smart-ass."

He slid a single finger across her cheek, collecting the tiny particles of floury residue on his fingertip.

"Next time you decide to cover yourself in something, let's try sugar instead." He ran that same finger across her mouth, and she had to restrain herself from visibly shivering when he slipped it between her lips.

Isabella sucked on it as she twirled her tongue around, forcing a sharp hiss from Justin's lips. He tugged his finger from her mouth and cupped her cheek with his hand, tipping her head back.

She closed her eyes just as his mouth brushed against hers, his tongue teasing the seam of her lips. She inhaled deeply, dragging in the spicy masculine scent of him until he filled her lungs. He traced the shape of her mouth with the tip of his tongue, and she opened wider, her mouth eager for the taste and feel of his tongue stroking hers.

She linked her arms behind his neck and settled into Justin's warm embrace, her body flush against his. He pressed her deeper into the counter, his hips gyrating slowly, his erection nudging her belly. Fresh urgency plowed through her as every pore and nerve strained to absorb his essence. An arrow of liquid heat shot straight to her pussy, the slick folds growing heavy and full with need.

She trembled in his arms, every inch of her tingling with a smoldering heat that was quickly growing out of control.

She tore her lips from his, their breathing uneven as they stared at each other.

"We can't," she said to the question in his eyes. "The door's not locked. Anyone walking by can easily see us."

He nodded as he slid away from her, taking the warmth of his body with him.

"So will I see you at my place later?"

"And what do you expect me to tell my mom?"

"I don't know." Justin shrugged. "Just tell her the truth."

She was incredulous. Did Justin hear himself? He acted as if he hadn't met her mother. It wasn't that she would disapprove—quite the opposite, and that's what she was afraid of. Maggie would be planning the wedding if she found out Isabella was spending her nights with Justin.

"No. My mom does not need to know what's going on. At least not now." Or ever.

His eyes flashed with mischief as the corner of his mouth lifted. "You could always sneak out."

She couldn't help but grin at his outrageous proposition. "Are you suggesting I sneak out of my mother's home at the wizened age of thirty-three as if I were a naughty schoolgirl fleeing in the night to meet her boyfriend?"

"Hey, this should be old hat for you. You used to do it all the time."

"Uh, don't remind me. I almost broke my leg twice jumping out of that window."

He drew her into his arms and leaned down, his mouth just inches from her ear as he whispered, "That's what bad girls get when they break all the rules."

Yeah, and she knew all about breaking rules.

She shuddered as his warm breath fanned across her skin. Damn it, she was already panting in anticipation of what Justin had in store for her tonight. Maybe he'd decided to accept her proposition—twelve wicked nights of exploring all their fantasies.

Maggie or not, she would find a way to make it to Justin's house.

"I just need to go home and grab my stuff. I'll meet you in an hour," she said, practically breathless.

She couldn't get out of that bakery fast enough.

Justin was almost done preparing dinner when a soft knock against his front door interrupted him. He opened the door, a smile spreading across his face as he swept his gaze over Isabella. Tiny snowflakes dotted her hair and clung to her long, sooty eyelashes.

"It's snowing again," she said by way of explanation as she slipped past him.

He glanced outside, frowning as he followed the swirling flurry of snowflakes until they settled onto the ground.

"Why didn't you call me? I could have picked you up." He didn't like the idea of her driving in a snowstorm, with that crap-ass, clearly unreliable car of hers.

"And chance the Italian inquisition? Uh-uh. Thankfully, Mom was asleep, so I didn't have to explain, but fate has a way of screwing with me. If you'd shown up, she would have been sitting right there in the living room, wide-awake."

"I still don't see the big deal," he said as he helped her out of her coat. "If she asks, just tell her the truth."

She rolled her eyes, leaving him standing there in the foyer as she marched across the living room toward the kitchen.

"You don't get it, Justin. I can't tell her we're just sleeping together. She'll be on your doorstep with a shotgun."

He stilled as an unfamiliar and unwelcome emotion surged through him. Just sleeping together? He glowered at her from across the room, but she was oblivious to the change in his mood as she rummaged through the pots and pans on his stove.

"Mmmm, something smells good," she said, carefully lifting the top off the simmering pot of spaghetti sauce.

"Yeah, help yourself," he muttered under his breath, although it really wasn't necessary, since she was already spooning the sauce onto a plate.

Her words continued to gnaw at him. Justin had no idea what they were doing, but he certainly would never characterize their situation as *just sleeping together*—even if that's what it was.

Isabella's flippant remark was a potent dose of reality. They were two very different people, who lived vastly different lives. Sure, they'd known each other forever, but when he left for South America in two weeks, whatever they were doing would have to come to an end. He didn't regret sleeping with Isabella, but this was why he'd never wanted to cross this line with her—his relationship with her was already complicated enough.

"Woo hoo, Justin. Where are you?"

He glanced up and nearly lost himself in her wide hazel eyes. His body began to stir, and he wondered how just moments ago he'd thought of Isabella as too much of a complication. Now that he'd had her, he couldn't seem to stop wanting her. And that's what scared him the most. "Huh?"

Her eyes narrowed. "Are you on drugs?"

"Izzie, I've never done drugs a day in my life."

"Yeah, well, just checking. The first sign of addiction is the loss of mental clarity."

He bit back a smile as he shook his head. No matter what happened between them, Isabella wasn't likely to ease up on the smart-ass digs.

"Thanks for your concern, but I'm perfectly lucid."

She snorted. "Right. You're perfectly lucid, if we don't count the little incident a few seconds ago when I asked if you were still coming over for Christmas and you stood there like a stoned scarecrow."

"Of course I'm still coming. I always go to your mother's when I'm home for the holidays."

She shrugged. "I was just checking," she said. Then she shoved another spoonful of sauce into her mouth, but he didn't miss the subtle flickering in her eyes. He was probably one of the few people in the world who could catch the tiny shift in her gaze and understand what it meant.

Studying her with narrowed eyes, Justin walked into the kitchen. Whether she realized it or not, she'd given voice to the small doubts that lingered inside him. He was almost relieved to know she wasn't as unaffected by the change in their relationship as she pretended to be.

"Why would you think I wouldn't come this time?" He spoke softly as he slid behind her, his body lightly touching hers.

She set down her spoon, her shoulders heaving when she released a tiny sigh and turned around.

"I just didn't want you to feel obligated or uncomfortable about being there."

His brow wrinkled. "Would *you* be uncomfortable with me being there?"

She shook her head. "No. I actually think I would feel uncomfortable if you *weren't* there," she said with a small smile.

He slipped his hand into her hair. "To tell you the truth, it would feel strange not being at your home for Christmas." Lonely, too. His brothers didn't come back to Jacksonville for the holidays anymore, so he'd just gotten used to going to Maggie's whenever he was home.

"Well, now that we know *where* you're spending Christmas day, I think we should talk about how you're spending Christmas night."

She was backing him toward his bedroom, her fingers lingering on each button as she took her time undoing his shirt.

"What would you like to discuss about Christmas night?" He was surprised his voice came out strong and masculine, rather than breathless and needy, which was exactly how he felt.

Both their shirts were off by the time they made it to the bedroom, and she was making quick work of his pants.

"I think my gift Christmas night should be a spanking. What do you think?"

"You seem to be obsessed with spankings."

Fire twinkled in her gaze as she slid his pants down his legs, and he helped her by stepping out of them and kicking them aside.

"I guess I always thought spankings were for *naughty* girls."

And Isabella was nothing if not naughty.

She shrugged out of her own pants, and they both stood there in just their undergarments. He allowed her to maintain control, and when she shoved against his chest, he fell back onto the bed, spread-eagled.

He grinned up at her. "Yes, spankings are for naughty girls like you, but I will decide when you deserve one."

She straddled his body, the warmth of her femininity pressing intimately against his chest.

"You're a control freak; you know that?"

He would have replied, but she lowered her head and pressed her lips to his. Her mouth was soft and teasing, her tongue probing gently against his lips until he finally opened to her. The taste of her was sweet and spicy, and he took control of the kiss, his mouth hungrily devouring hers.

She trailed the soft pads of her fingertips along his arms before settling on his wrists, grasping them in her hands and pulling his arms high above his head. He chuckled against her lips as he arched into her, thinking it was adorable how she was trying to exert her dominance over him, when they both knew that all he had to do was breathe if he wanted to break her grip.

He let her hold him imprisoned beneath her, and lost himself in the hot, wet cavern of her mouth. An explosion of pleasure and need bubbled over inside him as anticipation thickened the air in his lungs. The passion coursing through his veins overrode all sense of rational thought—this was the only explanation he could give for not noticing the cool press of metal against his wrists until it was too late.

She smiled as she sat back to admire her handiwork, pointedly ignoring the lewd curses that poured from Justin's lips. She was thoroughly impressed at how slyly she'd managed to handcuff Justin to his headboard.

"Get these handcuffs off me right now."

She slid back down his body, her hands lightly tracing patterns across his chest.

"You're sexy like that. All pent-up and angry."

Did he really just growl at her? She chuckled as she continued to run her hands all over him. The muscles in his arms strained against the cuffs as he clenched and unclenched his hands, but he didn't buck beneath her or try to toss her off. He remained completely still as the tiny glimmer of moonlight slipping past the curtains illuminated the hard muscles of his body.

His eyes never left hers, their smoky green now a fiery emerald as he fought to hold on to his temper. He may have been angry with her, but his body didn't seem to notice, especially when she rubbed against him and the large bulge inside his boxers grew harder.

"Let me guess. You've gotten me all tied up so you can spank me?"

She'd never thought of that. Definitely had some interesting possibilities, but that wasn't her goal at the moment.

"No. I've gotten you all tied up so *you* can spank *me*."

He shot her a quizzical look before glancing above his head at his restrained arms.

"That's going to be awfully hard to do in my current state."

"Not right now." She smiled. "Right now I'm going to have my wicked way with you." And to emphasize her point she scraped one nail across his nipple. He sucked in a sharp breath, dragging her attention to his face, where his eyes simmered with lust.

"But later, after I'm done having my wicked way with you, I want you to have your wicked way with me."

"So this is your way of bargaining, huh?" Justin said sarcastically. "You chain me to the bed, force me to agree to your 'terms,' and then later I fulfill the promise I made to you."

She grinned. "You were always a smart one."

Desire burned in his gaze, but she watched as he fought to temper it, pushing it behind the fury that leapt in his eyes.

"You don't know what you're asking, Isabella."

He seemed nervous and hesitant, which made her wonder if the things Justin did were a little dangerous. "Will I need to be hospitalized when we're done?"

His expression was horrified. "No. Why would you think something like that?"

"Well, you seem reluctant to do this, so I wondered if it was because you thought you would hurt me."

"I would never hurt you, Izzie."

His whispered words made her smile, and she didn't even mind that he'd called her by that ridiculous nickname.

"Then why are you being so resistant?"

His chest heaved as he sighed, and for just a moment he looked away. When his gaze returned to her, it was intense and brooding, and it made her nervous all over again.

"This won't work, Izzie, if you're not a true submissive—if you can't follow my commands."

She nibbled on her bottom lip, thinking that he had a good point there. She'd never been particularly good at taking orders.

"What if I promise to try?"

He sighed again, as if she was a lost cause—and maybe she was.

"This is for you, Izzie. This is what *you* want. You can promise to try, but if you can't submit to me when I command you to, it *won't* work."

She gave him an impish smile. "But we'll never know what I'm capable of if we don't try." She teased her finger across his bare chest, her voice low and seductive as she leaned into him. "You can't tell me that the thought of indulging in our deepest fantasies, exploring the exciting new places they take us, doesn't excite you, doesn't turn you on?" When he shuddered beneath her, she had her answer. Whether she could submit to him was really unimportant, and they both knew it. No matter what, they would have fun over these twelve nights, exploring each other's most intimate desires.

She winked at him. "Come on, Justin. We'll indulge in every carnal fantasy we can imagine."

He still hesitated, so she leaned closer, her lips poised just above his, and she delighted in the slight tremor that raced through his body at the nearness of her lips. His body's reaction only further confirmed her earlier assessment. While it would certainly be a thrill, Justin didn't need her to submit to him in order for him to enjoy exploring their most forbidden desires together. "So, do we have a deal?"

He frowned. She knew he didn't want to agree to this, but what choice did he have? He was still all tied up with no place to go.

"I'm going to make you pay for this later."

She grinned. "You better."

Chapter Six

Isabella pressed her lips against his. The taste of her mouth was silky and warm. She was in control, but she allowed him to lead the kiss, and he arched into her, plunging deeper inside with his tongue until their mouths were seemingly fused together.

Justin groaned when she broke the kiss and slid down the length of his body. Her movements were sensual, her lush figure soft against him. Her eyes twinkled as she clasped his boxers in her hand and slowly peeled them from his body.

She tossed them aside and crawled between his legs. Her gaze was fixed on him, her luminous eyes heavy with desire as she licked her puffy pink lips with that wicked little tongue of hers.

He groaned low in his throat, his cock growing harder as the evidence of his arousal seeped from the tiny slit at the tip. He held his breath as she held his gaze, her soft hands stroking through the hair on his thighs, inching their way closer and closer to the center of his body.

When Isabella slid one hand through the nest of dark curls surrounding his cock, he rasped out her name. She cupped the heavy sac between his legs, but did not bring her hand anywhere near his hard shaft.

She massaged him gently, rotating his flesh in her palm. He arched off the bed, pressing deeper into her hand until he couldn't stand it anymore.

"Isabella. Touch me." His voice was broken and hoarse, and she giggled in response, but she rewarded his plea by curling her slender fingers around his thick length and pumping gently.

It was like velvet sliding across his sensitive skin, and he closed his eyes, savoring her silky touch. She gripped him tighter, her strokes quickening, and he released a strangled moan as tremors began to rock his body. Liquid heat swirled in his gut, sending bolts of pleasure sizzling across his skin. He wanted—no, *needed*—her lips on him: that hot, wet, bow-shaped mouth of hers that looked as if it had been made to accept his kiss, his cock.

His eyes flew open, the erotic images behind his lids too intense. He didn't want to come just yet, but she was working his body into a frenzy with her hand, and he didn't think he would be able to stop the rush of pleasure that was already surging through him.

She seemed to sense the urgency that roared through his blood, and he had to fight not to explode when she swiped her tongue across the broad head of his dick, licking up a tiny droplet of precum. Air whooshed from his lungs as she swirled it around his entire length, all the way to the base, before she settled her puckered mouth on him and slowly sank down.

She jerked his length with one hand while the other massaged his balls as she worked the warm cave of her mouth up and down his shaft. He was bursting with sensations, and he desperately wanted to rip his hands from the cuffs to tangle them in the silky black strands of her hair.

He found himself balling his hands into fists, his blunt nails digging into the flesh of his palms until he was sure he would draw blood. She moaned against his cock, sending tiny vibrations skating all over his body. He panted beneath her, every inch of him on fire. He was mesmerized by the sight of her as she sucked him, her head bobbing vigorously. Her eyes were closed, her face twisted in pleasure as she moaned around his flesh.

She released him to snake one hand inside her panties, settling it between her legs to finger her pussy. She was the most beautiful sight he'd ever seen, her entire body pulsing with desire as she pleasured him.

The sac between his legs drew tight to his body, and blood pounded louder in his ears. He was close, but as wonderful as her mouth was, he wanted to be inside her when he found release.

"Ride me."

A strangled moan bubbled from her lips, as if she'd been waiting for him to give her permission to do just that. For a moment he wondered about that. He knew instinctively Isabella wasn't any more submissive than he was, but he hadn't protested her dominance over him, and just now she'd waited for his command. He'd never considered submitting to a woman, and he knew Isabella would not play the role of an obedient submissive when the time came. They were both dominant by nature in every way, which had him curious about the possibilities their arrangement would offer. What would it be like to wrestle with Isabella for control in the bedroom? The mystery of that question excited him, and now that he'd finally given in and agreed to her little game, he was more than eager to find out.

The rustle of clothing drew his attention back to Isabella, who had quickly cast aside her bra and panties. Her body was poised just above his aching cock as she straddled him. She braced her palms flat against his chest and arched back, her gaze locked with his. He wanted to grab her hips and thrust himself into her, but since he couldn't, he just lay there, completely still, not moving a single muscle, not even to lift his hips off the bed.

He didn't have to wait long as she slowly lowered herself onto him, the warm, wet tunnel of her pussy enveloping him in its tight grip. They both cried out in unison as she seated herself fully on him before rocking off his body to take him inside her again.

Over and over, she impaled herself on his shaft, her heavy breasts bouncing before him, her coral nipples like ripe berries. He couldn't watch her, not when she cupped her breasts and began to stroke her delicate fingers across those perfect, pink nipples. He shut his eyes, savoring the heat of her pussy as it coated his dick with the evidence of her arousal.

She moved faster and harder, and the bed creaked loudly in time to the rhythm of her hips. Sweat dotted his flesh. The scent of their salty skin combined with the heavy musk of sex permeated every inch of the room.

She called his name, and his eyes flew open just as she threw her head back and arched toward the sky. Her dark hair caught a glimmer of the silver moonlight, and a crimson flush spread across her entire body as she let out a long, tortured moan, her sheath drenching him with her sticky warmth.

He was powerless to stop his own climax as her pussy clamped tightly around him. A loud roar rumbled from inside him, splintering against the walls as semen rushed from his cock and he spurted his milky warmth into her.

Neither of them moved for a long while, their breathing labored, but his arms began to ache, and when his lids grew heavy he stirred. He didn't want to fall asleep still cuffed to the bed.

"Izzie."

"Hmmm."

The side of her face was nestled against his shoulder, and he turned to kiss the top of her head with a smile.

"I need you to unlock me."

"Oh." She yawned as she slowly slid off him, her eyes still bleary with the first brush of sleep.

She threw on one of his shirts, and he watched her search the floor for the tiny key. He wasn't worried at first, but when she abandoned the floor for his nightstand, and then the bed, he frowned.

"Please tell me you know where the key is."

She marched across the room and flipped on the switch, forcing him to blink a few times as the harsh light stung his eyes.

"Um, I did."

What the fuck! "What do you mean *you did*?"

If she noticed the gravel in his voice, she ignored it as she tossed pillows and clothing across the room, her search growing more frantic.

"I swore I left the key right under your bed where I found the handcuffs."

Great. Just great.

"Go into my closet and look on the floor. There is a black case with another set of cuffs in there along with a key. Let's try that."

She found the case and tried the other key, followed by a nail file, a screwdriver, and even a kitchen fork. But nothing worked, and he refused to let her near the saw in his shed.

She'd been in the middle of trying to pop the lock with the sharp end of a pair of scissors when Justin finally conceded the inevitable.

"I think we're going to have to call Caleb."

Her head popped up. "At this hour? What are we going to tell him?"

They wouldn't have to tell him a damn thing. As soon as his best friend walked in, he was going to know what the hell they'd been up to.

"Yes, at this hour. I'm not going to spend the night with my hands cuffed to the bed."

She seemed to consider his words for a moment before she nodded. He was relieved that she at least agreed it was just a tiny bit cruel and inhumane to leave him chained to the bed all night, because if she hadn't, it wasn't like he could get up and dial Caleb himself.

"Do you think Caleb will be able to get these things off?"

He had no idea, but Caleb was the sheriff, and he knew a thing or two about handcuffs. Justin just hoped Caleb could figure out how to jimmy these cuffs, but even if he couldn't, Justin trusted his old friend with the job of sawing them off. He didn't have the same faith in Isabella, who would probably maim him in the process.

"I don't know, but he's the only one I trust right now to see me like this.

If he doesn't get them off, then we'll have to call Bill." He cringed at the thought of old Bill Wiley, the town locksmith, coming into his bedroom— leering at Isabella with his beady eyes and rotten yellow teeth while he made lewd and raunchy comments the entire time.

Isabella shuddered. "Eck, Bill gives me the creeps. I'll go call Caleb *right now.*"

Thirty minutes later, the doorbell rang just before Caleb let himself in with his key. Justin hadn't warned Isabella that Caleb had a key, so she was glad she hadn't waited until the last minute to clothe them both. If he'd walked in on them naked, it would have only made the situation more awkward.

"Hey, Isabella," Caleb drawled in his faint Southern accent. He strolled into the bedroom and kissed her gently on the cheek, and she smiled up at the handsome man, whose tousled blond hair told her he'd been fast asleep when she'd called. She hadn't seen Caleb in a couple of years, but she'd heard from Justin that he'd moved back to town a few months ago. They'd all been friends since they were kids, although Caleb and Justin remained close even after Caleb's parents moved from Jacksonville when Caleb graduated from high school.

"Thanks for coming. I didn't want to wake you, but Justin insisted."

He turned his attention to the bed, a crooked grin spreading across his face. "Well, I can see why.

"Hey, buddy. Got yourself in a bit of a bind?"

Justin glowered at Caleb as he sauntered toward the bed. "No jokes, Caleb. I'm serious."

Caleb shrugged his large shoulders, the corded muscles in his back shifting beneath his shirt. He heeded Justin's warning and didn't crack another joke, although the grin remained plastered across his face.

Caleb brandished a key from his pocket as he bent over the bed.

"Sooo, I didn't know you two were *close*."

Isabella hadn't been expecting that statement, so she wasn't prepared for it when it came. She stood there speechless, helplessly meeting Justin's gaze. She had no clue how to explain what was going on between them exactly, especially when she didn't quite know herself. And when Justin spoke up, she let out an inward sigh, relieved that she didn't have to.

"It's a recent development."

Caleb arched a single brow as he twisted the key in the tiny lock.

"Interesting."

That single word conveyed nothing to her. She didn't know whether he was upset or pleased by these recent developments. In the same way that Justin and Celeste had trouble "sharing" her, she'd always felt as if she had to battle Caleb for her own place in Justin's life. They'd both been boys of the same age who shared similar interests. Even though she'd long since moved past her feelings of jealousy, she'd always felt left out while they were growing up, an outsider whenever Caleb was around. She wondered how Caleb was feeling now. Did he imagine himself as an outsider, intruding upon this intimate relationship she and Justin now shared? Well, whatever he was feeling, he didn't let it show.

He easily released Justin from the handcuffs and unhooked them from around the headboard of the bed.

Justin sat up, rubbing his hands across his wrists.

"Thanks, man. I really appreciate your coming out here so late." He glared at her then. "I owe you big-time for Isabella's little prank."

Caleb chuckled, his voice rich and hearty, but she didn't find any humor in Justin's words, not when his green eyes promised retribution later. "Don't mention it."

Caleb pressed a tiny key into Justin's hand before shuffling toward the bedroom door.

"That's a spare key. It can pretty much unlock any set of cuffs. Keep it for as long as you need it," he quipped with a tiny grin and a wink.

He disappeared out of the room, and moments later Justin and Isabella heard the front door bang shut.

Now that Justin was free, Isabella realized she was all alone with him and his fury, but he didn't seem to pay her the slightest notice. He ignored her as he bustled into the bathroom before returning to the bedroom to pull back the covers on the bed.

"Are you still mad?"

He slipped into bed. "Very, but I'm more exhausted than angry right now." His eyes were gentle as he stared up at her. "Come to bed, Isabella. I'm not going to bite." His eyes flashed with fire. "At least not yet."

She clicked off the light and then slipped into bed beside him, nestling her body against his. She sighed when he wrapped his arms around her, holding her closer as he gently nuzzled her neck.

"I really am sorry, Justin."

"I know you are, which is why you won't say a word when I punish you."

She didn't know about that, but she did know that whatever punishment he decided to mete out, she certainly deserved it for her embarrassing blunder.

Whatever Isabella was dreaming about, it was certainly very pleasant for her. Every so often she sighed, and a smile would spread across her face.

Justin had to admit he was a bit curious about her dream, but more than that, he was thankful it held her so enthralled that he could do everything he needed to do without waking her. He glanced around the room at the flickering candles. He was pretty much done. All he needed to do now was tie her up. He tugged on the taut leather in his hand as he walked toward the bed. With careful movements, he grasped her wrists, wrapped the leather ropes around them, and secured them to the headboard. It was exactly what Isabella had done to him—minus the cuffs, of course.

He stared at her for several minutes, trying to decide if he should wake her or just wait for her to come to on her own. As if she'd heard his thoughts, her lids began to flutter open. She still wore a sleepy smile, but not for long.

He knew the moment she realized that she was bound because her eyes darkened to chocolate pools and her gaze darted nervously around the room. She couldn't see him; his entire body was draped in the dark shadows of the room. He figured that was one of the reasons why she began to struggle against the ropes.

"Relax, Isabella. Before you hurt yourself."

She stilled, her head twisting back and forth, searching for him.

"Justin?"

He waited for just a moment before stepping into the glow of the burning candles.

Her eyes widened, desire igniting her dark gaze. His body hardened instantly, but she didn't seem to notice, as her attention was drawn to the object in his hand.

"I would never hurt you, Isabella," he assured her as he glimpsed the disquiet in her eyes. But it was obvious she didn't quite believe him when she smiled nervously.

"Um, yeah. So—the whip? That's just for show, then?"

He grinned at her innocence. He would tell her later that what he had in his hand was a flogger, and he never used a whip, but he did prefer a crop to a flogger when he was going to strike her backside.

"Not quite." He moved closer to her, absently toying with the flogger in his hands. "Remember, you asked for this, Isabella. You asked—no, demanded—that I share the darker side of my nature with you." She gulped, and he figured that, by the way she was staring at the braided leather in his hand, she was probably regretting her earlier enthusiasm.

"You know I must punish you for that stunt with the handcuffs earlier," he said quietly, the hushed tone of his voice drawing her gaze back to his face. And once he had her full attention, he flicked the braided leather across her rosy breasts, to prove his point that indeed he planned to punish her.

She yelped, the tiny red slash bursting across her smooth creamy flesh. He watched her, gauging her reaction, carefully assessing her tolerance for pain.

The strike had been light, meant to arouse both pleasure and pain. He knew he had succeeded in doing both when moisture glistened on the dark thatch of curls between her spread legs.

He struck her again, the black leather whipping across her breasts. He did it over and over until she was writhing and panting against the bed, her slit dripping with her juices.

She was breathtaking, her head thrown back against her shoulders, her eyes closed. He knew she wasn't quite aware of all the sensations flooding her body. The pain burned across her sensitive skin, but he could tell from the expression on her face that her body also hummed with pleasure—she couldn't stop herself from wanting more. Learning to move past the natural inclination to separate pleasure from pain was usually difficult for first-time submissives, but Isabella eagerly accepted everything he gave her.

Maybe she would prove him wrong after all.

"Do you want me to stop?"

She lifted her head. Her eyes were drunk with lust, and sweat plastered her hair against her forehead.

"No."

Her voice was hoarse and dry, and he heard the desperation just beneath the surface.

"You are on the edge of climax, but you can't find release, can you?"

Her eyes widened as if she couldn't believe he'd read her mind. But in order to ignite lust, even as he wielded pain, he had to be able to anticipate her needs, her desires, even her fears so he could give her pleasure.

He struck her with the flogger again, but this time the leather did not touch her breasts. She cried out as it whipped across her clit, and more juice trickled from her sheath.

"Justin, please."

Her voice rasped with need, and he knew she now begged him to give her release, to end her torment.

"You will not come," he commanded as he tossed the flogger aside and stalked toward the bed. She whimpered low in her throat as she jerked against the bindings, but she did not voice her protests.

He rewarded her obedience by sliding between her legs. He gripped her thighs roughly, and settled them over his shoulders.

His face was poised at her entrance, and with every breath he took he filled his lungs with the scent of her arousal.

"You will not come, Isabella, until I say so. Do you understand me?"

She nodded.

He grinned up at her. Yes, Isabella was certainly proving him wrong in so many ways, he thought as he lowered his head and swiped his tongue through her folds.

She cried out, her body jerking against him, but he held her still and devoured her. He sucked on her hardened clit for a long time before plunging his tongue inside. Over and over he alternated between tongue-fucking her and sucking her with his mouth until her juices dribbled over his chin.

She was close, barely hanging on to the edge, and she clamped her thighs around his head, desperately trying to stave off her climax as her legs trembled.

"You will not come," he warned.

"I—I can't—"

"You will not come." He repeated against her mound, but the words were barely out before she was exploding all around him. He didn't even touch her. He didn't have to; she'd already tumbled over the precipice.

Tears leaked from her eyes, and she continued to erupt, her body breaking apart as convulsions shook her. He'd held back his own climax, but as he watched her he felt that familiar tingling gather at the base of his spine.

He jerked on his cock, pumping wildly, his fist tightening around his shaft. It took only a few seconds for him to erupt, and he came violently, pouring his seed onto the bed sheets with a heavy grunt.

He fell across the bed, his arm draped over the middle of her body as he nestled beside her. He would untie her before he fell asleep, but for just these brief moments he wanted to keep her like this, naked and at his mercy.

He leaned into her, his mouth barely inches from her ear.

"You came without my permission. That means I'll have to punish you again."

She turned her head, her eyes dancing with mischief, a naughty smile on her face.

"You better."

Chapter Seven

Celeste Hamilton slowed down her two-door, fire-engine red Mercedes as she neared Jacksonville. The closer she got to the small town, the heavier the snow became. She was almost there, no more than twenty minutes out, but with the falling snow, she probably wouldn't reach Isabella's home for another forty-five minutes.

She considered calling to let Isabella know she was coming, but decided to just surprise her. She'd talked to Isabella every day since her engagement had been called off, and aside from the day they'd talked about the breakup, Isabella hadn't mentioned Harry even once. Not that Celeste could blame her. The simpering fool really wasn't worth mentioning. Still, it had been less than a week since she'd broken up with him. Isabella should have been sort of heartbroken, or at the least she should have mentioned that she missed the wimp just a little bit, but she hadn't. It was just odd that Isabella hadn't so much as whispered Harry's name, and even odder that her friend kept telling her she had a juicy secret to tell her, but refused to spill it over the phone.

They'd known each other for more than fifteen years, and they'd *never* kept secrets. Besides, Maggie and Isabella were the only real family she had anyway, and ever since she'd known Isabella, they'd never spent a

Christmas apart. Isabella also kept complaining about how they needed more help at the bakery. Celeste was a *far* better cook than Isabella, and what were a few days off work when her best friend could use her help? Besides, what else would she do anyway? She was bored out of her mind back in DC without Isabella.

Celeste gunned the engine. She was just too damned impatient to get there, which explained why she didn't see the black ice until it was too late.

She kept the wheel steady as she took her feet off the gas and didn't touch the brake. Her car jerked a little, swerving off to the right. She steered it left, being careful not to overdo it.

As the car moved past the sheet of ice and began to slow, she let out a small sigh of relief. When she was sure there wasn't another patch in front of her, she pressed down on the gas again.

She'd been so focused on the ground right in front of her car that she didn't realize two things—she was still riding halfway on the shoulder, and there was a car parked not more than ten feet in front of her.

Caleb Hirsch released a string of curses when the tiny red sports car clipped him in the back—and then kept going.

He flipped on his siren and followed after it. When the car didn't immediately stop, he started to call for backup, but just as he pressed down on the button to his radio, the car slowed and pulled off onto the shoulder.

He called in the plates and a description of the vehicle before piling out of his squad car. He noticed the car was registered in DC, and wondered for just a second if this was one of Isabella's friends. Maybe even her fiancé—no, after what he'd seen the other night, make that *ex-fiancé*.

He sidled up next to the car, his hand on his sidearm. He couldn't be too careful. The driver had already tried to flee the scene. He was either running from the law, or drunk, or both.

He relaxed when he got to the window. *He* was a woman—a very pretty woman, from what he could tell—and she was pissed as hell to see him. He tapped on the window, and she rolled it down, her almond-shaped golden eyes meeting his gaze.

"Good evening, ma'am. Do you know that you just hit my car?"

She glanced over her shoulder, a grin curling her full, pouty lips.

"You call that hunk of metal a car?" She slid her gaze over the inside of her vehicle, her French manicured nails running along the smooth leather. "That is not a car, Officer. Now, this—*this* is a car."

Great. Just what he needed. A snobbish city girl who came with jokes.

"Your license, registration, and insurance please."

She rummaged through her purse and wallet until her hands closed around two cards.

He frowned when he saw what she'd handed him. "You're missing your insurance."

She shrugged, her rose-stained lips furling into a smile. "I don't have insurance."

He didn't need this. Christmas was just days away. He didn't have the energy to do any last-minute paperwork, but if this woman—he glanced at her license—if *Celeste* didn't have any insurance he was going to wind up buried beneath a mountain of paperwork in order to process her.

"Ma'am, do you know it's against the law to drive around without insurance?"

"Well, since I'm a lawyer I should, but I've just been so busy that I didn't have the time to renew it. I've never seen the need. Besides, I barely drive this car in the city."

He sighed. She didn't seem the least bit perturbed or upset that she was about to go to jail. In the back of his mind he wondered whether this was Isabella's best friend, the same Celeste whom Justin mentioned every now and then.

"Ma'am, please step out of the car."

Her long shapely legs, the color of rich sienna and as smooth as silk, were the first things he saw as she slipped out of the car, wearing a white sweaterdress that clung to every seductive curve of her figure. She flicked her hair over her shoulder, the auburn-streaked mane collecting tiny snow-flakes in its lustrous waves. Justin had never mentioned to him that Celeste was a beauty—but then, why would he? Until a year ago, Caleb had been "happily" married.

He brandished his cuffs and slapped them on her wrists as he read her her rights.

She grinned up at him, those dark gold eyes twinkling with laughter.

"Why didn't you put my arms behind my back?"

He didn't know what compelled him to do it, but he found his eyes stray-ing to her full breasts, and imagined them thrusting forward, her back arched as the metal cuffs imprisoned her arms behind her. He shook his head. What was it about Isabella and her friends—and this obsession with handcuffs?

He seized her by the arm and ushered her toward his car.

"Since you didn't exhibit any violence, I saw no reason to restrain you that way."

The corner of her mouth quirked into a small grin. "I usually reserve that type of aggression for the bedroom."

He bet she did. He shook his head at her shameless flirting and settled her into the backseat.

He returned to her car, grabbed her purse and keys, and locked it up. As soon as he got back to the station, he would make a call to have her car towed there. And right after he made that call, he would phone Isabella and tell her to get down to the station as soon as possible and bail her law-breaking friend out of his jail.

————

sabella's mother's eyes never left her as she bustled around Angelo's, working to catch up on orders as best she could.

She pretended not to see those hazel eyes, identical to her own, following her, and she dared not ask her mother why she was looking at her so strangely. That would only open up the floodgates.

Isabella had arrived home earlier that morning to shower and change, but her mother knew she hadn't spent the night. In fact, she was almost positive her mom knew exactly where she had slept. She didn't know how, but she suspected it was just mother's intuition. The silence was unnerving, and she wondered if that was what her mother was trying to do—wear her down until she crumbled and admitted all her dirty little secrets. Not likely. Maggie could stare at her and play the silent treatment all day long, but she would never crack under the pressure. Thankfully, she didn't have to—the doorbell chimed, and a guest sauntered in.

She smiled at the handsome middle-aged man as he walked toward the counter. Dr. Reginald Reynolds. He'd moved to Jacksonville two years ago after their old resident physician decided to relocate his practice out West. Where the weather was a bit warmer, he'd said.

She liked the doctor—or at least she had until she realized that his eyes had not once made it over to her. Instead they were glued to her mother, who was . . . *blushing*? She furrowed her brow into a deep frown, deciding her mom had some explaining to do.

"Good afternoon, Dr. Reynolds. Can I help you?"

He seemed bewildered as he glanced over at Isabella, and she realized that he hadn't even noticed she was standing there. Isabella glanced at her mother, her expression making it very clear that as soon as they were alone they were going to have a little talk. Maggie looked away, which only infuriated her more. How dare she meddle in her life all the time, with obvious interest in what was going on between her and Justin, when it was clear she had her own secrets to tell.

"Hello, Isabella. Good to see you today."

Yeah, she bet. The only person he'd come to see was Maggie.

"Good to see you, too. What can I help you with?"

"Well, I wanted to stop by to place an order for the New Year's Eve Festival."

She nodded as she jotted down the order. Every year Jacksonville held the annual Christmas tree celebration in the center of town and the New Year's Eve Festival at the high school It was a nice time for the entire town to come together and celebrate the passing of another year.

She was calculating the amount for his deposit when the store phone rang.

"I'll get it," Maggie said as she shuffled to the back of the shop to answer the phone. Isabella was just handing Dr. Reynolds his receipt when her mother returned, her face ashen and drawn.

"What is it, Mama?" Isabella asked, concern in her voice.

"That was Caleb on the phone. He called to tell you that Celeste is in jail."

Caleb Hirsch was not Celeste's type. She liked her men charming and flirtatious, with liquid brown eyes and silky black dreads. They were usually artists with lithe bodies, and impeccably dressed as if they lived and breathed *GQ*.

Caleb was none of those things. He was a mountain of a man, tall and stocky, as if he'd played on the offensive line of his college football team. Since he was now off duty, he'd changed into a pair of well-worn jeans and a gray Marines sweater.

There was also the little issue with him being white. Now, it didn't bother her that he was white—she'd dated white guys before. It was just that he was *really* white. He could have just stepped off a boat from Viking land, or something.

A giggle tore past her lips as she tried to fight the urge to call him *Thor*. But when he turned those piercing sapphire eyes on her, she stopped. A tiny shiver raced down her spine, and her body trembled. He must have noticed the slight movement, because he stood and reached for his coat.

"You're probably cold. I completely forgot about your coat when I locked up your car. I'm sorry." He handed her his coat through the metal bars, and she was forced to bite back a gasp when their fingers touched and a small bolt of heat shot through her body. She wasn't cold, certainly not anymore, but that didn't stop her nipples from tightening against her dress.

He'd noticed, too—both the tiny sliver of heat that shocked them, and her pebbled tips. He tried to play it smooth, clearing his throat and shuffling away from the bars, but he wasn't quite fast enough, and Celeste caught a brief glimpse of the large bulge behind the zipper of his jeans.

Now *that* was interesting. She hadn't come to Jacksonville looking for a quick tumble in the sheets, but she couldn't deny that he intrigued her. He was a quiet, brooding man, and she imagined he was hiding a wealth of mysterious secrets in the deep pools of his cobalt eyes. He wasn't her type, and she got the sense that if she tangled with him, he'd be some work. But *damn*—he'd awoken something deep inside her, and she was having a hell of a time ignoring it.

sabella cursed her unreliable Aston Martin and the mechanics who swore they'd "fixed" it as she rolled up to the sheriff's office in Justin's SUV. She'd been forced to ask him to take her down to the station when her car hadn't started—again. She could have taken her mom's car, but with the bakery closing in a half hour, she didn't want her mom to be stranded there waiting for her to return. After all, busting Celeste out of jail could take a while.

Justin had barely put his SUV into park before Isabella was jumping out. What the hell was Celeste doing in Jacksonville? But the better question was, what had Celeste done this time?

She pushed open the door to the sheriff's office and glanced up at Justin, who thankfully hadn't said a word on the drive over. She hoped Celeste and Justin didn't wind up in a bickering match, but she knew that was akin to wishing for pigs to fly and hell to freeze over, all in the same day.

The Jacksonville sheriff's office was nothing more than a two-room building. As soon as you walked in, you were met by a low counter, where the secretary sat. Off to the side of the counter was a swinging door that came to your hip, which led to the back of the building, where the sheriff's official office was located, along with the jail. Glancing over the swinging wooden door, Isabella could see straight into the jail, and she smiled when her gaze landed on Celeste.

Lucy, the secretary, was gone for the day, along with the two deputies, so she pushed past the door and walked toward the jail, with Justin at her heels.

"Celeste," Isabella cried. "What on earth are you doing here?"

She shrugged. "How I ended up in Jacksonville is an easy one—I came to visit you. Now, why I'm in jail—" She slid her gaze to Caleb. "You'll have to ask RoboCop here."

Isabella glanced at him. "Seriously, Caleb. Did you have to lock her up?"

"See—that's what I told him, too," she shouted, with her hands curled around the bars. "I think it's racial profiling."

Caleb looked as if steam would pour from his ears at any second. "Are you kidding me? You hit my car, then tried to drive off, and you don't have a lick of insurance."

Isabella turned toward her friend. "Celeste?"

She shrugged. "I plead the fifth."

"Ohmigod. I say just leave her in there," Justin quipped. "She's broken more laws than Nixon."

Isabella shot Justin a hard look from over her shoulder before turning her attention back to Caleb.

"What if we post her bail tonight and agree to pay for any damage to your car? Will you agree not to press charges?"

"She has to renew her car insurance, too."

"You're insane," Celeste sputtered. "Do you know how long that will take? I don't have time to do all that. Besides, I hardly drive my car in the city anyway."

"When you talk like that, it makes me think you shouldn't be driving a car at all, since it's obvious you're not only a terrible driver and dangerously reckless, but irresponsible, too. It's a wonder you even still have a license," Caleb shot back.

Celeste stared at Caleb as if he'd grown a second head. Hell, Isabella was shocked, too. Besides Justin, there was no man Celeste couldn't charm, and over the years, Celeste had even managed to find one or two ways to wrap Justin around her fingers. Caleb, on the other hand, had just met her. He should have fallen under her spell by now, but the fact that she was in jail already spoke volumes. And to add to that, he'd just done something Isabella had never seen a man do with Celeste before. He'd stood up to her, and she could tell by the fire in Celeste's eyes that she wasn't taking it so well.

"I can't believe I'm being insulted by some inbred country bumpkin." She tugged on the bars. "Get me out of here, Isabella."

Isabella guessed that now wasn't the time to tell Celeste that Caleb was a certified public accountant and wasn't the dimwitted "bumpkin" she made him out to be.

"You know what? I've changed my mind. She stays in jail," Caleb said flatly.

"What?" Isabella and Celeste shouted in unison while Justin roared with laughter behind Isabella.

"Ms. Hamilton could have seriously hurt someone. If she'd been in her *beloved* DC, she would have been charged with a felony hit and run, at the least." Caleb faced Celeste. "I think you need to spend a few nights in jail mulling over what you did."

Isabella could tell that Celeste was too enraged to speak as she spun away from the bars and kicked the wall with her high-heeled shoe.

"Caleb, please. It's almost Christmas," Isabella pleaded.

He glanced at Celeste. "If she behaves, then I'll let her out tomorrow."

Isabella opened her mouth to make one last-ditch plea for her best friend, but Justin's hand on her shoulder halted her words.

"Don't feel any pressure to let her out early on our behalf. After all, you're doing her a favor. She belongs in a pound."

Celeste glared at him. "What are you doing here? And why are you even talking? Shouldn't you be out saving hoes or something?"

The corner of Justin's mouth lifted. "Too late. Caleb got to you first."

Celeste's eyes flashed. "When I get out of here I'm going to—"

"Yeah, but you have to actually get out of jail first, and it doesn't look like you're going anywhere anytime soon, *Gotti*."

Celeste's gaze snapped to Isabella. "Next time leave this loser at home, would you?"

Justin's response was another round of laughter as he turned toward the front door.

"I'll meet you in the SUV, Izzie. Have a comfy night behind bars, Cruella."

Isabella sighed. Did Justin really have to antagonize her best friend? It was bad enough she was locked up for the night. "Do you want me to bring you anything? Some clothes, a blanket? Food?"

"I'll send one of my deputies to the store to get whatever she needs. She'll be fine, Isabella," Caleb said softly from behind her.

Yeah, physically, but when Celeste finally got out of there, Caleb was going to be at the top of her shit list. Even Justin didn't rank that high on the worst of days. Isabella almost felt sorry for him—almost. After all, he'd locked up her best friend.

She hugged Celeste through the bars.

"I'll stop in tomorrow after I finish up at the bakery. Hopefully, he'll have let you out by then."

Celeste smiled as she glanced sideways at Caleb. "Don't worry about me. I can handle country bumpkin."

"Keep it up, Ms. Hamilton, and you'll be in here until New Year's."

Celeste glared at him, but she clamped her mouth shut and didn't say another word. Isabella was relieved. She had no doubt Caleb would keep Celeste in there until New Year's if he wanted to, and nothing any of them could do would stop him. She just hoped Celeste would remain on her best behavior for as long as it took him to release her, because if she didn't, she would wind up spending her Christmas behind bars, locked in a tiny cell.

Definitely not Isabella's idea of a happy holiday.

Chapter Eight

"I'll talk to Caleb tomorrow."

Isabella's eyes brightened as she lifted her head from Justin's bare chest to meet his gaze.

"Thank you, Justin. That would help. Just as I was leaving she threatened him. I think he added another night."

He groaned. Of course Celeste threatened Caleb, and of course he added another night. They were like two bulls locked in a cage. Leaving Caleb and Celeste alone was like putting dynamite next to an open fire; it was only a matter of time before everything around it went up in flames. He just hoped the sheriff's office was still standing tomorrow morning.

"I doubt Caleb will keep Celeste for another night. Hell, I'd be surprised if he makes it through this one. As soon as she starts probing him with her incessant questions, he won't be able to get her out of there fast enough."

She sighed, her warm breath tickling the smattering of hair across his chest. "I hope you're right."

He peered down at her, his hands absently roaming over her bare skin. As soon as they arrived at his home, they'd wasted no time tearing off their clothes and sliding between the sheets, where they'd been ever since. He'd thought the situation with Celeste had left Isabella a bit on edge, so he'd set out to distract her. They'd made love for more than an hour. He'd even indulged her by allowing her to restrain him once again, although this time they used one of his ties and *not* the cuffs. She should have been satiated and relaxed, but her muscles were still knotted with tension, and he had a feeling her worries had less to do with Celeste.

"You want to talk about it?"

She lifted her head from his chest, her hair tickling his skin. "Talk about what?"

He slid a single finger across her cheek as he met her wide-eyed gaze. She seemed surprised by his intuitiveness, but he didn't know why that would shock her. He knew her better than most.

"You've been tense and distracted ever since I picked you up from the bakery. I thought it was Celeste, but I'm starting to suspect that this has nothing to do with her."

He knew he was right when her gaze strayed from his face and she chewed on her bottom lip with her teeth.

"Talk to me, Izzie."

She blew out a long breath, her eyes finding his once again.

"Did you know my mother was seeing Dr. Reynolds?"

He stilled. Damn, he hadn't been expecting that. She pinned him with her steady gaze, and he felt as if he were under a microscope.

"Not really. I've seen them together a few times, but I didn't think they were dating. I thought they were pretty much just friends. Does the thought of them dating bother you?"

She shrugged. "I'm not sure. On one hand, I want my mother to be happy, but on the other, I feel somewhat betrayed that she wouldn't talk to me about something like this."

"Maybe she didn't think you would care."

Isabella shook her head, her expression saying she didn't buy that.

"She had to have known I would have some type of reaction to the news."

He tightened his arms around her as her eyes clouded.

"Maybe she didn't think it was any of your business." He tried to soften the weight of his words by tempering his voice, but he knew it didn't work as well as he'd hoped.

"I know you're trying to play devil's advocate, but I can't really see her side to this. She knows how close I was to Dad. She could have at least asked me how this would make me feel."

"I don't think she's thought that far ahead. I really still believe they're just friends. I'm sure once she knows where things with Reynolds are headed, she'll sit down and talk to you, but I could see why she wouldn't want to worry you if they weren't going to move beyond friendship."

Isabella released a jagged breath and leaned her head back down on his chest.

"I don't know, Justin. You didn't see the way they looked at each other. They may be friends now, but I got the impression that they want to be more."

Her weary sigh made his heart lurch. He rolled over, sliding her beneath him.

"And if they do want more, would you deny them that, even if they are happy?"

Her eyes widened. "Of course not. I already told you that I want her to be happy."

"Then there is nothing your worrying and obsessing can do about it." She opened her mouth to disagree, but he silenced her with a single finger. "If Dr. Reynolds and Maggie decide to remain friends, then you have nothing to worry about. But even if they don't, and they decide to become more, then you've already admitted that you would be happy because your mother is happy."

"I just wish she had told me."

He grinned. "The way you've told her about us?"

"That's not the same."

He leaned down to kiss the hollow space at the base of her neck. "How isn't it?"

Her breathing grew choppy and uneven, the air coming out as shallow pants. "I can't think of a good reason when you do that."

He chuckled against her smooth flesh, his tongue peeking out to slide across the sensitive skin. "That's the whole point, my dear Isabella. Besides, we have far more exciting things to discuss than Maggie and Reynolds."

"Really? Like what?"

"For starters—that list you left on my dresser this morning."

Her eyes brightened. "Ah yes, the list."

He shifted off her to drag the sheet of paper from out of his dresser drawer. He'd found it that morning after Isabella left for the bakery. At the very top it read *Twelve Wicked Nights,* followed by twelve enticing bullet items. Apparently she'd been quite busy outlining in explicit detail how she wanted to spend their time together.

"Yes, the list." He ran his finger down the paper. "Now, let's see. You have some very detailed instructions on how you want us to spend our nights until I leave." He peered down at her. "Sure you didn't leave anything off?"

She was stretched out on her side, her head propped against her palm. Her smirk was decidedly very naughty. "Nope, I think that's pretty much it."

He bit back a groan as he skimmed the list again. She had a pretty vivid imagination and some very ambitious requests. He glanced down at her again. It would certainly be fun crossing off each and every one of her adventures.

"Okay. I've already tied you up. And we both know you've handcuffed me. So what would you like to tackle next?"

A tiny smile curled her lips as she leaned into him and plucked the piece of paper from his hands.

"Let's see." Her eyes roamed over the list quickly before she set it aside, an impish grin lighting up her face. "I think you still owe me that spanking."

And on their second naughty night, Justin gave Isabella her spanking. He returned her smile as he reached for her. Ten more nights to go—he couldn't wait to see what they did next.

"I've got to get out of here."

"Don't we all."

"This is ridiculous, you know. Keeping me in here all night."

Caleb glanced up from filling out the paperwork on his desk to meet Celeste's fuming gaze.

"The more you complain, the more I'm convinced that you need to stay in here longer and learn your lesson."

"This is not kindergarten, you know," she said huffily as she spun away from the bars and plopped herself down on the lone bed in the cell.

As if noticing her surroundings for the first time, she stared at the single commode in the cell, her eyes widening to tiny saucers.

"Are you really going to make me use that?"

He grinned at the horror in her voice. If he were a cruel man, he would have let her believe that he would not only make her go in it but that he would watch.

"No, when you have to go I'll escort you to the bathroom in the office."

She sighed and relaxed into the bed, her back against the wall. She fidgeted with the gray woolen blanket as she glanced around. It was as if she was brimming with nervous energy. He was sure she'd never been locked up before, and it was starting to wear on her.

He didn't know what made him do it—he always prided himself on following the rules. So he was more than a little surprised when he found himself crossing the room to unlock her cell.

"Are you letting me out already?"

He grinned at her hopeful tone. She wished. "No, but you can come out of there until it's time to go to bed."

She eyed him warily as she stepped out. "This one goodwill gesture does not even begin to absolve you of my fury."

"I'm sure," he said dryly as he turned back to his desk and sat down.

The sheriff's office had three desks, two for his deputies and a larger one for him. There was a bathroom farther down the hall, a small kitchen, and a television in the corner between the water cooler and the closet where the spare bed was stored. It wasn't fancy, but it was comfortable enough.

Celeste grabbed herself a cup of water and then sat down at the deputy's desk across from his. He felt her eyes on him as she studied him in silence. It was a bit unnerving having her assess him, but he pretended not to notice.

"So what's your deal?"

He looked up from the papers in front of him. "What do you mean?"

She scooted her chair forward so that her feet lightly touched his desk. "You know. How did you end up here in this town? How did you wind up becoming the sheriff?" She shrugged. "I'm just curious."

And bored. With the exception of the television, he was her only source of entertainment. He'd have to get Deputy Anders to buy her a book if she stayed another night.

"I grew up here. I've known Justin and Isabella since we were kids."

"Really? Isabella's never mentioned you."

"That's probably because I'm more Justin's friend than hers. Even after my family left Jacksonville, Justin and I remained close."

She scooted closer and began to lightly run her hand across the top of his desk. He set his pen down with a sigh. Now that Celeste had his attention, she was going to ply him with questions until her curiosity was satisfied.

"So you lived here, left, and then moved back. Why?"

"Why did I leave, or why did I come back?"

"Why'd you come back?"

There was open curiosity on her face, and he could tell from her expression that she was wondering why, after leaving such a small, sleepy town, he would then come back—but Jacksonville was home to him, and when his life had begun to fall apart, it was the first place he thought to go to seek refuge.

"A lot was going on at the time I decided to move back. I needed someplace that wasn't complicated and busy. My childhood hometown naturally came to mind."

She frowned up at him. "So what was it that made you move? It had to have been pretty bad to make you pack up your entire life and move home."

It took every ounce of will to keep his expression blank. She would probably never know just how close she was to the truth. How much he'd been hurting when he returned. How much solace he'd found in Jacksonville.

He stood and crossed the room to pour himself a cup of coffee. "My reasons for coming back are personal."

"Was it a woman?"

He glowered at her, but it didn't seem to have any effect. Her eyes widened. "A man? It was a man. I knew it. You're too pretty to be straight."

"Celeste!"

"It's okay. You don't have to tell me. I imagine coming out of the closet is hard to do."

"I'm not gay."

He stared at her in disbelief when she waved her hand and snorted, a gesture that said "Sure you aren't."

Although he felt the need to set her straight—literally—he couldn't stop the tiny smile from tugging at his lips. He'd been described as many things before, but *pretty* was never one of them.

"So what's your deal?" he asked, throwing her question back at her as he watched her from over the rim of his coffee mug. She'd dug deep enough into his life; now it was his turn to do the same.

"I don't live here."

"I mean, what made you decide to become an attorney? How did you end up in DC?"

She perked up. "Oh, that." Her smile was wistful. "Isabella and I went to college in DC; then we stayed for law school. Isabella's pretty much the only family I have, so when she took a job in DC, I did, too."

"And becoming an attorney? How did you know you wanted to go into law?"

Something flashed in her golden eyes. It was fleeting, so quick that if he'd blinked he would have missed it, but he'd caught a glimpse of a depth of emotion before she squelched it.

"I decided I wanted to become an attorney when I was a little girl. I was fascinated with the idea of knowing the law and putting bad guys away." She chuckled, the soft purr of her voice filling the empty space. "Over time, I guess I sold out. Instead of putting the bad guys away, I'm the one who fills the corporate pockets."

He wanted to probe just a little deeper—find out what had changed, why she wasn't the prosecutor she'd obviously wanted to be. But he already knew the answer to that. His gaze floated over her—the cashmere dress, the leather boots, and the designer purse back in her cell. He didn't get the impression that she was particularly shallow or materialistic, but he knew, probably better than anyone else, that the realities of life had a way of making some dreams fade away.

"It's time to get back in your cell. I'm ready to go to bed."

"Damn . . . and here I thought we were bonding," she grumbled as she dragged her feet, but she didn't protest when he locked her back inside.

Bonding? He chuckled to himself. Her idea of bonding felt more like an interrogation.

"Don't worry. We were, and now all this *bonding* has made me tired."
That wasn't a complete lie. His body might have been wide-awake, but he
was weary of the memories their conversation had dredged up. Celeste had
a strong intuition and was nosy as hell—a bad combination for a man who
had secrets to keep.

Chapter Nine

Isabella hummed softly as she put the finishing touches on one of the cakes for the annual Christmas Extravaganza. Considering that she hadn't gotten much sleep over the last few days, she was amazed by how cheerful she was. It was funny—just three nights spent in Justin's arms, and she was starting to believe that sleep was seriously overrated.

She started at the shrill ring of the phone. Setting aside the tube of icing, she reached for the cordless and settled it against her shoulder.

"Angelo's Bakery. How may I help you?"

"What are you doing?"

The deep baritone of Justin's seductive voice washed over Isabella, and her entire body roared to life. She shifted the cordless phone deeper into the crook of her shoulder and smiled.

"I'm just decorating a cake for the celebration tomorrow. Why? Whassup?"

"Do you have icing nearby?"

Her hand stilled around the tube of icing she was using to decorate the cake.

"Justin, I'm at the bakery."

"Are you alone?"

She was alone, at least for another half hour, until her mom arrived to help her finish these last-minute orders. But she wasn't so sure she should tell him that.

"Yes," she said, frowning at the breathless sound of her voice. So much for not telling him.

"I want you to go into the back room, and take the icing with you."

"Justin—"

"Are you disobeying me, Isabella?"

She didn't miss the subtle challenge in his voice, and she could imagine he was grinning in triumph on the other line. Every time she questioned one of his commands, he'd taunt her, remind her that she didn't know how to be submissive; but thus far she'd shown him that she was more amenable than he'd first thought.

"Isabella?"

"No, Justin. I'm not disobeying you."

"That's good. Are you in the back room with the icing?"

"Yes."

"Close the door and lock it."

She did as she was told and then stood there in the empty room, trembling with anticipation. "Justin, what number is this on the list?"

"Did you forget *everything* you put on that list, already?" He chuckled softly. "I seem to remember phone sex somewhere on there."

That's right. She had put phone sex on the list, but she'd never expected he'd call her in the middle of the day at work. But then again, she'd come to realize Justin was full of surprises.

"Now, I want you to turn on the speakerphone and take off your clothes."

"Even my underwear?" she asked as she pressed the speakerphone on and set the cordless down in its cradle.

"Everything."

Her apron was the first to go, followed by her baby blue T-shirt and snug-fitting jeans. She knew Justin could hear every single movement, because when she unzipped her pants his breathing became choppy.

She unhooked her bra and tossed it aside. The last item she removed was her panties; she slid them down her legs and stepped out of them.

"Are you naked?"

"Yes," she said in a breathless voice that was foreign to her own ears.

"What color is the icing?"

"Pink."

He groaned. "That makes this even better. Now I want you to sit down in the chair with the icing in your hand, open your legs, and close your eyes."

She followed his instructions, her hand gripping the tube of icing so tightly she worried for a second that it would burst.

"Open the icing and spread it all over your pussy, your nipples, your belly button. Imagine it's me touching you, Isabella."

She kept her eyes closed as she dropped two dollops of the sugary confection across the tips of her nipples and swirled it in her navel before dipping lower to spread it between the lips of her pussy. She moaned low in her throat as she imagined her fingers belonged to Justin. His fingertips skimming lightly across her skin. She sucked on the two fingers that were coated in icing, the sweet cream bursting on her tongue.

"Isabella?"

"Mmmm?"

"What are you thinking?"

"Not thinking—wishing. I'm wishing you were here, between my thighs, licking this icing off my pussy."

She smiled as a lewd curse filtered through the room. "God, Isabella, you're killing me."

That made two of them.

"Are you stroking your pussy?"

"Mmm hmmm."

"I want you to imagine that I'm there, eating you out." His voice was raspy, and she found it hard to concentrate on her own fantasy when all she could think about was that he was at home, naked and stretched across his bed, pumping his hard shaft in his hand.

"Are you touching yourself, too?"

She could see the crooked grin on his face when he said, "Yes."

"I wish I were there, too, licking this icing off your cock."

"Isabella."

The tortured sound of her name on his lips sent shocks of pleasure skating across her skin. She spread her thighs wider as she arched her back and rubbed her clit harder and faster.

"Are you close?"

She could barely get the single word out as her breathing grew erratic. "Yes."

"Wait until I say you can come."

She whimpered in protest as she clenched her lids tighter. She didn't know if she could—her skin was on fire, and she could already feel the slow heat building inside her womb.

"Now, Isabella. Come for me. Now."

She jerked against the chair, her entire body exploding into tiny pieces as she cried out Justin's name. In the distance she heard a harsh groan of pleasure and knew he'd found release only seconds later.

She panted deeply, her body a wobbly mass of jelly as she opened her eyes and relaxed in the chair. She could have stayed there all day, but the chime of the doorbell was like a bucket of ice water being dumped over her head, sending her reeling back to the present.

"Shit."

"What is it?"

"Someone's in the bakery."

She glowered at the phone when Justin chuckled on the other end.

"Well, you better wash your hands, then."

Her frown deepened as she struggled to hop into her jeans.

"Asshole."

He laughed a little harder in response. "I'll see you tonight. Oh, and don't forget to wash your hands."

She had another scathing name for him on the tip of her tongue, but he was already gone, and she was already planning her revenge. She straightened her mussed hair and left the room. Taking just a moment to rinse her hands in the bathroom sink, she headed to the front. She knew there was no time to get the drying icing off her body, and she grimaced at the gritty icing chafing her thighs. This was all Justin's fault, and she relished the thought of making him pay later.

She rounded the corner, but when she saw who stood on the other side of the counter she wished she'd just ignored the bell altogether. *Mrs. Billingsly.* She drew upon every single ounce of willpower inside of her and managed to keep her eyes from rolling to the back of her head. Why did she suddenly have the urge to drink?

"I want my money back."

Oh, here we go again. Isabella didn't even bother to ask why as she pressed her lips into a tight line, folded her arms across her chest, and waited for the ornery old woman to launch into another one of her tirades.

"I ordered three dozen doughnuts for church this weekend, and they were simply horrible. Ever since you started helping out at the bakery, things just haven't tasted right."

She let out a long sigh. For the past three days, Mrs. Billingsly had been in there with the same complaint. At first Isabella had been accommodating—after all, she was well aware of the fact that she wasn't the world's greatest cook. But now she was convinced the woman was just complaining to stir up trouble and listen to the sound of her own voice. Where the hell was her mother when she needed her? Had Maggie been there, Mrs. Billingsly wouldn't have dared to spout out this nonsense.

"I'm sorry to hear that, Mrs. Billingsly, but this is the third time you've asked for a refund, and I'm afraid I can't help you out this time."

A crimson flush spread across the woman's wrinkled face until it disappeared behind the hairline of her salt-and-pepper wig. "*What?*"

The old widow was clearly flustered by her response, but Isabella had had enough.

"I'm sorry you didn't like the doughnuts, but I am unable to offer you a refund." She couldn't believe that this would be her lot in life until the New Year. She was standing there arguing with an eighty-something-year-old woman over doughnuts. It would have been laughable had it not been *her* life.

"If Richard were here, he would give me my money back. I—" The woman never failed to mention her grandfather, or how much Isabella paled in comparison to him. She didn't bother telling Mrs. Billingsly that *her mother* had always done most of the baking, and still did.

"Look, Mrs. Billingsly," she said gently, cutting her off in midrant. "I can give you a twenty percent discount on your next order. How does that sound?"

Mrs. Billingsly grumbled something under her breath, but nodded slowly. "I guess that will do."

Isabella knew she was being had yet again, but it just wasn't in her nature to argue with old ladies—even old ladies who were borderline crooks. She plastered a smile on her face as Mrs. Billingsly mumbled a halfhearted good-bye and shuffled out.

As soon as the door closed behind the old woman, she let out a long, weary sigh. She was starting to seriously regret that promise she'd made to her mom. Thank God Celeste was there—and *of course* Justin. If not for them she probably would have pushed her broken-down Vanquish all the way back to DC.

Now that she thought about it, where the heck was her mother anyway? She glanced at her watch. Maggie should have been there ten minutes ago. She would give her a call, right after she cleaned off the rest of the icing.

Justin rushed into Jacksonville's only gym, a modest facility that doubled as a rec center. His spontaneous interlude with Isabella had set him back about fifteen minutes, although he certainly didn't regret it. He would trade fifteen minutes any day just to hear the soft hitch that always entered Isabella's voice just before she came.

He hurriedly dumped his stuff into a locker and headed toward the fitness area. As soon as he made it to the gym floor, he easily spotted Caleb, who was already lifting weights.

"Sorry I'm late—" He drew up short. "What the hell is she doing here?"

He frowned down at Caleb, who now sat astride the workbench.

Across the room, Celeste was cheerfully running on one of the treadmills.

"Shouldn't that little fugitive still be locked up?"

"She was getting antsy in her cell. When I told her I was going to the gym, she begged to come with me. Apparently she runs every morning."

Justin was incredulous as he stared down at Caleb. He felt as if he was seeing his longtime friend for the first time.

"What type of sheriff are you? The one who lets criminals out so that they can get some exercise? Are you crazy?"

"We both know she's not a criminal. Besides, I'm keeping an eye on her."

Justin glanced back at Celeste, who still hadn't taken notice of his presence, before returning his attention to Caleb. He studied his friend, who'd resumed bench pressing. Justin moved behind his head to spot him, and didn't say a word until Caleb finished his set and sat up again.

"I've known Celeste for fifteen years. In that entire time, her longest relationship has lasted six months, if you could even call it a relationship. She has serious commitment issues, and she's the worst workaholic I've ever met." He looked over at her again. "She's driven and ambitious, and she makes it no secret that slowing down long enough to settle with someone is not one of her priorities."

"Does this monologue have a point?"

Justin snapped his gaze back to Caleb, and grimaced at his friend's bored expression. "Don't say I didn't warn you. She's not your type."

Caleb chuckled bitterly. "Elizabeth *was* my type, and we both know how that turned out." Caleb stood to his feet, gesturing to Justin that it was his turn, and Justin took his place on the bench.

Caleb's hooded gaze told Justin to back off, so he did. His friend had been through a rough couple of years. He hadn't dated since Elizabeth left him two years ago, and Justin worried that Celeste was the type of girl who could turn Caleb off dating for life.

Damn, he couldn't believe he was about to give Caleb advice on how to handle Celeste, but if Caleb was determined to tangle with her, then Justin at least owed him a bit of insight.

Justin pushed out his set and racked the bar, then sat up on the bench to pin Caleb with his steady gaze. "Celeste knows how to wrap men around her fingers until they give her anything and everything she wants. She never has to work for it. If you want to get her attention, then don't make it easy for her."

"I don't see how I made it easy for her when I threw her in jail."

"Yeah, but then you let her out so that she could *run*."

Caleb grinned. "For the record, I'm not ready to date again. So all these warnings really aren't necessary." He shrugged as he glanced over at Celeste. "When I release her tonight, we'll go our separate ways, and that will be that."

Yeah, right. Caleb wasn't naïve, but he was certainly in denial. The tiny spark of fire that leapt in Caleb's eyes every time he looked at Celeste told Justin his friend was more than a little interested. Justin just hoped he listened to his advice.

"What are you doing for Christmas?"

Caleb shrugged as they moved to the next machine. "I don't know. I guess I was going to chill."

Caleb used to spend his holidays with Elizabeth, but after his divorce, that had naturally changed. He was an only child, and with his parents retired, and fans of taking exotic vacations over the holidays, he now spent the season alone.

"Why don't you come over to Isabella's? Maggie always cooks enough to feed an army."

His friend crooked his lips into a small grin. "Won't my presence take away from the quality time you want to spend with your new *girlfriend*?"

Girlfriend? Who? Isabella? He snorted at that thought. Izzie was almost as bad as Celeste, with her workaholic lifestyle and the pretense of committing to a man so wrong for her that everyone knew she would never marry him in the end. Hell, she'd stayed put in Jacksonville for the past week only because she was pretty much tied to his bed every night.

"Izzie and I aren't dating."

Justin almost fidgeted under the weight of Caleb's hard stare. It was so unnerving that he found himself blurting out, "We're not dating."

Caleb shook his head as he sat down on the apparatus and began to complete a set of incline presses. "Yeah, but you're not just friends any-more, unless the new definition of friendship involves handcuffing each other to the bed in the middle of the night."

Justin glared at Caleb, who wore a cocky smirk across his face.

"Okay, let's just say we're somewhere between dating and more than friends." That was all Caleb was getting, mainly because he hadn't stopped to define this new relationship he now shared with Isabella, although he'd thought about it more times than he was comfortable admitting.

"What you just said would have been fine had you not been so ada-mant over the years that Isabella wasn't your type."

"Is there a point to this?"

"My point is that maybe Isabella is more your type than you think."

"In what world is Isabella this jerk's type?" a feminine voice inter-rupted, and both men glanced up. Celeste had obviously finished her run and then made her way over to the weight area.

For the first time ever, Justin was relieved to hear Celeste's voice, but that relief was short lived when Caleb chose to open his big mouth and answer her question.

"Apparently this one. On the way back to the jail, I have to tell you a very interesting story about Justin and Isabella and a pair of handcuffs," he said with a smirk. Justin didn't crack even a tiny smile. Caleb had always been a bit of a practical joker. Justin had a good joke for him later—it was going to involve his fist in Caleb's gut. Now, that would be funny—at least for *one* of them.

"Handcuffs?"

Justin wasn't sure if Celeste was more horrified by the picture Caleb had just painted or if the thought of him with Isabella just made her sick, but her milk-chocolate complexion was starting to look pale. Apparently Isabella had some explaining to do—and he was going to let her.

Justin inched his way toward the door to the locker room. "You know what? I think I left the oven on at home—"

"But we're not done with our workout."

Justin glanced at Caleb. Oh, yes, they were. "I'll call you later about dinner tomorrow." He then turned his attention to Celeste, who was now eerily silent. "See ya, jailbait."

As he turned toward the locker room he expected to hear at least *one* "Captain Save-a-Ho." The fact that Celeste didn't say a word told him just how paralyzed with shock she truly was. He almost felt sorry for Isabella. He knew she was in for an earful when Celeste finally broke out of jail. As soon as he got to his SUV he would give her a call on her cell and leave a message—at least she would have a heads-up. But damn, he would hate to be in her shoes when Celeste finally cornered her.

"Say it ain't so. You and Justin?"

Thanks to the message Justin had left on her phone, Isabella knew the next time she saw Celeste she was going to have to come clean. When she'd discovered Caleb had released Celeste and dropped her off at Isabella's mother's home, she'd begun preparing her speech on the drive there. So as soon as she entered her childhood bedroom that evening, she wasn't surprised to see Celeste staked out, sitting with her legs crossed atop her bed, with accusation in her eyes.

"I wouldn't say it like that. Makes us sound like an item."

"But you're sleeping with him."

Were they! "We really don't get much sleep," she said with a grin.

"Oh, that's gross. Make it stop," Celeste wailed as she flopped back against the bed. "Was this the big secret you had to tell me that you refused to spill over the phone?"

Isabella crossed the room to sit in the rocking chair next to the bed. "Uh-huh."

"Now that explains it," Celeste said, popping upright again.

"What does it explain?"

"Why you never mentioned Harry the times we talked before I got here. Why you don't seem broken up at all. I thought you were having a psychotic break or something. That's why I came here. I thought you were just too upset to talk about Harry, but now I get it. Harry's not even on your radar. After all, you have Justin here to distract you. And what a distraction."

Isabella didn't like how that sounded. Celeste made it seem as if she was using Justin to get over Harry, when that couldn't have been further from the truth. Justin wasn't a rebound for her. She cared about him—she always had.

"Justin's more than a distraction to me, Celeste," she said quietly.

Celeste stared at her for several quiet seconds before she exploded. "Awww, hell! You're falling in love with the fool. I knew it. I've always known it. Although I will say I started to wonder, since it has taken you two so long."

Isabella frowned. "Nobody's falling in love. We're just having fun."

Isabella didn't like how Celeste was looking at her, as if she were clueless and dumb.

Celeste sighed as she stood. "Two people who meet on a two-week cruise and hook up are having fun. Two people who've known each other all their lives . . ."

Celeste let the words hover in the air between them, and Isabella found that even with all her education and training she could not come up with a good defense.

"Where are you going?"

Celeste stopped at her bedroom door and twisted around to face her.

"To take a shower, and then I plan to go to bed. The county jail isn't exactly the Wyndham, you know?"

Celeste started to turn around, but then hesitated. Her golden eyes were sparkling with laughter, and she curled her lips into a Cheshire grin. "The word on the street is you and Justin have a thing for handcuffs and lace. So, I take it that means I shouldn't wait up."

Celeste winked at her, and before Isabella could even gather her thoughts, she was gone. It wasn't until a little later that she began to wonder just how Celeste had found out about *that*.

Isabella made her way to Justin's soon after Celeste slipped off to shower. She marched inside, barely letting him close the front door before she rounded on him.

"How could you let Caleb tell Celeste about the handcuff incident?" she exclaimed.

"I didn't *let* Caleb tell her anything. He just blurted it out. Trust me, I'm just as pissed about it as you are."

She walked past him and shrugged out of her coat, her movements languorous, her lips lifting into a seductive smile. "I think *you* should be punished for letting it slip out on your watch."

Justin opened his mouth to protest, but then snapped it shut, and Isabella recognized the moment when he understood what she was asking—no, demanding.

He folded his arms across his chest and leaned against the breakfast bar. The corded muscles in his biceps strained the thin white cotton of his shirt.

"I take it you want to be in control tonight."

She closed the small distance between them. Running her palms lightly across his chest, she smiled when his muscles flexed beneath her touch. Each night their games became bolder, and she was enjoying giving her power over to Justin, but there were times she wanted to take it back.

This was one of those times.

"It's only because you deserve to be punished, and we need to cross an item off the list—the one where I get to tell *you* what to do."

He arched one brow. "Ah, yes. The list again. You know I don't make a habit of letting a woman dominate me in bed."

She leaned into him, grasping the lobe of his ear between her teeth. He groaned against her, his hands clamping down on her arms as he pulled her body against his. She released his ear, her tongue stroking across the outer shell.

"I know you don't like to give up your control in bed, but you'll make an exception for me. After all, I'm special."

She'd meant to tease him with her words, but when he leaned back to stare at her, she glimpsed a deeper, darker emotion in his eyes that trapped the air in her lungs for a full heartbeat.

"You certainly are," he whispered, just before leaning down to capture her lips with his.

For a moment, Isabella let herself forget that tonight was her night to hold the power. She melted against him, giving herself over to the intense heat of his kiss. His mouth branded hers, and he seemed to stake his claim on her with the sweep of his tongue between her lips.

She lifted her arms, twining them behind his neck as she held him tighter against her. His mouth plundered hers, and he deepened the kiss, pressing the hard bulge of his erection into the soft flesh of her stomach. Her nipples tightened against the fabric of her shirt, while liquid heat pooled between her thighs, making her ache all over. She wanted to rip his clothes off and fuck him right there on the floor. She'd practically been panting and distracted with need since their phone sex escapade earlier.

She tore her lips from his and leaned back, her hands lightly skimming across his chest. She trailed them lower and grasped the hem of his shirt. He shrugged out of it and tossed it aside. Her hands went back to playing again, teasing his broad nipples into tiny little peaks. She swiped her tongue across one, and smirked up at him when he released a low hiss. She loved how responsive he was to her touch.

"Where were you when you called me at the bakery? In your bedroom?"

"No."

"Were you out here in the living room?"

He nodded, his eyes slightly hooded as she inched her hand lower and lower.

"I imagined you were naked and stretched out across the bed."

He groaned when she slipped her hand inside his pants, her fingers curling around his engorged length.

"I was on the couch," he rasped.

She glanced over at said couch.

"Show me." She released him and stepped back. "I want you to strip naked and show me everything you did while you worked me into a frenzy on the phone."

She held her breath as Justin crossed the room, stepped out of his pants, and stretched his chiseled frame out along the sofa. His eyes never left her as he fisted his cock in his hand, working it up and down the length of his shaft. She was mesmerized by the sight before her, and more juice trickled from her slit.

"Take off your clothes."

"Uh-uh. This is my fantasy," she said with a smile, although she found herself removing them anyway.

She held his gaze while she stripped for him, although in her mind it was nowhere near as sexy as watching him strip for her. With each article of clothing she removed, he worked his hand faster, and his breathing became more labored. His excitement fed hers, and she lingered as she reached to remove her bra, her final article of clothing.

"Take it off."

Her hands stilled behind her back just as her fingers touched the clasp. "No, you take it off."

She didn't move a muscle when he stood to his feet and came up behind her.

"This is oddly nostalgic, don't you think?"

She tried for words, but nothing came out. His face was buried in the crook of her neck, the wet slide of his tongue heating her flesh. She moaned as she leaned against him, his cock digging into the small of her back. She didn't register that her bra was undone until his hands snaked around to cup her breasts.

He massaged the soft mounds in his hands, his fingers lightly plucking at her nipples until they stood at attention. Her eyelids fell shut as she leaned her head back against his shoulder, absorbing every tingle and whisper of pleasure that roiled through her body.

She called out his name, her body stiffening against his when he dragged his palm across her belly and dipped his hand between her thighs, spearing two fingers inside her dripping sheath.

She nearly came as bolts of lightning shot through her. She panted deeply and rocked her hips to the rhythm of his thrusting fingers. He worked his long fingers inside her slowly at first, teasing against the rough patch of her G-spot before moving faster. He kept going deeper and deeper inside her, his fingers more insistent, and when he pressed his thumb against the engorged flesh of her clit, rotating it back and forth, she splintered in his arms. She screamed his name on a long, tortured cry as her entire body burst into flames. He held her tight when she slumped against him, not once breaking the thrusting rhythm of his fingers, which plowed deep inside the clenching tunnel of her drenched pussy. He continued to play inside of her for a long time before eventually slipping his fingers from her body, his long digits now coated with the juices from her sex.

Again, she ignored the fact that she was supposed to be in control and let Justin lower her to the ground. He positioned her on all fours in front of him, and guided his hard length to her entrance.

She twisted her head around to meet his fogged gaze, a tiny, satiated grin on her face. "I thought I was supposed to be the one in control."

"Trust me. You are."

She didn't quite understand what he meant until he thrust inside of her on a single stroke, and she felt his entire body tremble against her as he fought back his building climax.

He grasped her hips and surged forward, stabbing through the tight walls of her cunt, which were still drenched with the evidence of her last climax. The sounds of his hard shaft sliding into her wet tunnel echoed all around them as their sweat-slick bodies slapped together.

His pounding thrusts grew harder and faster, and she pushed back against him, sending his length stroking deeper.

"Isabella." He called her name on a harsh groan, his fingers digging into her flesh as he continued to quicken his pace, slamming into her with brutal thrusts.

Her orgasm hovered inside her, just outside her reach, and she fell forward, the intensity of his movements making it hard to keep up with him. He leaned over her, his hands releasing her hips to lie flat on either side of her head as he drove into her. She spread her legs wider as he went deeper. Her hand found its way to her clit, and she began to strum it lightly with her fingers, tugging and rotating it until a wave of heat welled up inside her, gathering in her belly first before spreading out across her body.

She jerked against him, the intensity of her orgasm so overwhelming that she opened her mouth to scream, but nothing came out. Justin rode her through her climax; the guttural moans that slipped from his lips told her he was close.

She reared back, tightening the muscles of her pussy around him, matching him thrust for thrust until she felt him swell and harden inside her. He exploded with a harsh growl, and warmth flooded her pussy deep into her womb, their juices mingling together.

He slumped against her, the pounding rhythm of his heart matching her own until eventually the beat became steady and even once again.

He pulled out of her, and she fell flat as a pancake against the carpeted floor while he collapsed beside her. She reached out her hand, absently stroking his chest as it rose and fell beneath her palm. She listened to him breathe for a long time, until eventually its hypnotic rhythm lulled her to sleep.

Chapter Ten

"Merry Christmas, Mama."

Isabella shuffled into the kitchen still wearing her pajamas. For the past week she'd stayed at Justin's and gone straight to the bakery in the morning, but she'd left his place late last night so she could wake up early to help her mother with dinner—although she didn't know how much help she was going to be. She was bleary-eyed and exhausted from lack of sleep.

"Merry Christmas, Isabella," Maggie said, kissing her cheek, her eyes never leaving Isabella. "You look like you need more sleep."

Her mother's knowing gaze twinkled, and a small smile tugged at the corners of her mouth. Isabella knew she wasn't fooling her, but she still didn't part her lips to divulge any information to Maggie as she poured herself a cup of coffee. Maggie, however, refused to be stonewalled by Isabella's silence.

"I take it Justin is still coming today."

Isabella rolled her eyes. "Yes, Mama." She sat down at the kitchen table and waited. She could tell from the look in Maggie's eyes that she was determined to pry information out of her this morning, but Isabella was equally committed to holding her ground. Let her probe all she wanted. She was Alcatraz. No, even better—Fort Knox.

But Maggie locked Isabella in a piercing hawkeyed stare, a move that always made her break.

"Justin and I are sort of seeing each other, all right!" Yeah—way to go, Fort Knox.

She expected Maggie to gloat, or exclaim that it was about damn time, right after she got up off her knees from saying ten Our Fathers. So Isabella was particularly stunned when her mother simply smiled and returned her attention to the pie shell she'd been filling.

"Is that it? You have *nothing* to say?"

Maggie shrugged, her serene smile still plastered across her face.

"You and Justin are adults. As long as you're happy . . ."

Isabella narrowed her eyes. After all this time, all this poking and prodding she'd done over the years and her contrived attempts to throw them together, *that* was all she had to say? She was suspicious. There had to be more. It just felt so—so *anticlimactic*.

Isabella sighed and leaned back in the chair, reminding herself to be grateful that Maggie *wasn't* probing, since she didn't have much to tell her. The details of her fling wouldn't please Maggie. She and Justin weren't dating, and no matter what Celeste said, their situation would come to an end when he shipped out in a week. They were just having fun, and she knew that wasn't what her mother wanted to hear.

The muffled sound of footsteps coming from upstairs told her that Celeste was awake. Isabella stared at Maggie, wondering how best to broach the subject that had been gnawing at her for several days now.

"Mama, can I ask you a personal question?"

Maggie glanced up. "Depends on how personal," she said with a tiny smile, but her grin soon disappeared, her eyes darkening with concern when she glimpsed the pensive look on Isabella's face.

"What is it, Isabella?"

"Are you dating Dr. Reynolds?" She blurted it out in a rush before she lost her nerve.

Maggie set down the spoon in her hand, and wiped her palms on her apron. "No. Reginald and I aren't dating."

Isabella's eyes narrowed to slits. "But do you want to date him?"

"We enjoy each other's company, but right now we're just friends."

Isabella noticed that she hadn't answered her question, and she didn't miss the *right now* part, either. When her mother turned away from her, Isabella realized she should probably take notes from Maggie on how to keep a secret. If anyone was locked up tighter than Fort Knox it was her mother, so she was surprised by Maggie's next words.

"Your father has been gone for more than ten years, Isabella. You know I will always love him, but if I'm lucky enough to find someone special to share my life with again, then I plan to give that person a chance. I imagine it might be difficult for you to see me with someone else at first, but if I'm happy, I hope in time you can come to accept him and appreciate that he makes me smile."

Isabella was speechless. How the heck could she disapprove now? Not after a speech like that.

"I guess I should tell you now that I've invited Reginald to have dinner with us."

Isabella opened her mouth to protest, but immediately snapped it shut, reminding herself that she was in her mother's home. Her mother was free to invite anyone she liked. And besides, Maggie was right. If this guy made her happy, then Isabella would be happy for them—or, at the very least, she would give it a try.

Isabella started to tell her that, but Celeste chose that moment to rush down the stairs and sweep into the kitchen like the living hurricane she was.

"Merry Christmas!"

Like her, Celeste was still dressed in pajamas, although *unlike* her, Celeste's eyes were bright, her hair was freshly done, and she wore a radiant smile. Isabella must have looked like a living, breathing train wreck next to Celeste.

"Someone woke up cheery this morning," she grumbled.

"Yeah, that's because someone actually got some sleep," she said with a wink. "What did you do *all night long?*"

Isabella nearly choked on her coffee as she spewed several droplets across the counter. She glared at Celeste, who'd already turned her back on her to pour herself a cup as well.

Her mother chuckled softly, and Isabella glared at *both* of them; but neither paid her any mind as her mother went back to cooking and Celeste sidled up next to Maggie to help. It was all well and good. They could work on dinner while she took a shower and made herself halfway presentable. Besides, Celeste knew her way around a kitchen. She would actually be able to *help* Maggie.

"I'm going to go take a shower."

"Why don't you lie down, too? You look like hell."

Isabella glowered at Celeste, but she didn't say another word as she shuffled out, knowing that she would end up taking her friend's advice. After grabbing a shower, she ended up lying down for what was supposed to be a few minutes, but soon she was fast asleep.

She awoke a couple of hours later, and as she stood in front of the mirror to apply a dab of makeup, she noticed her cheeks were flushed red, her lips still full and puffy from Justin's kisses, and her hazel eyes sparkled as she fanned out her eyelashes with the mascara brush. She frowned at her reflection, wondering if this was what her mother and Celeste saw when they looked at her—she looked like a woman in *love*.

She jerked away from the mirror. This was all Celeste's fault for putting these thoughts in her head. Before her friend showed up, she'd been so sure of herself and her feelings for Justin. It was just a silly little crush. One that she'd had for as long as she could remember. But that wasn't the same as love. Not even close.

She pushed the nagging doubts to the back of her mind and made her way downstairs. As she entered the kitchen the tantalizing aroma of Christmas dinner made her stomach growl, reminding her that she hadn't eaten all day.

"I hope you're well rested, because you're just in time," her mother said.

Isabella was about to ask how she could help when Maggie started dealing out orders. In minutes she found herself scurrying about the kitchen, stirring this and stuffing that as she helped her mother and Celeste put the finishing touches on the meal. An hour quickly flew by, but Isabella was oblivious to the passing time until the doorbell rang and guests began to arrive.

J ustin smiled when the front door opened. Isabella stood there dressed all in white, like the naughtiest, sexiest angel he'd ever seen, her raven hair cascading in soft waves over one shoulder.

"Merry Christmas, babe," he whispered, and before she could utter a word, he swept her in his arms and kissed her soundly on the lips. He'd taken her by surprise, and for a moment she stood stiff as a board in his arms, until she let herself relax against him, the yielding curves of her body molding to his. He could have stayed there locked in her arms, his mouth fused with hers for hours, but the spell was soon broken when Caleb cleared his throat behind him, and Celeste simply opened her mouth.

"What is *he* doing here?"

Justin groaned against Isabella's lips as he pulled away, and a small smile tugged at the corners of his mouth when Isabella frowned. At least he wasn't alone in his displeasure at being interrupted.

"It's Christmas, Cruella. Can you *try* to be nice to my guest?"

Celeste glared at him before turning her honey brown eyes on Caleb, who pushed past him to stand before her.

"Merry Christmas, Robocop," she muttered as she raked her gaze over Caleb before twisting on her heels and stomping off toward the kitchen.

Caleb shrugged, a cocky grin spread across his face. "I guess she was overwhelmed by my good looks and charm."

Justin chuckled as Caleb followed after her, seemingly undeterred by Celeste's acid tongue. Caleb was a better man than him—he would never *voluntarily* subject himself to Celeste's company.

"I just hope those two don't ruin Christmas dinner with their bickering, or Mama is going to be furious," Isabella sighed.

"I'm sure they will behave. If they don't, I trust Maggie will bring them back in line."

Isabella returned his smile. "I can't quite say I share your optimism. I imagine she will be far too busy entertaining *Reginald.*"

He stopped at the slight catch in her voice. They stood within the foyer; just the two of them. He pulled her into his embrace and stared into her lovely eyes, his gaze firm and steady.

"Dr. Reynolds is a good guy. Don't you think you should give him a chance, at least for your mother's sake?"

Isabella looked to the floor. "I said I was going to try, but—"

He slipped his fingers beneath her chin, forcing her gaze to meet his. "It's Christmas, Isabella."

The greater meaning behind his softly spoken words must have been enough, because she nodded, a small smile spreading across her face.

"You're right. It's Christmas. I promise I'll *try.*"

He arched a brow. He wanted her to do more than just try, but he wasn't going to push her. He pulled her deeper into his arms, biting back a groan when the lush softness of her body stirred his own.

"Speaking of Christmas, I have a special present for you."

Her eyes twinkled, and a wicked grin teased the edges of her mouth. "Oh, really. So where is it?"

He leaned down to whisper against her ear, so close that his lips grazed her earlobe. "It's a *special* present. I have to give it to you in private."

"Mmm, I like the sound of that. So when do I get to unwrap this present?"

"Later. After dinner—when we're—"

"Isabella, I need you in the kitchen!"

They groaned, and he rested his forehead against hers. "Alone," he finished.

She stood up on her tiptoes and placed a gentle peck against his lips. "I can't wait."

She pulled out of his arms and disappeared into the living room toward the kitchen, leaving him to trail after her. As his eyes followed the gentle sway of her rounded hips, all he could think about was the end of the night, when he and Isabella would be able to make their exit and finally be alone again, without *any* interruptions.

"I didn't have to let you out, you know."

"So I should be grateful, then?"

Caleb furled his lips into a crooked grin, until one small dimple creased his cheek. Celeste wasn't sure what annoyed her more—that he was a pain in the ass, or that he was a *sexy* pain in the ass. She knew she couldn't ignore him no matter how hard she tried.

"If you'd pulled that hit-and-run in any other place, you would have still been sitting in jail." He reached around her to grab several plates, and she stilled at the slight brush of his arm against hers as rivulets of heat bolted through her body.

"What are you doing?"

"I'm helping you set the table."

She felt like an idiot when he stared at her, his expression puzzled, before he gave a casual shrug and resumed his task of doing just that—setting the table.

What was wrong with her? Caleb was *not* her type, and it baffled her that she was always so aware of him. But what was even more baffling was that he seemed completely unaffected by her. That just didn't happen—men *always* reacted to her. But Caleb had already proved that he was more than immune to her charms.

"Like I was saying. I can't believe you're still mad I locked you up."

"I'm not upset about that." That much was true. She'd accepted that he was only doing his job. After all, she'd *hit* his car.

"Really? You didn't seem too thrilled when I showed up with Justin." He leaned against the table, and she traced the corded muscles in his arms as he folded them across his broad chest. She didn't realize she'd done it until her gaze slid to his face, which now wore a smug grin.

She frowned, finally pinpointing what was really bothering her about him. He knew she found him attractive, but he didn't share her interest, and it angered her that he would be so obvious about it. Wasn't it enough that he'd already humiliated her once? Did he have to continue doing it by rubbing it in, too?

"I wasn't thrilled to see you because I believe you should spend Christmas with people you like—and I really can't say that I like you, Caleb."

That was a lie—a big, bold-faced one. When he crossed the small space between them and backed her against the wall, she knew he didn't believe a single word that had come out of her mouth.

"You liked me well enough yesterday."

Anger replaced her humiliation tenfold, and she lifted her chin to shoot him a hard glare. If Caleb had been a gentleman, he would have left her alone. He certainly wouldn't have brought up how she'd practically thrown herself at him last night in his squad car when he'd dropped her off at Isabella's. She'd never been rejected by a man she wanted, and she'd been so certain that Caleb was attracted to her. But she was pretty certain pushing someone away was definitely not how one demonstrated attraction.

"Must you be so rude? And so arrogant about it, too?" Her eyes flashed. "If you were a decent guy you never would have brought up this subject— you certainly didn't need to throw it in my face."

She stilled, realizing her mistake. Her anger had just given her away— it had revealed something she didn't want Caleb to know: that he affected her and his rejection had gotten under her skin.

"I wasn't trying to throw anything in your face," he said softly, but she didn't believe him.

She glowered at him as she pushed against his chest. He was tactless and rude, and all she wanted to do in that moment was get away from him, but he refused to budge.

"You're arrogant; you know that?" She pushed harder, but instead of moving away, he edged closer, trapping her against the wall.

"You already said that. And besides, I'm no more arrogant than you, don't you think?" He seized her chin in his hand, tilting her head back so that she had no choice but to meet his gaze. "If you hadn't sprinted out of my car, I could have explained. You took me by surprise yesterday. I'm not used to women coming on to me. And from your reaction, I take it you're not used to men rejecting you."

Her eyes dipped to the floor, avoiding his sapphire stare as her face heated with humiliation. He was right. Men didn't reject her. Handsome, powerful, wealthy men didn't reject her—and yet, Caleb had. Straitlaced, small-town Caleb. With her track record, it shouldn't have bothered her, but it had. There was just something about Caleb that was earnest and genuine. She found herself attracted to those qualities in him, and it stung when he'd pushed her away.

"But I didn't reject you," he whispered as he leaned forward, so close that with every breath she filled her lungs with the spicy musk of his cologne. So close that if she angled her head just right, his lips would touch hers.

"At the same time, I knew what I was doing when I pushed you away."

She frowned in confusion. Didn't he just say he hadn't rejected her?

"Have you ever thought of stepping back and letting a man take the lead?"

It was more of a statement, less of a question, and it explained everything now. But she should have already known. He was a traditional guy—so different from the men she knew, so different from her.

She narrowed her gaze. "Why would I do that when I know exactly what I want?"

"Do you?"

Well, she thought she did. But no one had ever questioned her like this before.

"You think you want a man who will come when you say come, and fawn all over you when you simply look his way."

She frowned at the image he painted. He made her sound like a dog-catcher. "So, I guess you're going to tell me *exactly* what it is I want, since you now seem to know me so very well."

"I don't have to tell you anything, because I think you already know." She gasped when he pressed his body against hers, the heavy evidence of his arousal nudging against her belly. He was such a conundrum. One minute he pushed her away, and the next he was chasing her down—seducing her against a wall.

He was going to kiss her. She could tell by the desire swirling in his eyes. He inched closer, and she lifted on her toes, straining toward his lips. She ached to taste him, to feel his sensual mouth flush against hers, so when the doorbell rang she ignored it.

"I better get that."

She was so startled by the abrupt change in him that her brain didn't begin to register his words until he moved away.

"What?"

"I was the only person not assigned a task, so I better get the door." He tipped his head in the direction of the dinner table. "I'll let you finish up."

She slumped against the wall, completely stunned by his exit. Once again, Caleb made her question if her pheromones were out of whack. He wanted her—that much she knew. But for the first time in her life she was going to have to *wait*. Caleb was in charge, and if she wanted their attraction to turn into something more, she was going to have to do just what he'd advised. She was going to have to step back and let him take the lead, which was something she wasn't so certain she could do.

Never once had she handed control over to a man—but then, Caleb was different.

Chapter Eleven

Jacksonville's annual Christmas Extravaganza was a time-honored tradition in the small town. After dinner, Maggie had insisted that they all head downtown to join in the festivities, although "festivities" was far too strong a word, and "extravaganza" was certainly a gross exaggeration. It started with the tree-lighting ceremony, which Isabella always thought was odd because it came when Christmas was practically over, but that was just how it was done. The mayor would make a few announcements, and then they would all sing a couple of holiday songs. That was about all there was to the Extravaganza. After that, most of the adults and teenagers would gather under several tents, where an array of Christmas desserts, courtesy of Angelo's Bakery, was spread out over the picnic tables. They would huddle there for a while, talking and eating, while the younger kids made their way to the skating rink that the town put up every year just for the holidays. The festivities were usually over in a couple of hours. People would begin heading home when it became too cold to stay outside.

Isabella glanced over at the ice skating rink, where dozens of children whizzed by, floating across the ice on their skates. She smiled as she watched them, her mind recalling all the vivid memories from a time when she'd enjoyed Christmas in her small hometown.

She hadn't felt this sense of nostalgia in a long while. Usually, her time in Jacksonville was spent in angst. She was always itching to get out of there and back to DC, but today she was actually quite content, and it didn't take a genius to figure out why.

Her gaze settled on Justin, who stood several feet away talking to Reginald. Her heart skipped a beat when he glanced up and smiled. She returned his smile before looking away.

As she watched the children zip past her on their skates a plaintive sigh fell from her lips. She'd gone and done what she'd vowed she wouldn't do. She'd allowed herself to fall for Justin when she should have guarded her heart. She almost couldn't blame herself. Justin was the type of man women fell for easily, and it certainly wasn't surprising that she'd succumbed as well. Never mind the fact that she'd been half in love with him for most of her life.

Justin liked to joke that they were having a twelve-day Christmas affair, but instead of the twelve days of Christmas, they'd put their own spin on the classic song. It was turning out to be more like the twelve wickedly erotic nights of Christmas, and they had only seven nights left. She'd fallen in love with a man who would leave in a week and then disappear into some South American jungle for the next six months. She was stupid, but there was nothing she could do about it now.

She glanced over at Justin again, but her lips quickly dipped into a grimace when she saw that Dr. Reynolds had walked off to join her mother, and it was now Monica DuPont who stood beside him. It had been Monica Likert back in high school, but, like Isabella, Monica had sought out bigger and better things and had used her classic good looks to get out of Jacksonville, establish a successful career as a model, and marry one of the DuPont heirs. Her escape from small-town Virginia hadn't lasted long though; she was now divorced, with two kids in tow. And by the way she was leaning into Justin, her breasts pressed against his arm, she appeared to be on the hunt for a new *baby daddy*.

Isabella stared at them, fuming. Justin should have pulled away from Monica to put a polite distance between them, so she was shocked when he leaned into her as if he were telling her a secret. When Monica giggled, the throaty purr of her voice singed Isabella's ears, and she saw red. She took one step toward them, but stopped when she realized what she was doing. Starting a fight in the middle of town was so not classy, or smart. Besides, Justin didn't belong to her. He wasn't her boyfriend, and by the words from his own mouth, they were having an affair—nothing more.

She started to turn away from them, but then Justin looked up and met her eyes. She couldn't read him, and she was careful to wipe her face clean of any expression. But when her façade began to slip, she spun away and disappeared into the crowd of people, fleeing his searching stare.

Isabella felt as if she'd walked for miles, although she probably hadn't gone more than a few feet when she found a quiet space in the shadows, hidden on the other side of the hefty Christmas tree. She fidgeted with her gloves, picking at the scratchy wool with her fingers. The rational side of her knew Justin hadn't done anything wrong. And while she was jealous, she knew that she didn't really have the right to be. He hadn't made her any promises—and neither had she, for that matter.

"There you are. I've been looking all over for you."

She stiffened as Justin wrapped his arms around her from behind. He lightly kissed her temple, and she closed her eyes for a brief moment, wishing his tenderness could lessen the dull ache in her heart.

He turned her around to face him. "Are you all right?"

No, she thought. But she heard the words "I'm fine" come out of her mouth instead. She couldn't meet his probing stare, her eyes darting everywhere but up at him. "We'd better get back. I'm sure everyone must be ready to leave."

He studied her for a moment longer, his forehead furrowed in concern, but thankfully he didn't question her.

"Everyone else is gone. Reginald took your mother home, and Celeste and Caleb went with them."

She wanted to ask how he'd managed to learn all that with Monica tucked under his arm, but she bit back what she knew was a bitchy retort.

"Well, it seems as if everyone is settled, then." She forced out a smile when Justin narrowed his gaze, scrutinizing her.

"Are you sure you're okay?"

"I'm fine," she insisted. Her response was a little too quick to be believable, but she avoided his searching eyes and clasped his hand in hers, tugging him in the direction of where his car was parked.

They had only seven nights left together, and she wouldn't ruin it with irrational insecurities. She wanted to enjoy what little time they had left.

When it was over, she would just have to figure out how to deal with the feelings that had crept into her heart when she wasn't looking.

sabella was probably the worst liar Justin had ever met. She'd been distant on the entire ride to his house. Now, as she undressed in his bedroom, her actions were mechanical, and her mind seemed to be somewhere else. It was clear something was bothering her, and while his nature beat at him to demand she tell him the truth, he restrained himself. Isabella was far too stubborn to be pushed. When she was ready she would open up, but until then, he refused to make love to a woman who was so detached from her body that she could have doubled as a zombie.

"Stop."

He was surprised Isabella even heard him, given how far away she seemed to be, but her hands stilled behind her back before they could unclasp her bra.

"You keep telling me you're fine when I know something is bothering you—"

"Really, I'm—"

"No, you're not," he said, silencing her with a single finger against her lips. "But I'm not going to force you to come clean. You are free to keep your secrets until you trust me enough to be honest."

She winced at his words. Good, because he'd been deliberate in choosing them. It aggravated him that she still didn't seem to realize just how much he cared for her and that no matter what, she could always trust him.

The silence between them was palpable as he gave her one last opportunity to open up. When she remained quiet, he sighed, realizing he had more work to do. Apparently she had no idea just how much she meant to him, but he was determined to show her. He spun away from her to dig into his dresser drawer. When he found what he was searching for, he turned around.

She shook her head as he lifted the black strip of fabric, but he ignored her silent protest, and she didn't resist when he secured the blindfold across her eyes.

"After all these years, and everything we've shared these past few days, you should be able to trust me." He circled behind her, undoing her bra and casting it aside. Slipping his hands beneath her arms, he cupped her breasts, dipping his head into the crook of her neck.

"I thought you would trust me after the night I restrained you, but I see now that I've failed." He smiled when she shivered against him, her back brushing his bare chest.

"W—what are you going to do?"

"That's for me to decide. But tonight I will take away your ability to see. It is considered the most valued of the five senses, and when it is gone, it makes one feel more vulnerable than with the loss of any other sense." He stroked his tongue across her silky skin until she gasped softly. Every single sensation would be heightened because she couldn't see—every whisper, every caress, every kiss.

"Tonight you will have to trust me, Isabella, as you've never trusted anyone else before."

Isabella stood in the center of Justin's bedroom, her hands lightly touching the soft velvet of the blindfold. His fingertips whispered across her skin, and she shivered as a deep sexual yearning stirred in her belly. With her vision now gone, she was at his mercy. She realized that she had no choice but to trust him, and she waited in anticipation for what would come next.

Every other sense was alive, straining to fill the void left by her absence of sight. The low hum of his voice trickled to her ears as he guided his hands down the length of her body, leaving a smattering of goose bumps in their wake.

He hooked his fingers beneath the elastic of her panties, dragging the lace down the length of her legs until they pooled at her feet. She grasped his shoulders as she stepped out of them, and kicked them aside.

She thought he would stand up then, but he lingered on his knees, raining tiny kisses across one ankle, before tracing an achingly slow trail up her leg to the inside of her thigh. She held a breath when he stopped just before he reached her pussy. His warm breath tickled her moist sex, and she yearned for him to kiss her there as well, but instead of touching her with his lips, he brushed his fingers across her silken folds. He played with her there, teasing her with his skillful fingers until she moaned.

He smeared something wet and slippery across the lips of her sex, and she started to ask what he was doing when her flesh began to tingle with burning heat.

She jerked away from his hands, the sensitive skin now aflame. "What the hell did you just put on me?" She sniffed the air, wrinkling her nose. It smelled like eucalyptus—felt like it, too.

"It's peppermint oil." He tried to touch her again, but she moved away at the first stroke of his hand. "It will burn for a few more seconds, and then it will start to tingle as it cools down."

"You could have warned me," she grumbled; but no sooner were the words out than the burning stopped, and her skin began to cool. It wasn't cold like ice; it was more like a cool jelly.

When he grasped her hips in his hands, this time she didn't pull away. "Every time I blow on you, the oil will heat up, and you will experience a rush of warmth."

"Like the first time you put it on?" She wasn't so sure about it getting warm again. The burning was something she would like to forget altogether.

"No, it won't burn anymore. When it warms, you will feel nothing but pleasure." As proof, he leaned forward and blew across her sex. She almost collapsed against him as sharp tingles of pleasure skated over her pussy and fanned out across her entire body.

"Oh my God." She'd never experienced anything quite like it.

He chuckled, his warm breath wafting across her sensitive mound, sending tiny shocks of heat surging through her body. "Wait until I'm inside you. You will feel every move I make, even the slightest twitch of my cock."

Well, she wanted to ask what the hell was he waiting for, but she knew that no matter how loud her demands, Justin would not be rushed. Tonight wasn't just about her pleasure. She had no doubt he would see to that as well, but that wasn't his only goal. He wanted to prove that he deserved her trust—and he would use her body to convince her.

She trusted Justin with her body. It was her heart that was a different story. But she couldn't—*wouldn't*—tell him that.

"Ouch—ouch!" She almost ripped the blindfold off when pricks of pain burst in her chest. She ran her hands across her nipples, careful not to disturb the metal clamps that Justin had secured to her sensitive buds.

"What is with you tonight? These things really hurt."

"They're supposed to." There was a soft rustle, and she knew Justin stood. His hands seized her hips, pulling her flush against him, although he was careful not to press his chest to hers.

"Don't worry. I won't keep them on for long," he said, as if reading her mind.

She forgot all about the stinging bite of the nipple clamps when he backed her against the bed, gently helped her down until she was stretched across it, and settled between her thighs.

Justin was right about the peppermint oil. She felt the first swipe of his tongue all the way to the tips of her toes. She arched against him, her fingers digging into his scalp as he sucked on the tiny nub of her clit. She panted softly, the muscles in her entire body tensing. The pleasurable sensations coursing through her were overwhelming, and she exploded before she even realized what was happening.

"You will come quickly and effortlessly until the effects of the oil wear off," Justin explained after her first climax. He then devoured her with his mouth, sending her hurling over the edge several more times.

She was a writhing mass of heightened nerve endings, each one straining toward that pinnacle of completion, until she erupted in his arms yet again. Already she was exhausted, her body completely boneless, and he hadn't even entered her.

He released her thighs and slid up the length of her body, the soft smattering of hair across his chest tickling her along the way. She whimpered when she felt Justin remove the clamps. Blood rushed to her tender peaks, and the pain was almost as intense as it had been when he'd restricted the circulation.

She didn't understand the point of enduring the pressure of the clamps, but when Justin swiped his tongue across one hardened tip, it was blatantly clear. She sucked in a sharp breath, an explosion of pleasure bursting inside her. The silky slide of his tongue was like a soothing balm to her flesh, and her gut clenched as sticky warmth flooded her sheath. The blood in her veins ran hotter, and she wondered if she would pass out, unable to stop the assault against her senses.

"Justin." She said his name on a breathless moan, begging him to cease with his brand of pleasurable torture.

He buried his face into the hollow space between her shoulder and neck, and laughed, the rich sound vibrating through her entire body.

"So, have you learned your lesson?"

For a moment she blanked, until it slowly started to come back to her. Oh, right—she was supposed to be learning how to trust him.

"I've always trusted you, Justin." That much was true.

"And yet you still hold back."

She stilled at his words, wondering if he'd somehow put the pieces together and learned the truth.

"You tensed up again. What are you afraid to tell me, Isabella?"

He nudged the tip of his erection against her moist heat, and she felt even that slight movement all over her body. She wondered if this was yet another method to his madness. Taunt her until she revealed all her deepest, darkest secrets.

"Justin, please?" Her words were as much of a plea for him to let this issue go as they were to beg him to enter her.

He shuddered against her, his breathing labored. A crackle of energy sizzled between them, hot and raw and carnal. She knew then that she'd won—for the moment, at least.

"Keep your secrets, Isabella, but just know this—I would never lie to you."

His words made her heart clench; the accusation was heavy in his voice.

Later she would dwell on them and wonder if she could open up to him, but in that moment all she wanted to do was feel. And when he reared back and drove into her, every single thought evaporated from her head.

The rhythm he set was hard—punishing—and his frustration poured off him in waves as he thrust inside her body. His strokes were rough and wild. The primitive rawness of his lovemaking turned her on even more, and she lifted her hips off the bed, matching his furious pace.

He crushed his lips against hers, his fingers digging into the soft flesh of her thighs as he pinned her against the bed. The headboard pounded against the wall, and she longed to remove her blindfold to watch him.

She imagined that the muscles in his tanned, hard body bulged with exertion as the blazing heat of passion swirled in the depths of his emerald eyes. A jolt of sexual energy slashed through her, and she buried her fingers in his tangled hair. Sensation after sensation bombarded her, and she tensed against him, staving off the pleasurable burst of her orgasm long enough to demand his own surrender.

"Come with me, Justin," she whispered into his ear as she rocked against him. The control he'd tried holding on to instantly slipped, and he pumped and thrust into her, his body quivering with strain.

She clung to him as she finally allowed herself to spiral out of control, dragging him with her. She screamed out his name, her silken sheath flooding with wet warmth while tiny convulsions rocked her body. He thrust into her one last time, his entire body heaving as he went rigid, a long, ragged groan of release tumbling from his lips. He poured his hot seed into her along with all his frustration as it finally drained out of him and he went limp against her.

With shaky hands, she removed the blindfold and tossed it aside. His cheek rested against her chest, and she brushed aside the sweat-dampened curls along his brow to place a gentle kiss atop his head.

He wasn't asleep, but he kept his eyes closed. She held him tight against her while his heart continued to thump loudly. Eventually it quieted, but neither of them said a word, too afraid to break the tenuous truce their lovemaking had brokered. She settled her head against the pillow and closed her eyes. She fell asleep with him still draped across her, their bodies entwined.

Chapter Twelve

fter all these years, and everything we've shared, you should be able to trust me. Justin's words had haunted her all day. It wasn't so much what he said but the expression on his face when he said it. No matter what she did or how hard she tried, the pained look in his eyes would not leave her mind. He seemed hurt that she refused to open up to him, but how could she tell him the truth? He was leaving in a week, and as much as she wished otherwise, he just wasn't capable of loving her—at least not the way she wanted him to. Justin wasn't ready to put down roots and invest the time necessary to have a solid relationship. She snorted at the thought of her own hectic lifestyle and endless hours at the firm. Hell, she wasn't so ready either.

"Isabella!"

She jumped at the sound of the shrill voice behind her and stopped kneading the dough beneath her hands.

"What is it, Mama?"

"The dough. There's far too much flour in it," Maggie cried as she pointed her finger toward the large lump in her hands. "I was going to bake a rack of cookies before I left for the day, but I can't use that dough." She glanced at her watch. "I have to be at bingo in half an hour, and there's no time for me to fix this. You'll just have to start over and bake them yourself."

Isabella cursed under her breath when she realized her mother was right. She'd added too much flour, and now the dough was hard and stiff—something she would have realized had she been paying attention.

Her mother clucked her tongue. "Where is your head, Isabella? You've been distracted all day."

"I know where her head is," Celeste crooned as she breezed into the kitchen, her tiger-gold eyes twinkling with laughter.

"*I know where her head is,*" Isabella mocked under her breath in a singsong voice. "Shouldn't you be out working the cash register?"

"I came back here to see if you need help, and obviously you do. Why don't you go hold down the register while I fix things back here?"

Isabella glared at Celeste, who pretended to ignore her as she slipped on an apron.

"I don't need any help—" She stopped midsentence when two pairs of wide eyes swung in her direction. All right, maybe she did. After all, she'd already spilled a sack of flour and broken a glass pie dish, and now she'd ruined a lump of dough. Handling the money was definitely looking as if it would be a bit safer for everyone in the end.

"I better get going if I don't want to be late," her mother said, looking at her watch again. "Do you two think you can handle things until closing?" Isabella thinned her lips into a tight line when Maggie directed her question to Celeste.

"*We* will be just fine," Isabella assured as she ushered her out of the kitchen and toward the front door of the bakery. "Have fun tonight." She waved her mother out and pulled the door shut before Maggie had a chance to protest.

Isabella blew out a long, deep breath as she twisted on her heels and marched back into the kitchen, where Celeste was already preparing another mound of dough.

She'd been trying to get Celeste alone all day, but her best friend had been hard to pin down, despite the fact that they'd both been working in the bakery. Every time Isabella tried to talk to her in private, Celeste would dodge her. It was almost as if Celeste knew what was on Isabella's mind and was determined to steer clear of the inevitable for as long as she could.

Now, thanks to her mother's standing weekly appointment with a bingo board, Celeste's time was up. Isabella leaned against one of the freezers and folded her arms across her chest, pinning her best friend with a hard stare. "It's funny. I've been trying to talk to you all day, but I get the feeling you've been avoiding me."

Celeste glanced up for a brief moment, but her expression was unreadable. "I haven't been avoiding you. I've just been busy. We've been swamped all day."

She was telling the truth there. Right after Christmas, New Year's orders always came flooding in. And yet, Isabella sensed Celeste was using their hectic day as an excuse.

"And here I thought you were avoiding me because you knew as soon as I got you alone I was going to ask what the hell is going on with you and Caleb."

If Celeste was put off by the sarcasm in Isabella's voice, she didn't show it. The only indication she gave that she'd even heard Isabella was the slight wrinkling of her brow as she frowned, but even then she didn't look up from her task of kneading the dough. "Nothing's going on."

"Really?"

Celeste stopped long enough to scowl at her. "Really."

She wasn't buying it. She'd seen the surreptitious glances Caleb and Celeste had given each other at Christmas dinner when they thought no one was looking. The fireworks they'd ignited when their gazes clashed had been so intense that the lights around the Christmas tree paled in comparison. Celeste didn't get to mock her for getting entangled with Justin when it was apparent her friend was somehow entangled herself.

"So you haven't done anything with Caleb?"

"Nope."

Isabella narrowed her eyes.

"So not a single kiss, then?"

Celeste faltered.

Aha! "You kissed him." When Celeste didn't lift her head, she knew she was spot on. "I knew something was up. Spill it."

Celeste huffed out a long breath and finally stopped playing with the dough in her hands to meet Isabella's gaze. "Some days I hate that you're an attorney. You just dig and dig—"

"We both know you're guilty of the same tactics, but I'm not going to let you change the subject. I want to hear about the kissing."

"That's really all there was to it—a kiss."

Isabella arched one brow. Her friend didn't *just* kiss men. Celeste was like a *manizer,* or a man-eater. Or whatever the term was. When it came to Celeste and men, there was more—there always was.

"No, really. What happened after all the kissing?"

"Nothing. And I wouldn't even call it a kiss, since a kiss generally involves *two* people and he didn't seem inclined to add himself to my one."

Isabella stilled. "What?"

"He didn't kiss me back," she said with a wry smile, but they'd been friends too long for Isabella not to notice the tiny flash of embarrassment in Celeste's warm gaze. It probably had been a blow to her pride. Men didn't tell Celeste no, and they certainly didn't reject her. It just didn't happen. But from what she'd seen yesterday, Caleb *definitely* wanted Celeste. So she knew lack of interest wasn't the reason why Caleb hadn't reciprocated.

"Caleb's not like the men you're used to—"

"So I've noticed."

Isabella returned Celeste's wry smile. "He's kind of old-fashioned. He likes to do things at his pace, and in his own way—"

"So he's controlling?"

"No, he's just"—she searched for the right word—"*methodical*. He's always been that way. He's not like you in the way he approaches things. If you want something you go after it, but Caleb is more strategic about it. He thinks everything through, and then he acts."

"Perfect. So by the time he decides to have a fling with me, I'll be back in DC."

Isabella studied Celeste, who appeared indifferent about their entire conversation, as if none of it mattered. She couldn't fool Isabella, though.

"You like him."

"So? I like a lot of men."

"But you *really* like Caleb. I can tell."

Celeste tilted her head to the side, pinning Isabella with those piercing golden eyes of hers. "Really? So we're psychic now?"

"No. I just know you—and I know you like Caleb. He's the first guy who won't jump just because you said so, and while I know you won't admit it, you like that you can't quite figure him out."

Celeste opened her mouth to protest just as the doorbell chimed.

Never was there a more literal example of being saved by the bell.

"I gotta get that." And before Celeste could utter a word, Isabella floated out of the room, with a smug grin on her face.

Justin furled his lips into a small smile as he watched Isabella sail into the front room of the bakery, her hips swaying gently. Her jeans rode dangerously low, revealing just a small peek of the creamy skin along her midriff.

"Hi," she said breathlessly as if she'd been jogging.

He ambled across the room and leaned against the countertop. "Is this a bad time?"

"A little. We're getting ready to close, and I just have a few things to get done before I leave today."

He frowned as his narrow gaze sharpened on her face, noting how her eyes didn't quite meet his. He'd called her once on her cell today, but she hadn't picked up. He knew it was a busy time at Angelo's, and from the rumpled mess of her clothing and disheveled hair, he was sure she was in fact busy, but he sensed it was more than just that. She'd been guarded that morning, and she was the same way now.

He didn't say a word as he walked around to the other side of the counter and tugged her into his arms. She gasped softly but didn't pull away. If nothing else, Isabella could not fight her body's response to him. His fingers brushed her cheek, cradling her face against his hand as he tipped her head back. Her eyes drifted shut just as his lips grazed hers in a soft, searching kiss.

A sharp spike of heat pierced his gut, and he groaned against her mouth. He twisted her around, pinning her against the counter. She moaned into his mouth, the soft sigh whispering through his entire body. His gut clenched tighter at the needy sound, and he inhaled her unique scent, savoring the taste of her on his lips.

"Eck, gross."

He brought an end to the sweet kiss and rested his forehead against hers, releasing a low groan of frustration. Celeste interrupting them was becoming a far too common and unwelcome occurrence.

"Get lost, Cruella."

"Can't. Isabella needs me to help her finish up here."

He ignored Celeste's smug expression and peered down at Isabella, a single brow lifting in question.

"She's right. I need to close out the receipts while she finishes up in the back."

"What if I finished up for you? You could send Celeste home and—"

He frowned at Celeste's derisive snort. "Yeah, right. And as soon as I'm gone, you two would be all over this place frolicking in whipped cream and dough."

Despite his best intentions, an image of Isabella covered in whipped cream and wearing nothing but a smile flashed into his head.

"Ugh, that's gross—both of you." He glanced at Isabella, who wore a similar dreamy expression, and grinned. That was definitely being added to the list before he shipped out—*sex at the bakery.*

"That's nice of you, Justin, but we're almost closed. I'll be finished in about an hour."

"But—" He stopped. He didn't want to push her. Just because he was on vacation didn't mean she was, and it was obvious she was swamped.

"What is it?"

He shrugged. "I just had a surprise planned for you, and hoped we could leave right at closing. I can help out if that means you'll finish up sooner."

"A surprise? I bet it's something kinky—"

"Celeste!" Justin exclaimed.

Celeste shrugged, but the grin on her face told Justin she wasn't the least bit contrite.

"Oh, go on and get out of here. I can close up," Celeste said with a wave of her hand.

Isabella shook her head. "I'm not going to leave you here. There's too much left to do, and—"

"The cookies are already in the oven, and I can do the receipts while they're baking." Celeste was already pushing Isabella toward the door, for which Justin was grateful. They rarely saw eye to eye on anything, but it was nice to know that when it came to Isabella, he had Celeste's approval. He hadn't thought much about that, but Celeste could have chosen to make things difficult between him and Isabella if she'd wanted to.

"Celeste, I couldn't leave you. How will you get home?"

"Just leave your car." She gave him a small wink. "Justin can take you on whatever kinky adventure he has planned in his SUV. And I'll drive your car home."

She smiled as she shoved Isabella toward him. He never thought he'd say the words, so they stuck in his throat for a moment, eventually coming out awkward and stiff.

"Thanks, Celeste."

"Yeah, thanks, Celeste. I owe you one," Isabella said.

"Whatever, girl. It's fine. You deserve a break."

But just before the door clicked shut, he swore he heard Celeste murmur under her breath, "Besides, if I can't get laid, then at least *somebody* should."

C eleste was just pulling the cookies out of the oven when a knock sounded against the door. Setting the tray aside, she wiped her hands across her apron. A quick glance at her watch told her it was almost six o'clock. Isabella and Justin had left about an hour ago. She hoped they hadn't forgotten something and been forced to double back.

The murky darkness outside made it hard to see who it was until she reached the door. Standing there glaring at her visitor through the glass, she debated whether to even open the door, but quickly decided that was just childish as she twisted the knob.

"The bakery is closed."

Despite the fact that she'd blocked the entrance with her body, Caleb effortlessly pushed past her with his large frame.

It was either let him in or get bowled over.

"I know. I stopped by to make sure you were all right. Justin called to let me know you were here alone."

She wanted to roll her eyes and smile at the same time. Who said chivalry was dead? She'd lived in a big metropolitan city all by herself for years, but Justin and Caleb somehow thought she needed an escort in the small town of Jacksonville, where a crime hadn't been committed in the past five years—that is, if one didn't count her *itty bitty* hit and run.

"That's nice of you, but as you can see, I'm fine."

He ignored her as he crossed the room with three easy strides and sat down on the stool behind the counter. "I'll wait until you finish and then escort you home."

She opened her mouth to protest, but thought better of it and snapped it shut. Caleb was stubborn—probably as stubborn as they came. He was also a gentleman. There was no way he would leave her alone at night, no matter how much she said otherwise.

"Fine. I'll be done in a second."

She marched past him into the kitchen, pretending not to notice his eyes on her as he followed her every move until she disappeared from his sight. As soon as she was alone in the safety of the kitchen, she blew out a long, uneven breath. Whenever Caleb was near, he seemed to suck the air out of the room. With his size and presence, he was impossible to ignore. Even now, when they were separated by a room, the spicy scent of his aftershave still lingered in the air around her.

"Do you need any help?"

A tiny yelp tore past her lips as she clutched her chest, trying to ease her racing heart.

"Sorry, I didn't mean to scare you. I thought you heard me."

She glared at him, but she didn't say a word. Instead, she backed away from him, trying to put some distance between them. How had she not heard him get so close? She took two more stutter steps away, and then another. It wasn't until her back was against the sink that she realized he was *stalking* her.

"I—I'm fine. I don't need any help back here."

He moved closer, his body inches from hers, and she tightened her grip on the sink. The tiny action didn't go unnoticed, and he smiled, his full sensual lips curling into a grin until a small dimple creased his cheek.

"I make you nervous."

That was the last thing she'd been expecting him to say, so she blinked several times before she could collect her thoughts. She didn't like the expression on his face—that smug smirk that said he knew exactly how he affected her. Yes, he made her nervous, but that didn't mean he was necessarily in control. She knew that if she turned the tables on him, he would find himself equally out of his element. She smiled at that thought. Maybe it was time to do just that.

"Nervous?" Mischief twinkled in her gaze as she removed the clip at the back of her head and let her hair fall to her shoulders. With a gentle shake, she loosened her auburn-streaked curls and noticed how Caleb's eyes followed every sensual move of her head.

"There is little that makes me nervous." She removed her apron, silently taunting him with the possibility that she was about to take off something else as well.

"What are you doing?" She smiled at the harsh rasp of his voice, her fingers stilling on the third button of her blouse.

"I'm proving that men have little effect on my nerves—not even you, Caleb."

"I know what you're up to."

"Just as I know what *you're* up to, but it won't work."

He arched one brow. "But you think wrestling control from me will somehow get you what you want?"

She didn't like the way he made it sound, as if she was battling for dominance. She didn't need to be in control, but she refused to be the one always out of her element.

"It's always worked for me in the past."

"But not this time, and not with me."

She detested that self-satisfied air about him—as if he knew she wanted him, and that eventually he would teach her how to behave. All she wanted was a little fling, not a head trip. She was starting to think that sex with Caleb really wasn't worth all the effort.

She twisted on her heels and started to slip past him. "Why am I even playing this game with you?"

"Because you want me," he said softly, trapping her against the sink between his splayed hands. The warmth of his breath against her ear caused tiny frissons of heat to slowly wind their way along her spine. She struggled to find her voice, but somehow she managed.

"I won't lie. I do want you, and you know that. But you're too much work, Caleb. When I see something, I go after it, but you—you—"

He traced a single finger along her cheek until it reached her chin, and he tipped her head back. "I take my time."

No kidding. "Well, I don't have time. I'm a busy woman who has needs, and if you can't fulfill them, then I will find someone else who will."

His blue eyes darkened to deep cobalt and he pushed away from her. For the first time since he'd arrived at the bakery, she could finally breathe without absorbing every single molecule of his essence. And yet, for some peculiar reason she felt bereft of his nearness.

"You know what you are? You're a coward. Real intimacy scares you, so you do everything in your power to avoid it."

She drew back at the sharpness of his tone. She was many things, but she wasn't a coward, and he had no right to make grand sweeping statements about her character when he didn't even know her.

"Who says I want to be intimate with you? I don't want to get to know you, Caleb. I just want to sleep with you. Two very different things."

As soon as the words were out, she wanted to snatch them back. That wasn't how she felt at all, but she couldn't tell him the truth—that he was right about her. She *did* fear true intimacy.

A tiny muscle in his jaw twitched, but that was the only indication he gave that he'd even heard her words.

"I will wait for you outside until you finish up."

A pang of remorse shot through her, but before she could even offer so much as an apology, he stalked out of the kitchen, leaving her standing there feeling like a world-class bitch.

She sighed as she shoved a hand into her hair, wishing she could take back her words. Caleb had called her a coward, but what she'd said had been so much worse. If a man had ever told her that he wanted her only for sex, she would have told him to kiss her ass and then shown him the door. She owed Caleb an apology. He was a good guy—probably one of the few truly good guys still left in the world.

She busied herself with cleaning up, silently arguing with her guilty conscience. As much as she hated her despicable words, the outcome was probably for the best. Their attraction to each other was ill fated from the beginning. Caleb would have wanted more from her than she could give, and he would have given her more than she wanted. In the end, she knew this was for the best. So why did she feel so miserable?

Chapter Thirteen

"Oooh, my ears just popped. I knew it. We're up in the mountains. I want to see—"

"Don't touch that," Justin warned Isabella when she started picking at her blindfold. "We'll be there in thirty seconds. Do you think you can restrain yourself until then?"

He grinned at her long-suffering sigh, but his words must have placated her, because she settled back against the seat and folded her hands in her lap. He stared at her for a single heartbeat before turning his gaze back to the narrow winding road that led up to a small log cabin. As a child he'd spent many summers at his family home in the mountains, but he hadn't been back since the deaths of his parents. He glanced at Isabella. She was the reason why he was there now. He knew she loved it up there, and if anyone could dull the pain of the bittersweet memories that this place conjured, it was her.

He slowed his SUV down to a steady crawl as he pulled into the driveway and cut the engine.

"Can I take it off now?"

"Nope." He slid out of the SUV and walked around to the other side to help her out. He glanced around at the jagged snow-capped mountains in the distance, and the looming pine trees, their branches weighed down with sprinkles of white snow. It was beautiful, even pristine, and he inhaled the crisp air, the fresh scent of pine filling his lungs.

Gripping their hands together, they walked toward the pier, which stretched out across a small lake that was now completely frozen over. He stopped just at the edge.

"You can take it off now."

The words were barely out of his mouth before she whipped off the blindfold. A small smile spread across his face as he watched her admire her surroundings beneath the iridescent glow of the moonlight.

"I forgot how beautiful this place is."

"Me, too." He wrapped her in his arms, her back against his chest, and rested his chin atop her head.

"I wished we could have gotten here sooner to watch the sun go down. It's an amazing sight."

"I remember."

He knew she would. A grin furled his lips as he recalled the last time they'd watched the sun go down over the lake more than ten years ago.

"I'm surprised you even saw the sun, with all the commotion caused by your little skinny-dipping stunt."

She twisted around, her eyes twinkling with mischief.

"I must admit it was hard to focus with all those hot, hard, naked men around me. I got into so much trouble with your mom for that."

"I remember. I was there." He'd just finished up his first year of law school and was home for a few weeks over the summer. His parents had let him and Isabella bring some of their friends up to the lake for the weekend. Everything had been fine until his parents went into town for the day and Isabella got the idea of skinny-dipping in her head. Soon everyone was naked—*except* him. And when his parents returned from their trip hours earlier than expected and found the rest of them in the lake naked, all hell had broken loose.

"Yeah, but you didn't do anything wrong. You never got in." He didn't bother reminding her that his parents had been furious with him for letting the incident happen in the first place. For some reason they refused to accept that Isabella was a force of nature. Like a hurricane, she was hard to predict and impossible to control.

"Ah, but I did plenty wrong. Mom caught me staring, and I can tell you I wasn't looking at the sun."

She chuckled as she turned her head back around to gaze out over the lake. "I bet. All those young nubile girls frolicking about. You probably didn't even notice the sun was out."

He frowned as he glanced down at the crown of her head. She said *girls*—but there had been only *one girl* he'd been caught staring at that day.

"You're right. I didn't give a damn about the sun going down because I was too busy staring at you."

She whipped her head around again, her eyes wide. "Me?"

"Why is that so shocking to you?"

"Because you couldn't stand me back then."

"Is that what you think?"

When she nodded, he released a long breath, his arms tightening around her. Of course that's what she would believe. Until a week ago, he hadn't said or done anything to make her think otherwise.

"Have you ever wondered why whenever you're in trouble, I always seem to be there?"

She snorted. "Um, because if you weren't, then who else would my mother call to save me?"

"If I didn't care, Isabella, I wouldn't come, no matter how many times your mother called me."

"Of course you would," she said with a small smile. "You're a hero by nature. If someone needs you, you're there. Hell, you fixed Monica's car, and now every time she needs something else fixed, you're there to do it. That's just who you are."

"You really believe that? If *anyone* calls, I just come running?"

He glowered at her when she shrugged, as if to say that was exactly what she thought. That stupid nickname Celeste had coined had always rankled him, but he never believed Isabella saw him that way, too. At some point, he thought she would come to realize that he *always* came to her rescue because he cared about her, because she was special to him.

"The other day when you were stranded on the side of the road in the middle of the blizzard, Monica called—" It didn't go unnoticed by him that she stiffened in his arms when he said Monica's name. He knew she didn't particularly care for Monica, but if she thought she was in competition with his long-ago ex, she was mistaken.

"—She wanted me to come over to check the circuit breaker—"

"I bet she did," Isabella muttered under her breath, forcing him to bite back a grin.

"She was afraid there was something wrong with it, and was worried that she and the kids would be stranded in their home with no lights if the power failed. I told her if that happened, she should call me and I would get the fire department over there immediately, but that I couldn't leave because the roads were too dangerous at the time—"

"But that was true. You could have been hurt driving over there to check on something she wasn't even sure was broken. Besides, she has neighbors. She didn't have to stay there if the power went ou—"

He cut her off in midrant when he lifted her chin with his finger, gently tilting her head so that she could meet his gaze. "Your mother called five minutes later. The roads were still dangerous, but I didn't hesitate to go after you."

"But that was different. She was safe at home. I was stranded on the side of the road—"

"Dammit, Isabella. It's not that different." Frustration washed over him. Why was she being so damned obtuse? "When it comes to you, I never hesitate or offer excuses. I'm always there whenever you need me, regardless of whether you want me there, because I lo—" He cut himself off and started again. "I care about you. You're special to me, Isabella. Always have been."

She stood there, stunned speechless by his whispered words. In that moment, he was glad she didn't say anything, because he needed a second to come to terms with his own inner revelation. He loved Isabella—always had. For so long, his feelings had been purely platonic, more brotherly than anything, but at some point things had changed. Over time, what he felt for her had evolved, and it wasn't until he'd almost faltered and confessed something he hadn't quite acknowledged himself that he realized he was falling in love with her.

She'd always been a part of his life, sharing both the highs and lows with him. It seemed strange to people that they bickered all the time and still maintained such a close relationship. He'd gone to college and then law school in New York, and somehow she'd always managed to make her way up there about every other month to crash at his place—and then leave it trashed. He hadn't minded because he would repay the favor about a month later when he found some excuse to head to DC for the weekend, where Isabella went to school, with his rowdy frat brothers. One weekend she'd even thrown them out when they broke almost every piece of furniture in her apartment. She didn't talk to him for two weeks after that. When he joined the Navy, they didn't see each other as often, but they still managed to stay in touch. At the very least, they never missed the major holidays or each other's birthdays with cards or phone calls. And whenever he was in the States he always called her—just to make sure she hadn't finally ended up in prison, he would say. And she always managed to send him a letter or a care package when he was stationed in another country—

something she did only because Maggie forced her to, she would write in her letters. Their relationship was hard to explain, but it had always been this way, and it worked for them.

There was probably no one who knew him better, which was why she was the first person he'd brought out to the cabin since his parents had passed away. Isabella would understand. Without him having to say a word, she knew how much this place meant to him, and just how hard it was for him to return. She saw him in ways others didn't. He glanced out over the frozen lake before settling his gaze on her. He probably had the worst timing in the world. It wasn't every day a man discovered he was in love with a girl he'd known all his life. But he would be forced to leave her in less than a week, and he could only hope that when he returned, the feelings they now shared would still be there.

Justin was certain that he would still feel the same way six months from now, but he knew Isabella was another story. Right now, everything was magical between them. They'd been closeted off from the rest of the world, away from the stresses of work and everyday life. But what about after he left and she returned to her lavish life in DC—*and to Harry*? Would she even think about him, or just chalk up their time together as a brief Christmas affair?

Isabella was silent as she walked to the cabin with Justin, still trying to digest his words. She was too afraid to read more into them, because she didn't want to be disappointed when she finally had to face reality after he left. And yet, the silent message he'd conveyed made her wish they had more time—just a little bit longer to discover where this was all headed.

He opened the door to the cabin and ushered her inside. As soon as she stepped into the foyer area she came to a halt. She hadn't been there in years, and in that instant all the memories from her childhood and teenage years came flooding back. She'd spent several summers there just hanging out and getting into trouble—and, of course, driving Justin crazy.

The two-story home looked the same as she'd remembered, with its handcrafted wooden furniture, stone fireplace, and shiny hardwood floors still coverd with colorful handwoven rugs. Everything about the cabin was picturesque, as if it belonged on a postcard for a winter wonderland vacation.

But it wasn't the quaint beauty of the home or her brief trip down memory lane that caused her to hesitate—it was the trail of rose petals.

She glanced over her shoulder at Justin, who was leaning against the front door, his arms folded across his chest.

"Follow the petals."

Mischief danced in his eyes, and she knew that whatever lay at the end of her journey promised to be a sensual surprise.

He didn't follow her as she walked along the trail of roses. It wound its way through the house, up the stairs, then back down again. She was on a wild-goose chase, and it didn't end until she was outside. The firelight from the kerosene lamps flickered along the trail, illuminating her way, until she reached the hot tub.

Roses of pink and red floated along the surface of the frothy water, while off to the side sat a bucket of champagne and an assortment of fruit and chocolate. She heard Justin's footsteps behind her. Seconds later he turned the hot tub bubbles on, stirring up the petals.

He came up behind her, his hands settling atop her shoulders as he whispered against her ear. "Get in."

She started stripping out of her clothes, but stopped when Justin didn't follow suit.

"Aren't you getting in?"

He smiled. "I will, but later. Right now I just want to watch you."

A slow, steady heat coiled in her belly, awakening her desire as she imagined all the things Justin had planned for her. Sex in a hot tub wasn't on the list, but she was glad he'd added it anyway.

She took her time removing her clothes, her body twisting seductively as she gingerly peeled off each garment. Raw, sexual fire leapt in his gaze as he stared at her with a hungry, predatory look in his eyes.

The air stood still in her lungs when she was down to just her bra and panties. It was almost déjà vu—reminding her of the sensual striptease across a Scrabble board that had started all this. It felt as if that had happened so long ago, but it had been only seven days—seven naughty days and six wicked nights of erotic pleasure in Justin's arms.

She shivered as every single memory flashed into her head, and her entire body grew hotter with need.

"Are you cold?"

She blinked in confusion before realizing he was talking about her slight tremble. She glanced around at the heating lamps that surrounded the bubbling tub. Even if they'd been off, she was sure her own internal heat would have been more than enough to keep her warm.

She shook her head. "I'm fine."

He took a step toward her, one hand stretched out. "Do you want me to help you?"

Their eyes met, and energy crackled between them. She stepped away from him, just out of his reach.

"No, I just want you to stand back and watch."

A wicked gleam lit up his eyes. Obeying her command, he stepped back. Her lips furled into a small, mischievous smile, her hands slowly sliding across her body. She delighted in how his eyes darkened, never once leaving her.

She continued to caress her body, ignoring the small chill that slipped past the lamps to cool her skin and brush tiny goose bumps along her body. She wound her arms behind her back once again, pausing for just a moment to unhook her bra. She held Justin's gaze, her heart thumping harder in her chest as she let her bra fall from her shoulders.

Smoldering embers of desire raged in his eyes, nearly scorching her with their intensity. A low growl emanated from him as he took a step toward her.

"No," she commanded with a shake of her head, forcing him to halt his steps. "You stay right there until I'm done."

His chest rose and fell on short pants, his eyes boring into her. She knew it was a struggle, but he didn't move a muscle. She rewarded his obedience by hooking her fingers beneath the elastic of her panties. With slow, measured movements she slid the dark strip of lace down her legs. Stepping out of her panties, she kicked them aside, and before Justin could take a step she hopped over the side of the tub and jumped in.

The warm bubbles tickled Isabella's skin as they swirled around her. A naughty glint sparkled in Justin's eyes as he strolled toward her. He shucked off his sweater and cast it aside, along with his winter boots, and then his jeans.

Her gaze remained glued to the hard, chiseled muscles of his torso as he drew closer to the tub before stopping at its edge. He knelt down on the steps, his fingers lightly skimming across the surface of the water. She held her breath while he slowly stripped out of his boxers and slid into the tub.

He pulled her into his embrace, his arms wrapping around her waist.

"Do you want some champagne?"

She glanced over his shoulder at the bottle that sat in a bucket of ice, but then shook her head.

"No." She wound her arms around his neck, pulling him closer. "I have everything I need right here."

Her heart skipped a beat when he smiled down at her.

"This is beautiful, Justin. When did you have time to do all this?"

A small grin spread across his face. "I'm on vacation so I have a lot of time to be creative. As soon as I was done, I came for you."

She smiled up at him. "Thank you, Justin," she whispered, lifting herself on her toes to give him a gentle kiss. The moment their tongues touched, the innocent kiss quickly transformed into a mind-numbing explosion of passion and heat. She clung to him as desire clawed at her, hot and insistent.

He rocked his burgeoning arousal against her belly, stoking the flames of wanton heat that raged inside her. She rubbed her body against his, the friction driving them both wild, until they were panting with need. He claimed her mouth possessively, deepening the pressure of the kiss with his strong, hard lips.

She let out a slight whimper when he tugged his mouth from hers, his chest heaving, struggling to take in his next breath. She imagined she looked the same as her heart raced ferociously in her chest.

"Turn around." He issued the command, moving her body so that her back was flush against his chest. She gasped at the hard nudge of his length against the cleft of her ass. She wriggled against him, delighting in the harsh sound of her name on his lips.

"Open your legs." He murmured the words against the smooth skin along the column of her neck, and she found it difficult to follow his instructions with his fingers plucking at her nipples. As if he'd read her mind, he slid one hand from her breast across the taut muscles of her stomach, through the nest of curls at the juncture of her thighs. He parted her with his fingers, and at the same time he slipped one leg between hers.

She leaned her head back against his shoulder, her eyes closing as she arched her back like a hunter's bow. He positioned her so that she was spread wide before the water jets just beneath the surface.

She let her hands drift down to her breasts as he held her legs apart. She teased her nipples to stiffened buds, the furious streams of water stroking the hardened nub of her clit. Burgeoning heat wrapped around her, and she felt as if she was being consumed from the inside out.

Justin stroked his lips against her neck, and tingles of pleasure shot down her spine as he suckled her flesh. He placed a wet trail of kisses along her throat until he reached her ear, and she let out a long, low moan when he caught her sensitive lobe between his teeth. Heat throbbed within her core, the insistent need to climax beating against her.

"Come for me, Isabella," Justin whispered against her ear, the sinfully rich baritone of his voice making her toes curl. Everything inside her ached to obey his command, and her hips began to rock instinctively, meeting the pulsing surge of the jets until tiny tremors of sensation roiled through her like a cresting wave.

She stiffened against him; the heady rush of blood pouring through her made her dizzy. She shuddered and cried out his name, the muscles in her pussy clenching tight as she came hard, her entire body shaking from her tremulous release. Tiny convulsions racked her for a long time, but Justin held her firmly until the aftershocks of her orgasm began to ebb and flow from her satiated body.

Isabella slumped against him, her limbs boneless and heavy. He held her to him, her legs still spread, until her breathing grew even. After she had recovered, Justin set her down so that her feet touched the hot tub's bottom. She thought they would begin to wade out of the water, but instead, Justin nudged her upper body over the rim of the tub.

She glanced over his shoulder, meeting his twinkling gaze.

"I suggest you grab hold of the side," he said with a grin. Just as her fingertips gripped the edge, he surged forward, burying his hot, hard length deep inside her.

They cried out in unison, her name coming out as a tortured moan from his lips. His hands closed around her hips, his nails digging deep into the sensitive flesh as he pounded her pussy. He went so deep, so hard, she swore she could feel him nudging against the mouth of her womb. She winced, but she ignored the soft brush of pain as a fresh gush of wet heat flooded her sheath, renewing her desire.

His strokes were rough as he pummeled inside her, hard and demanding. She closed her eyes when he drove deeper, a feverish wave of pleasure building inside her.

"Justin." He seemed to sense her need, and he leaned over her, nuzzling the gentle curve of her neck.

"You want it harder?" He emphasized his words by plowing deeper within her, his strokes frenzied.

"Yes," she cried out, her eyes now clenched tight. The primal intensity of his wild lovemaking pushed her closer and closer to the edge. He grasped her shoulder with one hand while the other snaked down between her legs to strum her aching clit.

That was almost her undoing. He slammed into her from behind, the warm water splashing across her cheek, over the edge. She could feel him hardening inside her, his hurried strokes growing jerky and uneven as he pumped furiously.

He fucked her faster, his hard shaft going deeper, and she felt the pulsing vibrations through every inch of her body. She was so, so close, but his pleasure peaked before hers, and he let out a lewd curse under his breath just as he gave one final thrust. She bore down on him with her inner muscles, milking him as small spasms ran through her. Warmth pooled inside her, his seed drenching her channel, and his body quivered until finally he stilled and relaxed against her.

"I'm sorry," he said shakily, pulling out of her.

She spun around on wobbly legs, her hand lifting to cup his face. She brushed her lips against his in a quick peck, stroking her palm across his stubbled chin, the short hair tickling the sensitive pads of her fingertips.

"What are you sorry for?"

"I'm embarrassed to say this, but I've never lost control like that. Not since I was in high school have I finished befo—"

She placed a single finger against his lips, halting his next words as she wrinkled her nose at the thought of the other women he'd pleasured. She had no desire to hear how he'd driven them to ecstasy before finding his own release.

She let her hand fall from his mouth and twisted her arms behind his neck. "I like that I'm the first person you've ever lost control with." And she did. Justin was always so composed and in charge of himself. In the past, she'd always goaded him, trying to provoke him so he would break free of his shell. For once, it was nice to know that she'd shattered his control, not with her crazy antics, but in the most basic way that a woman could.

"I say we try and see if we can get you to lose control again."

He cocked his head to the side. "I must say my pride is wounded. The look in your eyes tells me you believe it will be so easy."

She chuckled softly at his teasing banter, drawing him deeper into her embrace. She didn't say a word as she kissed him soundly. She had no doubt Justin would work to maintain an iron leash on his control for the rest of the night, but regardless of whether he succeeded, she was bound to enjoy every minute of it.

Chapter Fourteen

"I think you've redeemed yourself," Isabella said with a sigh when she finally managed to find her voice.

Justin glanced down at her, his gaze following her fingers as they delicately traced a pattern across his chest.

"I'm glad. I would hate for you to tarnish my reputation."

She rolled on top of him, a wicked gleam lighting up her face, her hair spilling over one shoulder to tickle his chest. She was so lovely like this—carefree and uninhibited, full of laughter and an enthusiasm that was infectious.

He leaned up to gently kiss her nose before settling back against his pillow. He hated that soon he would have to leave her. For the second time that night, he wished he could somehow postpone his deployment, but he knew that wasn't possible. He blew out a long, jagged breath, exasperation and a sense of hopeless futility roaring through him.

"What's wrong?"

He fought to wipe his face clean and plaster on a smile, but Isabella's gaze only darkened, and he knew he wasn't fooling her—she knew him too well.

"Honestly? I'm wishing that I could delay my deployment."

A flurry of emotions flashed across her face, but before she could utter a response, he pressed his finger against her parted lips.

"I didn't say that to coax anything out of you. I was simply telling you what was bothering me." He shoved a hand through his hair when he realized that he didn't want to just delay his departure. It was more than that. "Hell, lately I've started to wish I didn't have to go altogether."

He realized his mistake too late, and when her eyes lit up, he knew he was going to have a hard time getting her to let this one go.

"I've always told you, you could go back to law—"

"Isabella—"

"Every time I try to bring this up, you always brush me off. Don't you think it's time that you finally dealt with the real reason why you walked away from JAG in the first place?"

Her words caused a low hum of fury to settle in his gut, and he rolled her off him as he sat up.

"I know why I left JAG; it's you who can't accept my reason."

"You can lie to yourself, but you can't lie to m—"

"Drop it, Isabella." The look in his eyes must have reflected the cold fury that pulsed inside him, because she snapped her lips together, her mouth dipping into a frown.

He slid off the bed and headed to the bathroom, but his steps almost faltered when she whispered behind him. Her voice was barely audible, but he heard every single word, and they burned a hole into his heart.

"It wasn't your fault, Justin."

He didn't reply, mostly because his voice was too choked up. With his back to her, he slipped into the bathroom and closed the door with a dull thud.

He slid into the shower and stayed there for a long time, wishing the water could somehow wash away all his memories. Isabella said it wasn't his fault, his brothers said it wasn't his fault, and he knew he wasn't ultimately to blame for his parents' deaths. But he still carried around a burden of guilt for what he considered to be his selfish actions.

If he'd just come home as his mother had asked, his parents would still be alive. The weekend his parents drove to Norfolk to see him, he'd been buried under a pile of depositions and case studies for an upcoming trial. He'd been too busy—he was always too busy. He lived less than an hour away, and yet he could never seem to find the time to come home.

His mother had been especially worried about him and about the toll his caseload was taking on him. So on a bright autumn Friday afternoon, just before rush hour, she'd set off to Norfolk with his father.

They'd never made it.

He'd blamed his job and himself. When he finally returned to work he knew he couldn't continue to do what he was doing, so he'd entered the SEAL program. Everyone had thought the change would be good for him—everyone *except* Isabella. To this day, she was the only person who'd known the real reason why he'd become a SEAL. He welcomed the danger and hazards of the job, because at the time, he'd felt there was little left to live for.

Isabella might have been right about his motivations, but as misguided as he'd been, he still didn't regret his decision. He'd needed something to anchor him at a time when he'd been lost, but now he wasn't lost anymore. And yet, he still didn't think he was ready to return to law—he doubted he ever would be.

He shoved a hand through his wet locks, letting out a long sigh. Damn Isabella for dredging up memories he'd buried long ago. He wished she would respect his decision and leave it alone, but he knew she couldn't. That just wasn't in her nature.

Why did she have to go and ruin a perfect evening with her prying and probing? They should have spent the rest of the night making love, but all he wanted to do was drive her home, drop her off, and forget about all the old wounds she'd just opened up.

The drive home the next morning was torture. Justin barely said a word to Isabella or spared her a glance.

Isabella had pretended to be asleep when he'd finally come out of the bathroom last night, because it would have been harder to face the painful silence of his rejection. She'd longed to apologize, but how could she? He'd lain down with his back to her, never once touching her.

She'd fallen asleep feeling miserable, but figured in the morning his anger would dissipate. Well, it hadn't, and she hated that he insisted on shutting her out. He always clammed up when people got too close to a sore spot, but things had changed between them. She wasn't the annoying Izzie, the constant pain in his ass. She was his lover, and it was frustrating that he refused to communicate with her.

She was contrite for most of the ride home, but was dwelling on the fact that he'd murmured tender words to her the night before and was now acting so cold that it made her angry. She didn't deserve this, not if he cared for her as much as he said he did. And by the time they pulled into her mother's driveway, she was irritated in her own right.

She thought that before he let her get out of the car, he would at least say *something*, but he just sat there stone-faced, his empty eyes staring straight ahead. Immediately, anger poured through Isabella, clouding her sense of reason.

"After all these years, is this still how you deal with things that upset you? You just shut people out." Her voice was filled with regret when she said, "After everything we've shared these past days, I guess I just expected more from you." She jumped out of the SUV and slammed the door. She was so lost in her emotions that she didn't realize he'd followed her until his hand clamped down on her arm and he spun her around.

"Shut you out? Isabella, I asked you to let something go, and you didn't. How do you expect me to respond? How would you have responded?"

He had a point, and she knew it. She'd seen the error of her ways the moment he'd stalked out of the room last night, but he'd never given her the chance to admit that she'd been wrong. He'd stonewalled her with his silence, making it nearly impossible for her to offer even the smallest of apologies.

"I would have been upset, but I would have given you the chance to apologize. You never even gave me the chance; you just froze me out."

He drew back, and his eyes clouded over as comprehension dawned on him. Her anger began to wane when she realized he'd never even considered that she would admit she'd been wrong.

"I'm sorry, Justin. I should have backed off when you asked, but I won't apologize for what I said." She almost stopped when his green gaze turned to stone, but she forced herself to tell him the truth. Even if he didn't want to hear it, she had to be honest with him. "I think you enjoy being a SEAL, but I know you loved practicing law. I just hate to see you give up your dream because you believe punishing yourself will somehow erase the guilt that you feel. It won't—and you know that."

He started to back away from her, his expression blank.

His face told her he was agitated all over again, and now she seriously wondered if he would speak to her before he shipped out. That was how Justin was. In his mind, her actions were disrespectful. He'd asked her not to do something, and yet again she'd gone and done it.

She sighed, wishing for the first time that she'd left this alone. She didn't want to argue with him—not when they had only six days left together. "You're brilliant at everything you do, so I know you're a brilliant

SEAL, but I can't pretend that I don't hate your job. I hate that every time you leave, it may be the last time I see you, and I hate what you do even more n-now that things have changed between us." She stumbled over her words, her voice shaky, and she wanted to say so much more, but when not one single emotion crossed his face, she lost her nerve. If Justin couldn't already tell that the reason why she pushed so hard was because she cared—*no*, because she loved him—then nothing she said would make a difference.

Regret filled her at the thought that this was how they would leave things, but there was nothing she could do about that. She'd apologized and explained herself; the ball was now in Justin's court.

She slipped inside her home without another word. Seconds later she heard the roar of his engine as he pulled out of her driveway.

"Women—they don't make any sense," Justin muttered.

Caleb raised his bottle of beer. "I'll drink to that."

"I mean . . . I don't get Isabella. She invaded my privacy, and yet now she's the one who's mad at me. I think there's something in their DNA that allows them the power to turn the tables on us until we feel like it's our fault, even though it's not." He hadn't seen or spoken to Isabella since their fight a day ago. Yesterday he'd still been upset at her, but today— today he felt *guilty*. And he wasn't even sure why.

"But it is kind of your fault, don't you think?"

Justin frowned as he watched Caleb take a deep swig from his bottle of beer.

"What do you mean it's my fault? How is any of this my fault?"

Caleb shrugged. "Not your fault so much, but Isabella thought she had the right to say what she said."

Caleb must have glimpsed the disbelief on Justin's face because he added, "What I'm trying to say is that you gave her the right to cross those boundaries of friendship and go deeper when you started sleeping with her."

Justin raked a hand across his face when he realized Caleb was right. But damn it, he didn't want Isabella poking around inside his head, searching for his darkest secrets, because once she found what she was looking for, she wouldn't let it go. He'd made up his mind about his life and his career. Why couldn't she respect his decision?

Justin's gaze followed Caleb as he stood.

"I'm going to get us another couple of beers," Caleb explained as he grabbed their empty bottles and headed to the bar.

While Caleb replenished their drinks, Justin decided to head outside to get some air. He just needed a second to clear his head, but as soon as he stepped outside his eyes were instantly drawn to the tiny bakery across the street. He narrowed his gaze, hoping to catch even a glimpse of Isabella through the glass, but the harsh, blinding rays of the sun made it impossible to see into the store. He let out a long, uneven breath and then walked back inside, his mind still clouded with thoughts of their fight.

"Justin?"

He stopped when a small hand closed around his arm, and his gaze swung in the direction of the soft feminine voice.

"Monica? Hi. I'm sorry. I didn't even see you there."

She chuckled, her purring laughter delicate to his ears. "I'm sure. You would have walked right on by me had I not stopped you."

"Sorry about that. My mind was somewhere else." He wasn't really in the mood to make small talk, but he didn't want to be impolite, so he gestured for her to have a seat, and slid in across from her. "How are you?"

She puckered her surgically enhanced, red-stained lips into a tiny pout that most men would have probably found sexy. He might have too, but every time he looked at her he couldn't help but see the girl he'd known in high school, who hardly resembled the artificially constructed woman before him.

"I've been well, although I'm a bit disappointed that I haven't spent any time with you lately." She settled her hands over his, her lashes fluttering softly over her clear aquamarine eyes. "I'd hoped we could catch up."

He wasn't stupid. He knew that Monica's version of catching up had little to do with meaningful conversation. He'd always been polite to her, but he also thought he'd been clear that he wasn't interested.

He did his best to disentangle his hands from hers without seeming rude. He didn't want to hurt her feelings, but he also couldn't allow her to think that at some point he would reciprocate her interest. What they'd had in high school was nothing more than a classic teenage relationship—superficial and immature. He didn't harbor any deep-seated feelings for her, and he knew that she didn't have any real feelings for him. Monica was newly divorced and simply looking to have fun, but he wasn't the guy for that.

"I'm sorry we haven't had a chance to get together; that's entirely my fault. With me leaving in a few days and Isabella in town for the holiday . . ." He shrugged as he let his voice trail off, the weight of his words settling between them. When her eyes narrowed, he knew he didn't have to spell it out.

Caleb returned with two beers in either hand, and Monica took that as her cue to leave. She stood, a brittle smile plastered across her face.

"Hi, Caleb. Good to see you."

"Likewise," said Caleb as he slipped into the booth she'd just vacated.

"Well, I must be going. I have a few errands to run. It was nice seeing you both," she said with a slight wave before she twisted on her heels and walked out of the diner.

"Let me guess. You finally had a heart-to-heart with her and broke the sorrowful news that you weren't going to become another notch on her bedpost?"

Justin grinned from over the mouth of his bottle, but he didn't say a word as he took a quick sip of beer. He didn't have to. Monica's hasty exit had said it all.

I sabella could feel Celeste's eyes on her, but she was grateful her friend didn't say a word. She'd been in a foul mood ever since she'd returned from her trip to the grocery store. She was furious with Justin. No, fury was too tame a word—she was *enraged*.

She'd walked past Joe's Diner on her way back from the store and just happened to glance inside. She now wished she'd let Celeste go to the store instead. At least she wouldn't be forced to replay the image of Justin sitting there in a booth with Monica, his hands clasped in hers.

One day. They hadn't spoken in one day, and already it seemed that he'd moved on. How long had he waited to get over her? Five hours! The jerk. She couldn't quite blame him, though. Justin liked pliable and accommodating women, and Monica was definitely that. Monica wouldn't butt in where she didn't belong or assert her opinion when he didn't ask for it. She would stand by his side and look pretty, which was obviously what Justin wanted.

"Isabella, give me the rolling pin."

She stopped in midroll and glanced up at Celeste. "Huh?"

"The rolling pin. Give it to me, then back away from the counter and go up front to the cash register. You've murdered that poor lump of dough."

She stared down at the piece of dough that had been rolled and flattened within an inch of its life. She sighed as she set the pin aside.

"I'll go out front."

"Do you want to talk about it?"

Isabella wrinkled her nose and shook her head. Right now she was too furious to talk to anyone, even Celeste.

"All right. Suit yourself," Celeste said with a shrug, thankfully letting her off the hook, and Isabella spun around and marched toward the front of the store before Celeste could change her mind.

Since the later hours were always slow and there were few customers to ring up, she busied herself with cleaning up. She was in the middle of sweeping the floor when Celeste barreled into the room thirty minutes later.

"Hey, I'm going to head back to your place a bit early to get a little work done. Do you think you can handle things tonight?"

Isabella glanced up at the clock. They had about fifteen minutes to go before they could close and go home. She didn't expect any more customers to arrive this late in the day, but if they did, she would just grab her mother, who was in the back office doing inventory.

"Sure. Take off. Mom can help out if I need it, but I doubt I will. Besides, you've already done more than enough. I have no idea how I would have managed this place without you here."

"Girl, please. This is nothing," Celeste said with a wave of her hand as she grabbed her purse from under the counter. "So if I see you tonight, great; but if I don't, have fun for both of us." Celeste gave her a tiny wink and then bounced out the door, leaving Isabella standing there shaking her head. Celeste was incorrigible. But unfortunately, she wouldn't be having fun for both of them—at least not anytime soon.

She'd just finished sweeping up when the doorbell chimed again. She set aside the broom and turned toward the door, expecting to see Celeste returning for something she'd forgotten. But as soon as she saw who it was, her smile instantly died on her lips.

"We're closed."

Isabella twisted on her heels and started to march into the back, but drew up short when she nearly collided with her mother.

Maggie gave her a sharp look before her gaze softened and she turned her attention to Justin.

"Hi, Justin. Come on in. I was just about to leave for the night, but I'm sure Isabella can help you."

Ummmm—no. She bit her tongue to keep from uttering the words.

"Thanks, Maggie. You have a good night," Justin said politely as her mother breezed past him and sailed out of the store, leaving her there alone to deal with Justin.

She folded her arms across her chest and glared at him. "What do you want?"

If he was put off by her rudeness, he didn't show it. "I came to apologize for my behavior and the way I reacted the other day. I know you were only trying to help, and I'm sorry that I treated you like that."

Oooh, he was good. He was *Tom Cruise, show me the money* good. Her carefully constructed defenses began to crumble, but she refused to let him off the hook that easily. There was still the teeny, tiny issue of Monica.

"Is that all you have to apologize for?"

He wrinkled his brow. "Uh, did I do something else? If I did, I'm sorry for that too," he said swiftly.

He didn't realize she'd seen him. He had no idea she apparently knew he'd phoned up his ex, undoubtedly to dump all his problems at her dainty little feet.

"I saw you today at Joe's with Monica."

For a moment he appeared dumbfounded, which only made her madder. He knew what she was talking about.

"I wasn't there with Monica—"

She was incredulous. "I saw you, Justin. I saw you sitting there across from her, with her hands clasped in yours as you stared lovingly into each other's eyes—"

"Then you were hallucinating, because I wasn't staring into her eyes lovingly, or any other way. And *she* put her hands over mine, not the other way around. If you'd snooped for just a little while longer you would have seen me pull away from her."

"Snooped? I wasn't snooping! I was walking down the street—"

"So, from that brief glance you jumped to all these conclusions? I was at Joe's with Caleb. We were having a couple of beers and watching the game when Monica came in and sat down. She probably wasn't even there for more than two minutes."

Their gazes locked, and as seconds ticked by, some of her anger began to wane. He was telling the truth. She read it right there on his face.

He tunneled a hand through his hair, disappointment in his eyes, his jaw tight. Her anger might have faded, but *his* was just igniting.

"I don't know why I bother." Justin gave her a bitter smile—if it could even be called a smile. It was so hard, she swore his face would crack at any moment.

"Justin—"

"You don't trust me, Isabella. I don't know who you trust, but it isn't me." He backed away from her toward the door, and she felt as if she should say something, but the words were slow to come. *Really slow.*

"I—um—"

"You don't have to explain, Isabella, because it's clear to me. Your trust issues would have always been a problem for us. I guess it's for the best that we discovered this now."

She frowned. He was *dumping* her because she had trust issues, but she wasn't the only one with problems. He had some nerve. His inability to communicate was what had started this in the first place. She didn't even take a moment to register the hurt as her anger fueled her words.

"Whatever, Justin. If it wasn't my trust issues, it would have been my pushiness. You would have found some excuse to end things before you deployed because you have to be in control of everything and everyone around you. You had to end things on your terms, your way, before you got hurt. After all, it would have been that much harder to stick it out and see where this was headed, and we both know what you do when things get hard—"

"Isabella."

The warning in his voice and the feral look in his eyes should have been enough to stop her, but it wasn't. "Every time things become too difficult, or you can't control the situation, you run, Justin. That's just what you do."

Chapter Fifteen

Anger erupted inside of him as he stalked toward her. She looked like she wanted to run, but she didn't. Instead, she remained rooted to her spot, her eyes wide. She had no right to hurl insults at him and judge him, not after everything he'd done to show her how much she meant to him.

He was too furious to speak as he backed her against the wall, trapping her with his body. He hadn't set out to kiss her, but her full lips parted in a sexy O drew his heated gaze, and he crushed his mouth to hers, channeling his fury into the kiss.

She didn't fight or resist him, but she didn't yield, either. Anger poured off her in waves, mingling with his own. A deep tremor of raw sexual need pulsed between them, carnal and instinctive. For a moment he forgot all about the fury that roiled inside him as his body took over and sexual hunger pumped wildly through his veins.

His tongue dueled with hers, demanding her complete surrender, but she refused to submit to the urgency of his kiss. Her hands plunged into his hair, pulling him closer, deepening the pressure of her lips, battling him for dominance. He tore his mouth from hers, his chest heaving, and spun her around, the swift action forcing a soft gasp from her lips. He bent her over the counter, his hands fumbling with their clothing until she was bare from the waist down, her ass high in the air.

He leaned over her, his breaths coming in choppy and uneven pants, brushing against her neck when he spoke.

"You're right. I like to be in control—I *can* admit that. So why can't you just come clean and acknowledge the fact that you don't really trust me," he whispered against her ear. She shivered, the warm air from his mouth skating over her sensitive skin.

"I—I do trust you."

Her softly spoken words wormed their way inside him, but he wasn't fooled. Her entire body was rigid with tension.

"You're lying," he growled out in frustration before plunging into her, plowing through her hot, tight heat until he was buried to the hilt. The silken vise of her pussy wrapped around him almost made him forget his anger . . . almost made him forget everything.

She rasped out his name as he thrust inside her, but not once did she deny his accusation.

She'd just admitted the truth with her silence—she *didn't* trust him. Anger mixed with frustration fueled his strokes and he plunged harder and deeper inside her, his jaw clenched tight as he gritted his teeth. He loved her, but she was willing to throw everything they had away because she was too afraid to trust him with her heart—too afraid of getting hurt.

Sweat dotted his forehead and trickled down his cheek as he pushed past the clenching muscles of her pussy. Her soft mewls of pleasure spurred him, and he gripped the counter with one hand, his knuckles turning white, while the other tangled in her hair, twisting the lustrous mane around his palm.

He quickened his strokes, tunneling through the sticky warmth that flooded her sheath. He tugged her head back and rested his lips against her neck. He could already feel her beginning to splinter around him.

She moaned loudly, the tremors pulsing through her. He slammed into her wildly, giving her just what she needed to send her over the edge. And in that last moment, just before she exploded, the husky purr of her voice calling his name stroked his ears, and he shattered with her.

He closed his eyes, groaning out her name as he erupted inside her, pouring his essence into her channel. At the same time, her pussy squeezed around him, and convulsions rocked her body. She milked his cock, her searing heat bathing him in its velvety warmth.

Neither of them stirred for a long while, but he was the first to recover as he drew away from her and righted his clothing. Her hands were shaky as she dressed herself, and he helped her as best he could with his own trembling fingers.

She averted her gaze and began to move away, but he snagged her around the waist before she could take a step. He'd made mistakes—they both had—but with his deployment just days away, this was not how he wanted to leave things.

He cupped her cheek with his other hand, dragging her gaze to his face as he gave her a small grin.

"That's another off the list: *two*, I think."

She furrowed her brow.

"Sex in public *and* at the bakery," he offered, and she smiled when she realized that they'd unintentionally crossed more items off her list. But if he had his way, they would make love in the bakery all over again, because this didn't count. In his fantasy, he'd envisioned spending hours licking whipped cream and icing from her body.

"I will give you a call tomorrow," he said, hoping to ease the tension that still hovered between them.

"Okay." She nodded, but despite what she said, her hazel eyes were still clouded with uncertainty, and he couldn't blame her. They had many issues to work out, but what he had with Isabella was special—complicated, but special nonetheless—and he was sure Isabella felt the same way. But with all the obstacles that stood between them, he was just as uncertain as she was about what lay ahead for them.

"Are you serious, Isabella? You let the man go home alone right after you had what you just described as the most amazing sex of your life. What's wrong with you? He's leaving in a few days. You could have at least spent the night with him." Celeste stared at her as if she were a moron. Well, Isabella couldn't blame her. Apparently, she was.

"I know. I know." She hung her head in her hands. Things had just been so tense after their argument and then their heated lovemaking. She'd figured he'd wanted space, or else he would have asked her to go home with him that night. "What am I going to do?"

Celeste patted her shoulder as she stood up from the dining room table to pour herself another vodka and tonic.

"Just relax. I'm sure everything will turn out just fine. You said neither one of you left angry, right? So tomorrow, after you leave the bakery, just head over to his place wearing something super slutty. Any grievances between you two will be long forgotten." Celeste winked. "Trust me. It works every time."

Isabella snorted. She bet it did.

But Isabella was skeptical. She didn't quite share Celeste's optimism, because she knew that at the end of the day sex was just a cover, just as their arguments were. She and Justin argued about his demons from the past, his future career, and her trust issues, but it was all a distraction from what they really needed to talk about—and that was them: where they were headed, if anywhere, and how they really felt about each other.

She sipped from her drink as she leaned back into the chair with a sigh, the warm liquid settling in her belly and relaxing her. She didn't want to think about Justin and everything that was wrong between them anymore, not when there was always tomorrow to do that. Right now, all she wanted to do was enjoy a nice quiet evening at home.

"Hey, where's your mom? Shouldn't she have been back from her date by now?"

Isabella glared at Celeste. That was another thing she didn't want to think about.

"Oh," Celeste said as she stared down at her drink, now seemingly fascinated by the contents. "Well, at least *someone* is having a good time."

"That's gross, Celeste. I really was trying to avoid that thought."

She shrugged. "Sorry." The sheepish grin on her face told Isabella she wasn't sorry at all, but she knew something that would wipe that grin off her face in record time.

"Sooo, are you ever going to tell me what happened between you and Caleb, or are you going to just continue dodging the subject forever?"

"Dodging. I like that idea—"

"Spill it, Celeste."

Her friend sighed, her hand raking through her hair.

"Oh, it can't be that bad. What did you do, try to jump him again?"

"Worse," she muttered.

Isabella sat up straighter. She was listening now. Celeste toyed with the napkin in her hand, and she wondered if her friend was ever going to speak. Finally she said, "I might have told Caleb that I wanted to make him my human vibrator."

She tried to suppress her laughter but a giggle bubbled out.

"I knew I shouldn't have told you. You think this is funny."

"I'm laughing *with* you."

She glowered at Isabella. "But I'm not laughing."

Isabella shrugged. "I'm sorry, but how did you expect me to react? I'm just picturing the look on Caleb's face when you told him that all you wanted was a living, breathing sex toy."

"Believe me, there was nothing funny about it."

"Not to you, but I can imagine Mr. Straitlaced, By the Book was pale as snow. He must have been shocked by your proposition."

"That's just it. He wasn't shocked. He was hurt."

Isabella's jaw dropped open, and it stayed that way for a full five seconds before she recovered long enough to snap it shut. She didn't know what was more surprising—that the unflappable, seemingly impenetrable Caleb had actually been hurt by Celeste's words, or that Celeste was *upset* because she'd hurt him. Celeste went through men like underwear—she never stuck around long enough to actually *care* if she'd hurt their feelings.

Isabella shook her head, the corner of her mouth curling into a small grin. "You and Caleb—I never would have imagined it." She shrugged. "But I don't know what to tell you, really. It's obvious he deserves an apology, but if you're not interested, then I would just drop it and avoid him until it's time to head back to DC."

Celeste nibbled on her bottom lip as she considered Isabella's words. Celeste could mull over her words all night if she wanted to, but in the meantime, Isabella was going to get some sleep. Isabella stood to her feet and finished off her drink.

"I have a long day tomorrow, so I'm headed to bed. Cheer up. I'm sure Caleb didn't really take it all that seriously," she said, trying to be optimistic. But the look on Celeste's face told her otherwise, so she decided to just let it go.

Celeste murmured good night, but from her distant expression, Isabella knew her mind was miles away.

She bit back a smile as she ascended the stairs. Celeste had man trouble? Now, *that* was unheard of! She'd been telling the truth moments ago—never in a million years would she have guessed Celeste would be interested in Caleb, but maybe he would be good for her.

Maybe in Caleb, Celeste had finally met her match.

The next day Justin did call, and Isabella found herself doing just what Celeste suggested—minus the slutty gear, though. She pulled into Justin's driveway and parked beside his SUV.

She grabbed her purse and piled out of her car and was halfway up the steps to his porch when her cell phone rang. Digging through her bag, she frowned at the number flashing across the screen.

Harry?

She pressed ignore and dumped the phone back into her bag. Why was he calling now? Hell, why was he calling, period? She hadn't spoken to him since he'd dumped her, and she liked it that way.

Pushing thoughts of Harry out of her mind, Isabella started to press the doorbell. Then she remembered that Justin said he would leave the door unlocked for her, so she twisted the knob to the front door and stepped inside.

She'd expected to enter the foyer to see him in the living room watching television or maybe in his kitchen cooking dinner. What she never expected was to enter the darkened room and close the door to see a black leather contraption hanging from the door that could only be described as—

"It's a bondage swing."

Yeah, of course it was. That had pretty much been her first guess, too, she thought sarcastically as she studied the four leather loops hanging over the door, two of which she guessed were for her legs, since they hung lower, while the other two would naturally be for her arms.

She turned as Justin strolled toward her, dressed casually in a T-shirt and sweats, and even as sexy as he looked, his muscles rippling with each step, her gaze remained fixed on the strips of black leather in his hand.

"I want you to put this on," he said, holding his hand out for her to take the garment.

"What is it?"

"It's one of many bondage suits."

She held it up. Calling it a suit was being far too generous. It was basically two strips of black leather that would barely cover her breasts, merging to make a deep V between her thighs, where the strips would then crisscross so that there was a small opening in just the perfect place. The two straps would then come around up her back and along her shoulder blades. It looked like a cross between a harness and a swimsuit.

She took the suit in hand and began to strip out of her clothes.

His gaze darkened as he watched her slowly peel the suit on, his erection tenting against the soft material of his sweats. Sexual excitement curled in her stomach at the intensity of his gaze upon her, her entire body warming under his regard.

Isabella slipped on the suit and pulled the first strap, and then the second, over her shoulder. When her body was finally encased in the snug suit, she ran her palms down the length of her body, loving the feel of the leather beneath her fingers. Every inch of her tingled with anticipation as she skimmed her hands across the skintight material. She felt sexy, naughty, like a wanton temptress.

"You like how the leather feels against your skin, don't you?"

She nodded as Justin moved toward her. She'd never been into BDSM, and it excited her that Justin, the seemingly good guy next door whom she'd known all her life, was introducing her to this darkly provocative world. She waited in eager anticipation of what he would do next, what he would demand of her, what pleasures he would bestow upon her body.

"Get in the swing," he commanded softly, his voice a seductive whisper, and even though it was low, it still rang with authority.

Her body instantly responded, that secret part of her that craved Justin's dominance over her, that relished his arrogant commands. She slipped her arms through the top holsters first, and lifted herself slightly to slip her legs through the other two. A fresh wave of heat rushed through her veins at the leather straps pressing into her skin, and she shivered at the erotic feel of the soft material against her naked skin. As she held herself suspended she was glad she hadn't done her workout DVD that morning; her muscles would have been sore, and it was taking some serious upper body strength to hold herself up.

"Lean back against the door," Justin said.

As he said that she relaxed against the door, and while it took most of the weight off her arms, she had to wrap her hands around the leather to steady herself.

Justin smiled as he watched her, and she soon forgot about what her arms were doing when she realized how she must look to Justin with her legs spread wide, the tiny opening in the suit leaving her pussy bare before him, her breasts straining against the confines of the black leather.

A shudder raced through her as she glimpsed the lust that burned in Justin's gaze. Every nerve ending was alive, and her body tingled as her nipples tightened and her pussy grew moist with her arousal.

Her time with Justin had awakened a side of her she'd never known she possessed. When he commanded her, she easily slipped into the role of his submissive, but then there were times when she took control, and she also liked it when he let her have power over his body. Submission and domination were two sides of the same coin, and she enjoyed exploring them both with Justin.

Each and every time they were together, Justin exposed her to something new, pushed her to places she'd never been, took her body to heights she'd never experienced. Justin's fantasies knew no bounds, and she eagerly followed wherever he led.

Justin stepped between her spread legs, one hand absently stroking his erection while he let the other hand roam over her body, sometimes caressing her bare skin, other times fingering the leather. Her body heated in every place he touched her, and she fought back a moan when he seized her thighs and pressed her flush against the door as he ground the bulge of his cock against her wet sex.

"You like that?" He panted, and all she could do was nod with a low moan. "You want me inside you, don't you?" he teased, pressing his erection harder against her.

"Please, Justin."

He kissed the skin along her neck, the shell of her ear, his warm breath caressing her flesh when he said, "That's right, Isabella. Beg for it."

She closed her eyes, her head falling back against the door as she bit her lip in sexual frustration. If she'd learned nothing else from their nights together, she'd learned that when she and Justin played their roles, none of her demands would be met with action. She could beg or she could wait, but in the end Justin would fulfill her only when he was ready.

She cried out in relief when she felt his hand slip between them, and seconds later he grasped his cock to feed her his thick length. His movements were slow, achingly so, until he was seated fully inside her, but when he pulled completely out again, she released a ragged cry.

"Justin," she gasped, but before she could take her next breath he slammed his full length inside her. Over and over he gave her all of himself and then fully retreated, until she was a writhing, panting bundle of nerves against the door.

The way she was positioned in the swing, she couldn't hold on to him. Her arms and legs were splayed wide—a vessel for his lust, his seed.

He drove into her with deep, brutal thrusts, pinning her body against the door until she just couldn't take it anymore. Her orgasm hit her so quickly, so strongly, that she could barely take a breath before she shattered completely on a ragged cry.

Her pussy clenched around him as he continued to pound his way inside her, her slick passage coating his thrusting dick until she knew he could no longer resist the demands of his body.

His fingers dug into her spread thighs, and he buried his face against her neck. At the same time he buried his shaft to the hilt inside of her and erupted on a harsh cry.

"Isabella," he gasped as he flooded her with his semen, his body trembling against hers until she felt as if he'd emptied all of himself inside her.

He rested against her for several moments before he somehow found the strength to pull out of her, and she noticed that his fingers were shaking as he helped her out of the swing.

"We still need to talk," he said as he gathered up her clothes and she grabbed her purse. "But right now we should probably rest."

She was in agreement as she wobbled behind him on shaky legs toward his bedroom.

Later that night she lay in Justin's arms, silently staring at the wall. They both knew they needed to talk about what had happened on their drive back from the cabin, and then their argument in the bakery, but neither said a word. If Justin felt the way she did, then he didn't want to ruin this blissful moment between them, where everything was perfect, and none of the realities of their lives and the outside world could intrude upon the solace they found in each other's arms.

On one hand she wished she could go back to the day when she'd come up with that list and they'd embarked on two weeks of spending their nights indulging in every fantasy imaginable. Everything had seemed so simple then, but that's because it had been. It was all about having fun, but then all these feelings that hovered just beneath the surface between them had begun to creep in. Just as much as she wished she could go back to that day when their only worry was what fantasy they would explore next, she also wouldn't trade what she now had with Justin for the world.

Justin did things to her no man had ever dared—things she'd never dreamed of but now craved each and every time he touched her. Every time his eyes darkened with lust, her heart would pound faster in anticipation of what he would command her to do for him, or what he would command her to do *to* him. She felt as if she'd blossomed sexually with Justin, and she knew no other man would ever be able to give her what he gave her. No man would ever be able to fulfill her the way he fulfilled her, and that was because she loved him with all her heart.

No, she didn't want to go back to the time when their affair was nothing but carefree sex, because then she would never have discovered what it was like to truly give her all to a man—her body, her heart, her very soul.

Chapter Sixteen

The Christmas Extravaganza really was nothing compared to Jacksonville's New Year's Eve Festival. Now, *that* was an extravaganza. Every year it took place inside Jacksonville High's gymnasium, and practically the entire town packed inside, where there would be games and food to entertain folks until everyone spilled outdoors to watch the fireworks at midnight. And even Isabella had to agree that the fireworks were pretty spectacular. The New Year's Eve Festival was worth all the fuss, and she was certainly looking forward to it, but she could do without the manic panic leading up to the big event.

The day had only just begun, and already Isabella wanted it to be over. The New Year's Eve Festival was tomorrow, and even with Celeste, her mother, and herself all slaving away at the bakery, they were still behind on orders. And it certainly didn't help that her unresolved issues with Justin still hovered over her like a dark cloud. They hadn't talked last night or that morning. They'd tried to convey with their bodies what their lips refused to say, but she knew that as his time to deploy drew near, they would not be able to avoid what they so desperately needed to discuss, and that was *them*.

"Isabella, can you run down to the store? I'm out of lemon juice, and I need a bit more to finish up this cake."

She started to ask if Celeste could do it, given how badly yesterday's grocery store run had turned out, but Maggie was already gone by the time she opened her mouth.

With a heavy sigh, she wiped her hands on her apron, grabbed her purse, and headed out. This time she stayed on her side of the street all the way to the store. As she walked back she breathed a sigh of relief when she neared Angelo's. She'd managed her trip without incident. Considering the frantic chaos she now called her life, she didn't know if she could handle another shock to her psyche.

The roar of an engine drew her attention, and she glanced up. Moments later, she realized she might have been too hasty in her thoughts, and she cursed under her breath when she glimpsed a shiny black BMW in the distance. She held on to a tiny granule of hope that it belonged to someone else until it rolled up to the curb beside her and stopped.

She cast her eyes heavenward, shaking her head. *You would do this to me today of all days.* The car door slammed shut, and a tall, slender man headed straight for her. He was the epitome of modern male sophistication—the classic metrosexual. His angular face was obscured by his aviator shades, and his sandy blond hair whipped in the wind. She couldn't believe she'd once thought that his equine features and the chiseled planes of his body were handsome. Compared to Justin, he was too gaunt and lanky, his face too pretty, and his nasal voice irritating. And to think she'd almost married this man. Isabella had to suppress the shudder at the thought of the mistake she would have made.

"Isabella," Harry gushed, his arms stretched wide. Before she could react he pulled her into his embrace, smashing his mouth against hers. She was trapped in his arms, her eyes bulging as she struggled against him. And when he finally released her, she was too shocked to speak.

"Isabella?"

Her heart plummeted at the sound of the familiar baritone, and she spun around to meet Justin's questioning gaze. This couldn't be happening—not now.

"Justin—"

"Justin, hello. It is good to see you," Harry said as he stood up straighter and draped his arm over her shoulder. She managed to get his limb from around her, but she could tell Justin was angry.

What was she supposed to do? She didn't want to outright humiliate him. She silently implored Justin to understand, but his eyes had already left her and were now focused solely on Harry.

"I didn't know you were coming to visit Isabella for New Year's," Justin said.

Harry gazed down at her, but this time, when he reached for her, she was far enough away to avoid his touch. He raised his eyebrows at the not-so-subtle distance she put between them, but Harry was always dignified and composed. If he was ruffled, he didn't let it show. He beamed at her before turning his professionally whitened smile on Justin.

"I couldn't let my fiancée ring in the New Year alone."

Justin arched a brow. "Really? But it was all right for you to leave her alone for Christmas? I got the impression that you two had parted ways."

Harry stiffened. "You and Isabella have always been close, so I'm sure she told you we had a bit of a break. But I assure you it was only temporary. I got cold feet, but we're still getting married—"

"Harry!" She glared up at him. She couldn't believe he would show up out of nowhere and outright lie.

"Justin. What Harry said—it's not true. I—"

She reached out for him, but he held up his hand, halting her next words.

"He seems to be convinced that your breakup was a misunderstanding, so apparently you two have a *lot* to talk about—"

"Justin—"

He turned away from her and hopped into his SUV. Her pride refused to allow her to break into an all-out sprint after him, so as soon as his car pulled away from the curb, she did the next best thing.

She rounded on Harry, unleashing the full weight of her fury upon him. "What the hell was that about!"

Harry stared at her, his expression incredulous. "I could say the same thing. I come to apologize to my fiancée for getting cold feet, but it seems my *fiancée* has found another love interest in the *very* short time we've been apart."

She wasn't even shocked Harry had discovered the truth. Anyone with two eyes could see that something was going on between her and Justin.

She could understand his dismay, but he had no right to feel betrayed. He'd dumped *her*. He couldn't just decide that he wanted her back and expect her to rush into his open arms. She wasn't a yo-yo he could yank around on a string.

"You told me to get lost over the phone the other day. Do you remember that?" She jabbed her finger into his chest. "I assumed you were serious. You can't just show up and take it all back."

His eyes hardened to tiny sapphire chips. "I never expected you would move on so *fast*," he said tightly.

"You broke up with *me*, Harry, not the other way around. You were done with me, so why does it matter if I decided to move on?"

"If you're doing this to punish me, then I completely understand—"

She abruptly silenced him with a single finger against his lips. They both knew their relationship had never been a love match, but she felt they deserved to have proper closure, despite the way he'd ended things.

"Harry, I need to get back inside, but if you're free later maybe we can grab a bite to eat and talk."

He nodded, a smug smile spreading across his face. She could tell by how quickly he'd acquiesced that he still thought he could worm his way back into her life. After all, he'd done it many times before. But this time, he would discover that he was wrong. Closure—that was all she wanted, nothing more.

"All right. I will meet you later this evening." He leaned in to kiss her cheek before he pivoted gracefully on his heels, got into his car, and drove off.

It was amazing—the stark difference. When Justin had driven away, all she'd felt was despair and the deep-seated need to tear after him and explain herself. With Harry, she felt only an overwhelming sense of relief that he was gone.

"Was that who I think it was?"

Isabella blew out a long breath as she let the front door to Angelo's bang shut behind her.

"Yep."

"Oooh. Where's that knife I had earlier? I will cut him—"

Isabella shook her head at Celeste, a smile worming its way across her face. "He's gone."

"A good thing, too. I would have been merciless. The pathetic fool. What the hell is he doing here anyway?"

"Good question." Isabella dropped down onto the stool behind the counter and set the bottle of lemon juice aside. She would take it back to her mother in a few minutes. Right now, she just needed a minute to pull herself together.

"He told Justin that we were still engaged."

"What! Why would he do that?"

She shrugged. "I don't know. I tried to set Justin straight, but he rode out of here without giving me a chance to explain."

"And what about Harry? Did you set him straight?"

"Sort of." She wrinkled her nose. "I don't think he really gets it. I think he believed he could just show up here, and I would be happy to see him."

"Of course he did. That's what he always does, and usually you are."

She sat up straight. "What do you mean, that's how I usually am?"

Celeste sighed, taking the stool beside her. "I didn't mean it as an insult. It's just that as long as Harry has been in your life, he's always been ... well ... inconsistent. He shows up to your birthday parties late. He occasionally forgets your anniversaries. He cancels dinner plans at the last minute. He's inconsiderate and selfish, but you've always brushed it off and forgiven him. He probably figured he could get away with doing the same thing this time around."

Celeste was right. She'd let Harry get away with one selfish act after another because his many hours at the firm had often been to blame for the cancellations and tardiness, and if anyone knew about how much pressure he was under to make partner, *she* did. So why would he think this time was any different? Why would he think this excuse wouldn't cut it this time around, when all the ones before it had? "Wow. I sound so—so *pathetic.*" She was ashamed of herself. When had she become so complacent?

"You're not pathetic. You're busy. Harry is easy for you. He may be inconsistent and inconsiderate, but he doesn't complicate your life. If he doesn't show up, you don't care, and if he does—well, then, that's nice, too. You stopped dating because you just didn't have the time. I think you and Harry just fell into a routine where neither of you had to try anymore."

"But I was all set to marry him. I was entirely prepared to marry a man

I was with only because he was . . . how did you put it? The path of least resistance?"

Celeste hopped off the stool and stood to her feet, grabbing the bottle of juice. "Really, Isabella, don't beat yourself up over this. You wouldn't have married him. It was just a matter of time before you came to your senses and ended that travesty."

"How can you be so certain?" It was horrifying to think that work had driven her to slip into a relationship that left her unfulfilled—and all because she was too busy and too lazy to try and find something better. She'd faulted Harry for many of their problems, but it was clear that her own inertia was also to blame.

"Trust me, Isabella. You would never have married him." A small grin spread across her face. "Because as long as I've known you, you've been *not so secretly* in love with Justin. It was only a matter of time before you wised up and followed your heart."

Celeste winked at her, and then she disappeared into the kitchen, leaving Isabella sitting in stunned silence.

Isabella was on a mission. Her talk with Celeste had propelled her into action. It was apparent that when it came to her love life, she'd been idle for too long, just letting life pass her by. But now she was determined to clean up the mess she'd made and set things right with Justin.

Her talk with Harry had gone pretty well. As expected, there had been no tears or accusations—just a polite, civil good-bye. Given the late hour, he'd decided to stay at the local hotel, but she hadn't been too thrilled with his decision. The longer he stuck around, the harder it would be to convince Justin she and Harry were truly done. But then Monica had walked into Joe's Diner, and getting Harry to leave immediately became a lost cause. That old adage had never rung truer than in the moment she'd glimpsed the instant connection between Monica and Harry—like attracted like. They were both self-interested opportunists. It was a match made in heaven.

She marched into the sheriff's office, her gaze instantly landing on Caleb. She'd called earlier to tell him she would be stopping by to ask a favor. Justin wasn't answering her calls, so he'd left her with few options. She just hoped her plan didn't backfire. She also hoped Caleb would help her, because if he didn't, she would find herself following in Celeste's infamous footsteps—but instead of a hit and run, she would wind up behind bars for breaking and entering, and possibly misdemeanor stalking.

"Hey, Isabella. You seemed upset when you called earlier. Is everything all right?"

She smiled at Caleb. He was such a good guy. She hated to involve him, but he was the only person who had a key.

"What if I told you everything wasn't all right, but you could be the answer to all my prayers."

His eyes widened, and she had to bite her lip to keep from laughing. "I didn't mean it *that* way, Caleb. I need your help with something, but you're going to have to bend the rules a bit."

He folded his arms across his chest, his eyes narrowing. "I'm listening."

Justin slammed his front door shut and kicked off his shoes. He'd spent the better part of the day up at the cabin, but when nighttime fell he'd decided to drive home. Everywhere he looked he saw Isabella—her ebullient face and the dazzling sparkle of her hazel eyes.

But as soon as he stepped inside his home, he realized that it would be equally difficult to escape the vivid images of Isabella. Well, at least he would be surrounded by the familiar comforts of his home. Here, he didn't feel quite as alone as he did out in the woods, where he was surrounded by the picturesque beauty of the mountainous landscape—and nothing else.

He heaved his weary body toward his bedroom. All he wanted to do was fall asleep and forget about his run-in with Isabella and Harry that morning. He must have replayed the scene a thousand times in his head. He'd stood there numb with shock when Harry announced that he was still engaged to Isabella. He believed Isabella when she said they'd broken up. He knew without a doubt that she was telling the truth, but the reality of their situation was she and Harry had a long history together. And with Harry showing up that morning, it was certainly evident that there were still unresolved issues between those two. Something had held him back last night—something that had made him hesitate to discuss the changing nature of their relationship—and now he was glad that he hadn't revealed his feelings to her then. If he'd thought through this ill-fated affair, he would have realized she was still on the rebound.

He pushed open the door to his bedroom, but stopped when he saw Isabella. Candles lined the room, their golden flames casting shadows along the wall as the burnished glow of the firelight illuminated her dusky skin.

She sat in the center of the room, her hands bound behind her back, her heavy breasts jutting forward. She was completely naked, with her legs primly crossed in front of her and her raven hair streaming across her shoulders to curl around her breasts.

"How did you get in here?"

"I broke in."

He stared at her dumbfounded. He couldn't do this with her right now. He was in love with a woman who was still entangled with her ex. He needed to be alone to sort this out. But right now he was battling his need to stalk across the room and drag Isabella into his arms until she forgot all about Harry.

He glanced around his room, searching for her clothes. A frown spread across his face when he didn't find them.

"Isabella, you need to get dressed and go home."

A tiny flicker of disappointment flashed in her gaze, but it was quickly replaced by determination. She jangled her arms, and Justin realized then that she wasn't bound as he'd originally thought, but was actually hand-cuffed to the chair.

"I wish I could do that, but unfortunately I'm cuffed to this chair, and I have no idea where the key is."

She was lying. He folded his arms across his chest and glared at her. He didn't have time for games. He was exhausted. All he wanted was to go to sleep and forget that she was the number one reason he was weary and worn out in the first place.

"What do you want, Isabella? Why are you here?"

"To talk."

One brow lifted. "And you had to take your clothes off and cuff your-self to a chair to do that?"

Her smile was sheepish. "No. I did that to get your attention."

Well, it had worked. She certainly had his attention. He was deter-mined not to be swayed by her enigmatic allure, but already he could feel his resolve weakening as she wove her seductive spell around him.

"You have my attention, so I'm listening."

She blew out a sharp breath and pinned him with those lovely hazel eyes of hers, her gaze unwavering.

"I wanted to apologize for Harry. We are not engaged, and after I spoke with him this evening, I think he understands that I have no desire to reconcile."

He nodded. "Thank you, Isabella, for clearing that up. I appreciate it."

She expected him to say more, so when he didn't, she sat there startled, her eyes wide.

"Is that all you have to say?" she finally choked out.

He raked a hand through his hair, a sickening mixture of weariness and frustration settling in the pit of his stomach. He loved Isabella. He certainly didn't want to hurt her, but he had to be honest with her.

"No. I have a million things I want to say to you, but I know you're not ready to hear them—" He held up his hand when she opened her mouth to speak. "You had how many days to process your breakup with Harry? Two? Even if you *think* you're over him and your engagement, you're not. Pretending that you weren't engaged just a week ago isn't fair to either of us."

"But I don't love him."

Her whispered words pierced his heart. Justin wanted to say she didn't love *him* either.

He forced out a sharp breath, past the ache in his chest. "This is insane, Isabella. Tell me where the key is so that I can unlock you."

"I can see it in your eyes and I know what all this means, but you didn't even give us a chance—"

"Isabella."

"Fine," she said stubbornly. "I'm sitting on it."

He blanched. He almost wanted to leave her sitting there naked. He didn't want to touch her, because in the hours he'd spent alone at the cabin, he'd promised himself that he would let her go. They were two very different people. He didn't belong in her world, and she didn't belong in his. And yet, every time he touched her, he forgot all about their differences, their problems. But life was more complicated than that. The reality was that as much as he wished otherwise, they just didn't have a future together.

He sighed as he stalked toward her and stooped down on his haunches. "Stand up."

"I can't. I'm chained to the chair," she said, as if she couldn't understand why he'd decided to take the short bus that day.

"How did you get yourself handcuffed in the first place?"

"Believe me; it took several failed attempts, but I was determined. I wanted to surprise you."

Her last words came out on a broken whisper, forcing Justin's gaze to her face. Her head was turned away from him so he could see only her smooth cheek. When a tiny crystal droplet slid down her face, he felt as if someone had punched him in the gut.

She'd come to him, offered herself to him in an attempt to show him she could be everything he desired, that she could give him complete surrender, even though he would have wanted her no matter what. Submissive or not.

He cursed under his breath. "Isabella." He reached out to take her into his arms, but couldn't because of the way she was cuffed to the chair. Damn it. Where was that stupid key? He slipped his hands beneath her, ignoring the spark of heat that shot straight to his groin when his knuckles brushed against her smooth skin.

Pulling the key from under her, he unlocked the cuffs and stood her to her feet. He dragged her into his embrace, even as tension emanated from her body. Several seconds slipped by before she relaxed against him, her hands stroking across his back.

He dropped his head to the curve of her neck and inhaled deeply, her soft, feminine scent curling around him. He closed his eyes, trying to ignore the urgent heat raking through his body.

"Isabella." His voice was desperate, needy, a perfect mirror of the tumultuous emotions that raged inside him. He wanted her, but he knew he shouldn't.

"Shhh," she whispered softly, placing a single finger against his mouth, as if she sensed the storm that spun out of control inside him, and with that simple word and even simpler gesture, she sought to quiet it. Her fingers teased his lips before dipping to his shirt to undo the buttons. He groaned low in his throat as her gentle fingertips slipped between the parted flaps of his shirt, lazily caressing his heated skin.

This was wrong. He'd come to the conclusion on his drive back from the cabin that they needed to put some distance between them while she figured out her feelings for Harry. The best thing for them would be to end things now, and then, when he returned in six months, maybe they could see where they stood. He'd planned to get a good night's sleep tonight and tell her that tomorrow. The last thing they needed was to fall back into bed together.

"Isabella." This time her name was a warning on his lips, but she ignored it and closed her mouth over his, effectively silencing him. Molten heat instantly exploded in his belly, blinding him to all reason.

He pulled her closer, his hands stroking everywhere. Her skin was like the softest silk, and he ached to run his palms across every single inch. He backed them to the bed, and she sat down, her hands going to his pants. He slipped off his shirt while she undid his jeans, and he held his breath as he watched her slowly drag the zipper down.

She lifted her head, her gaze meeting his. Slipping her hand into his pants and beneath the elastic of his boxers, she cupped his hardened length.

Justin sucked in a sharp breath, his lungs aching from the effort it took to breathe. She pulled out his cock and slid his jeans down his legs. When they gathered at his feet, he kicked them aside, his eyes remaining glued to her face.

A rush of desire surged through him, his heart thumping loudly in his chest. His next breath stuck in his chest when her lips closed around his dick. Searing heat slashed through him, insistent and sharp, and he closed his eyes, his head falling back against his shoulders. Her mouth was velvety warm, drawing him deeper and deeper inside its moist heat.

A shudder racked him when she swiped her tongue across the broad head. He slid his fingers through the silky strands of her hair as he fought to anchor himself to something—anything.

He called out her name in a raspy whisper, and hardly believed that the needy sound emanating from his lips belonged to him. She moaned around him, and the vibrations fluttered across his skin. He pulsed inside her, his cock swelling.

With both hands, he grasped her head, taking over the rhythm. He was careful not to go too deep or too hard, feeding her shallow strokes of his steel shaft. Her moans grew louder, driving him crazy and urging him on. He bit down on his lips, fighting to stave off his climax. The taste of copper exploded in his mouth, and he knew he was losing this battle.

He pumped harder, and she received every deep thrust. He could feel his control starting to wane, and he gripped the back of her head tighter.

He felt the urgent rush of desire burst inside him, and he gasped from the intensity of the assault.

"I'm coming."

He jerked his hips back, but she seized the cheeks of his ass in her hand, holding him firmly. He didn't have the power to stop her, and he clenched his eyes shut, a ragged groan of release spilling from his lips as he erupted inside her, shooting his seed down her throat. He could barely stand on his boneless legs, but she continued to hold him there, swallowing his essence until he was completely limp and soft in her mouth.

He slipped out of her, and she stood to her feet, her arms winding around him. He leaned down to kiss her lips, the salty taste of his cum still lingering inside her mouth. She leaned back from him, her eyes dark and mysterious as she swirled her fingers across his chest.

She started to pull out of his arms, but he found he couldn't let her go. He wondered if he'd ever be able to let her go after this night—or any other.

"Get on the bed."

A naughty gleam flashed in her eyes, but she did as he instructed, scrambling on top of the bed.

"Lie down against the pillows."

His heartbeat quickened when she leaned back, her full breasts thrusting skyward.

"Part your thighs." His eyes darkened as he watched those silky, creamy legs fall apart to reveal the treasure at its center.

"But don't touch yourself," he said when she slipped her hand between her spread legs and began to rub the tiny nub with her fingers. She mewled in protest, and he grinned as he crawled onto the bed.

He glanced up at her. "Tonight, that's my job," he said with a small smile before he dipped his head to slip his tongue across the smooth skin of her belly.

She made a soft noise deep in her throat, her back arching. He slid his tongue up the plane of her belly and swiped the underside of her plump breast. He cupped one with his palm, his thumb scraping lightly over her rigid nipple.

Her breathing was choppy and ragged, its staccato rhythm growing uneven when he drew a coral-tipped peak inside his mouth. She clutched the back of his head, her body writhing against the sheets.

He devoured her breasts, taking his time touching them, tasting them, until she begged him to touch and taste somewhere else.

He feathered a trail of kisses down the length of her body, slipping his tongue into the dent of her navel before dipping lower to her core, but he didn't stop when he reached the twinkling jewel at the apex of her thighs. He kissed his way down one leg, nipping at her ankles, her toes, even the gentle arch of her foot, before doing the same to the other. Her control snapped when he lingered at the back of her knee.

"Please, Justin."

He trained his eyes on her, on the pink flush of her cheeks, her lips parted slightly and swollen. She was delectable and enticing, and he found he couldn't deny her anything in that moment.

He slid between her legs, hooking his hands behind her thighs as he held her spread wide before him. His eyes never left her, not even when he leaned forward to curl his tongue around the gentle bud that was the center of her pleasure.

She cried out, her back arching even higher, her hands clutching desperately at the sheets. He licked her again, his tongue sliding between the creamy folds. Every breath he took was torture, the hot spice of her arousal filling his burning lungs. His body responded to her instantly, his cock hardening against the bed.

He loved her with his mouth, his teeth nipping gently at her clit before his tongue soothed her and dipped lower to probe inside. Her body pulsed and trembled around him, her hot pussy pouring forth the evidence of her arousal. He licked it up, but he refused to stop until she shattered in his arms, a trembling mass of sensual fulfillment.

Her eyes were clenched shut, her head twisting back and forth as she thrashed against the sheets. She was close, so close. The pulsing vibrations of her nearing climax rolled through him, shaking him to the core, and in that moment it hit him like a ton of bricks: She was a part of him, and he belonged to her.

She crested and exploded around him. Tiny frissons of heat whipped through him as she came against his lips, her sultry, slick warmth gathering at her center, and he licked every single droplet up, absorbing her very essence until it roared through his blood.

She slumped against the bed, her limbs completely limp. He covered her with his body, his mouth seeking hers. She kissed him deeply, her hand curling in his hair to hold him close. Her lips were silky and sweet, and he drew her tongue deep inside his mouth, tangling it with his. Their kiss was soft and languorous, full of unspoken promises and hidden desires, and when he finally lifted his head he found himself reluctant to release her.

He rolled off her, settling alongside her naked body. For the first time since they'd begun their affair, he didn't know what to say. His departure was just days away, and they both knew that unless they made promises they couldn't keep, their affair would have to come to an end. He'd tried to see reason and end things before they became more complicated, but Isabella had only to beckon him to her with a single look, and he was there, back in her arms.

She rolled over, her leg draping across his hips, reminding him that he still sported a hard-on. Her dark eyes smoldered with unspoken passion and the tiniest gleam of mischief.

"What do you say we put these on for old times' sake?"

He glanced at her right hand, where she dangled a pair of handcuffs.

"Isabella."

"I know where the key is this time. Come on. You're dumping me. I think you at least owe me this."

"I'm not dumping you." He wasn't. Ending things now was just the logical thing to do. He was leaving in only a few days. He wished she could understand how hard this was for him, too.

"Dumping, leaving—semantics."

He ignored the dull ache in his gut at her flippant response, and he found himself nodding, giving her permission to cuff him. It was probably guilt—that, or the secret wish that she would chain him to his bed and never let him go.

"You're sure you know where the key is?" It was too late if she didn't; the metal clasp fused together seconds later.

"Of course. Now shut up and let me have my wicked way with you."

A grin spread across his face as desire fanned out over his skin, dotting his flesh with tiny goose bumps. Her wicked way indeed.

He closed his eyes and imagined her sliding him inside her warmth, giving him the mind-numbing, toe-curling release that only she could. Instead, he felt a biting cold that seared the sensitive skin along the ridge of his cock.

"What the fuck!"

"Relax—it's just ice."

No sooner had she said the words than his skin began to warm.

"Where the hell did you get ice?"

"I stashed it in a cooler beneath the bed when I got here. You were taking so long, I was afraid it would melt."

He wished it had. He was surprised his erection hadn't withered from the traumatic shock.

"Relax, Justin."

Easy for her to say. Ice wasn't pressed against her most intimate parts.

He tried to do as she asked instead of focusing on the icy coolness, but then something strange happened. He found his body growing harder as she slid the cube of ice across his flesh, blowing in its wake.

His nipples, which normally weren't that sensitive, hardened beneath the cold square, sending shocks of acute pleasure straight to his groin. She numbed his flesh and then warmed it with her hot breath until he was begging her *not* to stop.

When the ice finally melted enough for her to close her lips around the cube, she slipped it into her mouth and slid her lips over him, taking his hardened length within the chilly cavern of her wet mouth. Pleasure burst inside him, the conflicting dichotomy of hot and cold sending tremors of desire shooting through him.

He'd never experienced anything so intense—the slight pricks of numbing pain, followed by the onslaught of pleasure that came in a rush seconds later. He tried to stifle his disappointment when the ice melted against the heat of his skin and her mouth, transforming into nothing more than a tiny gulp of water.

She let him slip from between her lips, and she slid up his body with the seductive grace of a courtesan. Straddling his hips, she held his gaze. What he saw in the depths of her eyes made his heart stop. He wanted to look away but couldn't bring himself to do it. The emotions on her face were open, honest, and raw, but he still couldn't force himself to trust them. A host of nagging doubts beat inside his head—*she was still in love with Harry, he was leaving, she still didn't trust him.*

He closed his eyes, shutting himself off from her and from the intensity of the emotions in her piercing eyes.

She slid down on him, slowly taking him inside her body, her hot pussy gripping him like a tight fist. His eyes flew open, and while she still stared at him, the emotions that had been there just moments before were now gone. In their place was raw desire, as well as a sultry passion that clouded her dark eyes.

She worked her body up and down his length, coating his dick with the evidence of her arousal. He ached to be free of the cuffs so that he could guide her hips, touch her breasts, stroke the hardened nub between her legs that called to him.

She bounced atop him, her hair whipping across her face, her head thrown back in wild abandon as she rode him. Her passion fed his, and he surged up into her, sinking deep within her tight sheath.

She called his name over and over again, until her voice grew thick and hoarse.

She quickened her pace, and her hands slid all over him, touching everywhere: his face, his shoulders, his chest. Her fingertips played across every inch of his torso, their feathered softness tickling him.

He wanted to watch her. He didn't want to miss a single moment of her climax, but he could already feel the heavy sac of his balls drawing up against his body. He couldn't watch her and beat back his own climax. He shut his eyes, the torture of the darkness worse than staring up at her. Every single stilted breath was like his name on her lips, and every slippery slide of her wet heat was like the sweetest agony.

She impaled herself on his hard shaft, her frenzied rhythm hurling him closer and closer to that place of completion. She pumped him hard and strong, the muscles of her sex clenching tightly around him. He wanted to wait; he thought he could, but the tingling at the base of his spine signaled his encroaching release.

"Isabella."

Her name was ragged to his ears, and she must have sensed his need, her hand reaching back to cup the sac between his legs.

"Let go, Justin."

His body had a mind of its own, bending not to his will but to hers. The words were barely out of her mouth, but he was already shooting up into her thick jets of his cum as a harsh bellow ripped from his lips to echo off the walls.

His heart pumped in his chest, and it was a short while before his breathing evened and his heartbeat eased into a steady rhythm.

Her hair tickled his face when she leaned forward to rest her head against his shoulder, her warm breath fanning across his skin.

"I'm sorry—again."

She turned to face him, her eyes already bleary with sleep.

"For what?"

"For losing control. For coming before—"

He stopped when her finger touched his lips. "I told you I enjoy watching you lose control. It turns me on." She yawned as she sat up, stretching her body seductively, making him wish he had just an ounce of energy still left in him.

"Besides, I will just have to make sure you make it up to me later."

Sadly, they both knew there wouldn't be a later, but he couldn't bring himself to ruin the moment.

Chapter Seventeen

The next day Justin invited Caleb over for coffee before his friend headed to work. He didn't really want to talk about Isabella—not when he was still trying to figure everything out—but he should have known that would be the first topic Caleb brought up.

"So, have you and Isabella decided what you two are going to do once you leave?"

He frowned. "It's funny you say that. With Harry showing up, it just added to our list of problems, so I *thought* we would end things before they got more complicated."

"But?" Caleb asked when Justin's voice trailed off.

He sighed. "But when Isabella left this morning, things still felt— *unfinished.*"

Caleb's brows rose. "You'll be here for only one more day. Not much time left to figure it out."

Caleb didn't need to remind him about how much time he had left; it had been weighing heavily on his every moment for the last several days. All that nagged him more was this "thing" with Isabella. Their affair had seemed so simple in the beginning, but now—now he didn't know who he was or what he wanted.

"If you love her, just tell her. I know she has feelings for you, too," Caleb said as he stood up to dump the remnants of his coffee into the sink.

Justin scowled at his friend's back. Caleb made it sound so simple, but it wasn't. Isabella didn't know what her feelings were right now. She might think she was in love with him, but when she returned to DC things would change. She might even realize that Harry was still the love of her life. The last thing he wanted was to come home after six months spent in a Colombian jungle to discover that the woman he'd dreamed of all those nights was now married to another man. That was his greatest fear, which was why he'd tried to break things off last night. But Isabella had somehow derailed him.

"It's complicated" was all he said when Caleb finally turned to face him.

Caleb grinned. "I can see that." He shifted off his perch against the kitchen counter and stood to his full height. "I gotta get to work."

Caleb reached for his jacket and shrugged it on. He was almost to the front door when he stopped. "Hey. Are you going to be at the high school later to help decorate?"

"Yeah, I'll be there. I promised Maggie I'd help set up the platform for the fireworks."

"All right. I'll see you later, then."

Caleb was almost out the door when Justin remembered the main reason why he'd asked his friend to drop by on his way to work.

"Oh, and Caleb. I forgive you for loaning Isabella my spare key and helping her break into my home."

Caleb's jaw dropped open, but Justin didn't wait for his friend's response. Instead, he headed down the hall toward his bedroom. Caleb probably hadn't expected him to figure it out, but it wasn't too hard to put two and two together. Isabella had a way of twisting men around her little finger, and he had no doubt Caleb had been unable to say no to her when she'd approached him with her harebrained scheme. He was sure Caleb would apologize later for his role in all this, but it really wasn't necessary. The thought that Caleb would stew over his actions until he saw Justin again gave him a perverse sense of satisfaction.

Not to mention the look on his friend's face just now, which could only be described as priceless.

"Soooo. How did it go?"

Isabella glanced up at Celeste. She'd been in the middle of balancing the accounts. Angelo's was back to normal, at least until the next holiday rolled around. All the deliveries had been made, and she planned to close up early in order to help her mother decorate the high school for the party that would begin later that night. Everything seemed to be in order—except her love life.

"*It* didn't go anywhere. Justin and I never got around to talking about *us*."

"Well, you better hurry up, girl," Celeste exclaimed, glancing at her watch with dramatic flourish. "You ain't got much time."

"You are such a big bubbly bundle of sunshine and inspiration today. No wonder you're my best friend," Isabella said dryly.

"I'm just trying to serve as a reality check. I really think you should corner Justin, tell him how you feel, and put the ball in his court."

"That's what I'm trying to do."

"Yes, but in your typical coy and fastidious way. Men can be slow and thick-headed. You need to spell it out for them."

"I'm trying. He's just not quite ready to listen. He still believes I'm in love with Harry, and no matter what I say, I can't seem to convince him otherwise."

Celeste snorted. "If he knew Harry, he would understand why it took you all of thirty minutes to get over him."

She frowned. "Yeah, well, he doesn't, which is why he's convinced that I'm just confused."

"I can't believe I'm actually going to agree with Justin on something, but I must say that you can't blame him. He's afraid to open up to you because he's not sure where your loyalties lie. That's why I keep telling you to just *say* that you love him. That way there is no room for doubt."

Celeste made it all sound so simple, so easy, but she'd never been forced to lay her heart out on the line for anyone. She didn't understand how gut-wrenching the prospect of being rejected could be.

"If subtlety doesn't work, then I will have no choice but to give your way a try. After all, he leaves for base tomorrow."

Celeste gave her a disapproving look, as if to say she was a fool, but Isabella knew that Celeste just didn't fully understand the position she was in. Celeste had no idea how vulnerable the uncertainties of being in love made someone feel, and right now, Isabella was as vulnerable and exposed as one could be. To tell Justin she loved him, without any assurances from him, would leave her stripped bare, and she wasn't so sure she would ever be ready to do that.

Isabella walked into the Jacksonville High gymnasium, which was teeming with volunteers. She'd locked up the bakery early and left shortly after Celeste, who was around somewhere, doing Maggie's bidding no doubt.

As if on cue, her gaze settled on Celeste—and then Caleb. They stood about as far apart as two people could get in the gymnasium, positioned at opposite ends of the room, casting baleful glares at each other. She shook her head. They probably thought they masked their attraction well, but they were so obvious.

An army of workers bustled around her, busying themselves by hanging lights and decorations. The biggest part of the celebration would take place outside, beneath a canopy of fireworks. Until about five minutes before midnight, though, the party would be inside.

She glanced around the room, searching for Justin. They hadn't spoken since she'd left his home that morning, and she really had no idea what she'd say to him. She just knew she couldn't let him leave town with so much left unspoken between them.

She was still searching for Justin when she saw Harry, who stood beside a very lovely and adoring Monica. They looked cozy together as they huddled close. Harry chose that moment to look her way, and she forced herself to plaster a smile across her face when he strolled toward her. It wasn't that she didn't want to talk to him; it was just that she didn't want to talk to him right then. She was on a mission to find Justin. Still, there was really no way she could politely walk away, especially now that he stood before her.

"Isabella."

"Harry." She glanced over his shoulder. "I didn't mean to take you away from Monica. You seemed, er, preoccupied."

He gave her a saccharine-sweet smile, but it didn't have the charming effect she knew he intended. "Monica's a wonderful woman. Thank you for introducing us."

She started to tell him that she actually hadn't introduced them—they'd kind of done that on their own—but she didn't see the point. They chatted for a few minutes, mostly about the firm and when he planned to return. She was just about to end their conversation when she caught a flash of movement from the corner of her eye.

She turned to her right and immediately spotted Justin, who was dressed in a gray sweater and a pair of jeans that fit his hard-muscled body perfectly. He gave her a grim frown before he turned away from her and stalked outside.

Was it her, or did Justin just happen to show up whenever Harry was around?

"Ahh, it appears that I'm at the center of your lovers' quarrel yet again."

She pursed her lips into a frown as she turned back to Harry. "So it seems. Would you excuse me for a moment?"

She caught up with Justin outside. His attention was focused on reinforcing the stage that had been set up for tonight. He pointedly ignored her, and she waited patiently until he finished his task. When he stood to his feet, he had no choice but to acknowledge her.

"Do you need something, Isabella?"

His expression was blank, and she hated that she couldn't read him, that he was so closed off from her.

"Can we talk?"

"I'm a little busy right now." To emphasize his point, he knelt back down and began hammering nails into the wooden structure. Seconds ticked by, and neither of them said a word. The only sound was the steady pounding of the hammer against the nails.

"This is ridiculous, you know," she said over the rhythmic pounding of the tool.

He pursed his lips into a frown, but didn't stop or look up. "What's ridiculous?"

"Your behavior."

That got his attention, and he stopped hammering again. "What's ridiculous about *my* behavior?"

She folded her arms across her chest and pinned him with a hard look. "The way you react whenever Harry is around."

"How do you expect me to react?" His brow furrowed with deep grooves. "It's . . ."

His voice trailed off, and she held her breath as she waited for him to finish. "It's what?"

He set down his hammer, dragging his other hand down his face. "It's nothing. Just let it go," he said with a weary sigh, as if simply talking to her pained him.

Let it go. *Let it go!* Her body began to vibrate with frustration at his flippant attitude. "It's *not* nothing. I'm trying to talk about what's happening between us, and you want me to let it go?"

He shot to his feet and hovered above her. "Yes, I want you to let this go," he thundered, the loud boom of his voice matching her angry tone.

"What are you so afraid of, Justin? Why is it so hard for you to open up and talk to me about us?"

"There is no *us*, Isabella. There's only you and Harry—"

"Justin—"

"I was convenient for you at a time when you were hurting. But let's be honest; we really don't have a future together."

She drew back as pain sliced through her heart. His words were like a slap across her face. Even worse than his words was the vacant look in his eyes. The truth of his statement was right there in the depths of his emerald gaze. When he thought of his future, he didn't see her in it, at least not the way she'd envisioned him in hers. She'd always known the truth—Justin was not interested in a woman like her. How had she allowed herself to forget that?

She felt like such an idiot—for hoping, for pushing for something more. She'd really believed he loved her, but it was obvious that he didn't. She should have listened to him from the beginning when he'd told her the deal—they were having a simple no-strings affair, nothing more.

She spun around and walked away. Not once did she look back, nor did she stop. Not even when he called her name.

————

"Caleb, I need your help."

Caleb was perched on a ladder, hanging up a string of lights along one of the gym's walls, but at the sound of his name his hand froze in midair. He twisted around to stare down at the only woman whose voice always managed to sound like a throaty purr as rich and silky as warm honey.

"Are you dying?"

She shook her head, her expression puzzled. "No. I'm fine—"

"Are you sick?"

"No—"

"Is anyone I know sick or dying?"

"As far as I know, no, but—"

He turned back around to finish hanging the lights. "Then you don't need my help."

"Caleb, I'm serious. This is important."

"Leave me alone, Celeste. I'm busy." He had nothing to say to her— especially since she had yet to apologize for basically calling him a gigolo. She'd made it very clear that he had nothing more to offer her than a quick tumble in the sheets.

The subtle shake of the ladder startled him, and when he glanced down at the rungs he saw Celeste climbing up behind him.

"What are you doing?"

"I'm coming up there to drag your ass down. I'm serious. I really need your help."

"What is wrong with you?" He glanced down at the floor. They were about fifteen feet off the ground. Not high enough to die, but if they fell, he imagined they would break some major bones. "All right. Stop, Celeste. I'm coming down."

The little imp had the nerve to smile as she made her way back down to the ground. He followed after her, and as soon as his feet touched the floor he seized her by the arm, dragging her out of the gym and down the hallway where they could be alone.

"One or both of us could have gotten hurt if that ladder had tipped over. Don't you ever stop to think?"

"I needed you to listen, and I couldn't do that from down here."

He sighed, releasing her so that he could run his fingers through his hair. "What is so important that you're willing to risk life and limb?"

"It's Justin and Isabella."

"What about them?"

"They had a fight—"

He rolled his eyes. "They seem to be doing that a lot lately."

"It's because your pigheaded friend won't admit that he loves her."

He thinned his lips into a tight line. He wanted to remind her that Isabella was also his friend, but decided he just didn't have the energy to fight with Celeste on more than one point.

"What do you want me to do about it? They're adults, Celeste. They'll figure it out when they're ready."

"But that's just it. *Your* friend has really pissed Isabella off to the point that she's decided to drive back to DC early tomorrow morning."

"That's her decision—"

"She can't drive back before she talks to Justin," Celeste wailed. "She can't let him ship out without telling him how she feels. I know she'll regret it, and so will that jackass friend of yours."

"Why are you so determined about this?"

Her eyes rounded, as if she couldn't believe he would ask such a question. "She's my best friend, and she's in love. As much as I hate the idea that the man she's in love with is Justin, the fool makes her happy. And I know if she doesn't tell him how she feels, she will never forgive herself. I don't know why you're giving me such a hard time about this. Don't you care that Justin is making a mistake too?"

He thought of how he'd let Isabella into Justin's home last night. It was a reckless move, but he'd found he couldn't deny her when she'd stood there pleading with him. As much as he hadn't wanted to get involved—*still* didn't want to get involved—he'd gone against his better judgment, thinking Justin would thank him later. Justin hadn't, of course, but Caleb still knew he'd done the right thing. As much as he didn't love the idea of joining Celeste in whatever harebrained scheme she had up her chiffon sleeve, he did agree with her. Justin would regret it if he let Isabella walk away without telling her how he felt.

He sighed. He knew he was going to regret this. "So why do you need my help?"

"Because without you, I won't be able to pull this off."

He stood up straighter. "Really? So . . . what exactly do I get in return for coming to your aid?"

Her golden eyes flashed with annoyance. "Let's see. The deep satisfaction of knowing that you did this one selfless act for your dear friend."

He cocked his head to the side as if he was pondering the idea. When he was done, he snapped his gaze to her face. "Uh, sorry. That's not enough." He twisted around and started to stalk off toward the gym, but stopped when her hand shot out to grasp his arm.

"Wait."

He peered down at her.

"What is it that you want? Whatever it is, I'll give it to you if you agree to help me."

She had his full attention, and he was sure she realized what she'd just promised when he furled his lips into a wolfish grin.

"All right. I'll help you."

"But you don't know what it is you just agreed to."

He stepped toward her, a wicked gleam in his eyes. "And neither do you."

Chapter Eighteen

I t was nearly pitch black outside. The faint glow of the moon lit Isabella's and Celeste's steps as they wandered around the grounds near the school's entrance. Isabella sighed as she trudged behind her friend, who was clearly up to something; she just couldn't figure out *what*.

"Celeste, have you been drinking?"

Her friend nearly jumped out of her skin, her eyes bulging. "No. Why?"

Because you're acting weird, Isabella wanted to say. She also wanted to ask if Celeste had been doing drugs, but she thought that starting with a discussion of the perils of overindulging in alcohol would be a smoother segue into that conversation.

"You seem on edge and a bit jumpy. I just wondered if maybe you weren't feeling like yourself."

"Nope. Fine."

She was lying, but Isabella didn't yet know how to prove it, so she just dropped the subject.

"Soooo, remind me again. Why are we out here?"

"I told you, Isabella. I think I dropped my wallet somewhere around here when I was outside earlier."

Isabella was skeptical. Everyone had been out back, near the gym and the recreation area, where the stage was now set up. No one had wan-

dered on the front grounds of the school near the entrance, except for
Celeste, apparently. It would also seem that the normally meticulous Celeste, who wouldn't be caught dead with a single hair out of place or a lip-
stick smudge on her perfectly even teeth, had somehow been careless and
clumsy enough to let her wallet fall out of her purse without noticing until
eleven o'clock that night. She didn't believe for a second that Celeste's
wallet was out here, but she pretended to look as she kicked around some
leaves with her foot.

With the exception of the tiny slivers of silver moonlight that managed
to peek through, the large elm trees made it nearly impossible to see. Their
dense canopy of leaves blocked most of the light.

A twig snapped in the distance, and she glanced over her shoulder, just
before her world went black.

She let out a muffled cry and struggled against her assailant as she was
scooped up and unceremoniously dumped over a hard shoulder. She sniffed
the air, but then instantly regretted it when the smell of wild livestock and
manure overwhelmed her. The noxious scent, coupled with her attacker's
jerky steps, caused her stomach to lurch and roil until she was sure she was
going to vomit.

"It's okay, Isabella. It's just me and Caleb," Celeste assured her.

"You know kidnapping and murder are real felonies, Celeste. And this
thing you put over my face—it really stinks."

"I'm sorry about the sack. It was the only thing we could find on such
short notice. And we're not going to murder you, Isabella. We're just going
to lock you up, but it's for your own good. You will thank us later."

Isabella doubted that.

It wasn't long before she found herself dumped into a jail cell.

Someone removed the sack from her head, and she took in a deep
breath of fresh air as she blinked furiously, struggling to adjust to the glare
of the fluorescent lights. As soon as she could see clearly, she glanced

around at her surroundings. Almost immediately her gaze landed on Justin.

She gasped and dropped to her knees beside him, her fingers tracing the purple bruise beneath his eye.

"What the hell did you do to him?"

"Justin put up a bit more resistance. We had to knock him out and handcuff him." Caleb tossed a small key into the cell, and it clanked loudly against the floor as it settled near her feet.

"Here's the key to uncuff him."

She reached for the key and unlocked the handcuffs. Justin groaned as he stumbled to his feet. He winced when he touched the small bruise that dotted his cheek, and anger leaped in his emerald gaze.

"You two are crazy, and just so you know, I plan to press charges as soon as I get out of here."

"Good luck with that. I wonder how hard it will be to press charges against a sheriff and an attorney when you have absolutely no witnesses," Celeste said, smirking.

Isabella glared at her. "How long do you plan to leave us in here?"

Celeste shrugged. "I don't know. Until you two can play nice." She wriggled her fingers in a delicate wave before turning on her heels.

"Bye-bye."

"Celeste! Caleb! Come back here right now!" She stopped shouting after them when she heard the front door to the sheriff's office close. "Damn it!"

She glared over at Justin.

"Don't look at me. I obviously had nothing to do with this," he said, gesturing to the darkening bruise beneath his eye.

He had a point. She sighed as she dropped down onto the single bed in the cell. This was certainly not how she'd imagined spending her New Year's Eve. Actually, that wasn't true. Before Justin had acted like a jerk, she'd imagined spending it with him, but her dreams had involved champagne, kisses, and lots of sex—just as she'd written it out on her list. Her eyes drifted around the room. She didn't see any champagne, and she certainly wasn't in the mood for any kisses or sex. This sucked.

He sat down beside her, and she scooted away, putting some distance between them, which didn't go unnoticed.

He sighed. "I don't think they locked us up in here for us to just continue ignoring each other."

She shot him a baleful look. "I have nothing to say to you—"

"Isabella—"

"Just *let it go*, Justin," she mocked. "Isn't that what you told me to do earlier?"

"Izzie—"

"Stop calling me that! Don't you get it? I'm not that little girl you once knew. I'm not that person who followed after you with nothing but foolish adoration in her eyes. My name is Isabella. That's who I am."

She stopped herself when she realized she was shouting, but she hated when he called her by that childish nickname. It made her think of the past, her stupid crush, and all her fruitless fantasies of one day growing into a woman he would notice.

"I don't want to talk, Justin. All I want to do is wait until this crazy trick Celeste and Caleb are playing on us is over and they let us out."

"Did you see their faces? Justin looked liked he wanted to pummel me." Celeste chuckled, her unbound hair catching the glow of the moonlight.

Caleb leaned against the squad car outside the sheriff's office, his gaze trained on Celeste. She was beautiful in that moment, her expression completely open to him, her eyes devoid of their usual guile.

"Thank you," she said breathlessly, advancing toward him. "I would have never been able to pull this off without you."

He shifted away from the car and closed the distance between them. "You're welcome."

"Do you think they will make up?"

Caleb shrugged.

"I have no idea, but with nothing else to do, I imagine they will at least have to try and have some type of conversation. That's really all we can hope for."

Celeste tugged on her bottom lip with her teeth. "But I don't want them to *just* talk. I want them to make—"

"Celeste—"

He hoped his friends could reconcile, but ultimately that was up to them, and worrying about it would not change that. Besides, right now Isabella and Justin were not foremost in his mind. Instead, he was focused on the woman standing before him.

"Have you given any thought to how you plan to repay me for helping you pull this off?"

Her eyelids fluttered, and it was clear she'd never thought he'd actually hold her to their agreement.

He reached out to cup her cheek with his hand, dragging her gaze to his face. "For starters, I want an apology."

"An apology? For what?" The words were barely out of her mouth before understanding dawned in her eyes. "Oh. That." She tried to dip her gaze to the ground, but the slight tip of his hand brought her attention back to his face.

She sighed. "I'm sorry about my comments at the bakery. They were rude, and you didn't deserve that."

He smiled at her earnest apology. That was a start.

"I also want dinner."

She furrowed her brow. "Dinner?"

"You know. The last meal people eat in the day."

He bit back a small grin at the hard glint in her eyes. "I got that part. I'm asking about the details."

"You're going to repay me by cooking dinner—"

"No—"

He arched one brow. "So you're reneging on our deal?"

She scowled at him as she shook her head. "No." She puffed out a long breath. "So, when do I get to cook you this dinner?"

"Now." She opened her mouth to complain, he was sure, but he didn't give her the chance to get a word out. "And while I'm enjoying dinner, I'll let you know the rest of my terms."

She wrenched away from him, her eyes glowing with fury. "You never said your favor would come with *multiple* conditions."

He leaned toward her, his mouth within inches of her ear, and he smiled when she shivered. "That's because you never asked."

"This is ridiculous." Justin shoved a hand through his hair in frustration when the silence between them became too much. "Don't you think we need to talk, Isabella?"

"Talk? Us? I tried to talk to you earlier— remember that? You told me to *let it go.*"

Those stupid words. She couldn't seem to get past them.

"I was wrong earlier—"

"You? Wrong?" She rolled her eyes. "Never."

His mouth tightened. He didn't blame her for not wanting to talk to him, but they were stuck there together for God only knew how long. It just didn't make sense for them to sit there in silence until Caleb and Celeste came back—not when they had so much left unsaid between them.

"Would you just listen to me, Isabella?"

Her eyes flashed. "As always, you're a control freak. You have to be in charge of the situation. Now that you're ready to talk, you expect me to be ready to listen." She glowered at him, her hazel eyes hard as stone. "Why should I listen to you when you refused to listen to me?"

He grimaced. Being in charge had nothing to do with this, but when she said it like that, even he had to admit she had a point. He needed to raise the stakes. He needed to *make* her understand.

He let out a shaky breath. "I'm asking you to listen, if only for just a second, because I'm trying to tell you that I love you."

He'd anticipated fireworks, right before her face lit up and she beamed at him with adoration. What he hadn't expected was an inelegant snort followed by a thunderous storm in those hazel eyes of hers.

"You don't love me, Justin." She shook her head. "At least not the way I need to be loved."

His heart squeezed in his chest at the sadness in her eyes. He would give anything to erase that look. She didn't believe him; she'd lost faith in him, but he *did* love her. He just had to make her see that. "And what way is that, Isabella?" he asked softly, his next breath lodging in his throat as he waited for her to answer.

His question stumped her, and her eyes clouded with an emotion he couldn't decipher before she turned away from him.

"It's not important."

It was important to him. He opened his mouth to tell her just that, but was interrupted when colorful blinding lights exploded outside the window.

Fireworks. It was midnight.

He glanced down at her. It was a new year, a time for a new beginning. They had a chance to start over. He just had to convince her it was worth it.

"I can't remember a time when I haven't loved you. Of course, it was different back then, when we were kids, less intense, but it was still there."

He looked over at her. She watched him with wary eyes, but he was relieved her focus stayed on him. That meant she was listening.

"I really never thought about how much you meant to me until I saw you with Harry at the funeral. I guess I always expected you to be here. It wasn't until I saw you with him that I realized I envied him. He had you. He had your love, Isabella—something I realized I wanted."

"I don't love Harry. I never have."

"And yet you were engaged to him."

The accusation in his words hung heavy between them. He needed to know that her feelings for him were genuine, just as real as his.

Seconds ticked by while he waited for her to speak, and he wondered if she would say a word when she shifted on the bed, the muffled sound of her fidgeting breaking the tense silence.

"You don't trust my feelings, and I can't blame you, but what I felt for Harry cannot even begin to compare to what I feel for you. You're not the only one carrying around a torch, Justin. I've done nothing but wear my heart on my sleeve for you. What more do I need to do to convince you that what I feel for you is real?"

"Say it." Her eyes rounded at the harsh rasp of his voice. For all her declarations, not once had she said the words he needed to hear.

Isabella's lips quivered and he held his breath as he waited, wondering whether she had the courage to be completely vulnerable with him, whether she could let her guard down and just trust him with her heart.

When she looked away, he felt as if a knife had sliced through his belly. Whatever her feelings, it was obvious Isabella wasn't ready to be honest with him. She might love him, but just not enough.

———

Fireworks of every color erupted outside the window.

Celeste stared at the flaring lights, mesmerized, bemusedly wondering how she'd ended up at Caleb's house, watching fireworks from his kitchen window.

"You're serious about me cooking—*right now.*"

Caleb shrugged, his eyes flashing with laughter. "I'm hungry—"

"It's midnight. I don't believe you're hungry at midnight."

"It's New Year's."

"So what?" She pointed the mixing spoon at him, flinging tiny droplets of pancake batter across the kitchen table. "You're doing this to punish me."

He smiled. "Of course I am."

She glared at him before returning her attention to the contents of the bowl. "I could be in my bed fast asleep right now—"

"You? Sleeping? On New Year's?" He shook his head. "I really can't see that." He shifted closer. The action was innocent enough, but his nearness made her heart beat faster as the heat of his body radiated toward her.

"If you were back in DC, you'd be partying. I bet you'd be dancing on a bar right now."

It took her a second to register his words; the blood pumping in her ears was so loud. She looked up, a smile on her face as she imagined all the crazy parties she and Isabella would have hit up had they been home.

"I'm sure Jacksonville on New Year's must be boring you to tears."

Not really. It was funny. A week ago she would have thought so, but she really didn't miss the club scene at all. She stared at Caleb. She was actually quite content. She jerked when she realized *why.*

"Shit." She liked this guy.

Caleb's lips dipped into a frown. "What is it?"

He reached for her, but that was the last thing she wanted him to do.

Damn it. Isabella had been right. She liked him. Not just for sex or a fun time; she really enjoyed being around Caleb.

As soon as she'd arrived in Jacksonville and discovered Isabella was all right—that Justin was taking good care of her—Celeste could have hopped back in her car and driven home, but she hadn't. Instead, she'd offered to help Isabella out at the bakery even though she had a shitload of work to do back home. At the time, she'd told herself that was because Isabella and Maggie were truly the only family she had, and right now they needed her. Besides, she always spent the holidays with them anyway, so what was an extra few days? But she knew that was only part of the truth of why she was still there. She'd stayed in Jacksonville when she could have been long gone, and she knew the *real* reason why.

The revelation was mind-numbing.

Caleb's hand seized hers, and she let the spoon fall from her trembling fingers as warmth settled in the pit of her stomach.

"Are you all right?"

No. "Yeah, I'm fine." She tugged her hand from his grasp and picked up the spoon, but he didn't move away. Instead, he inched closer, his chest brushing against her shoulder. She wanted to retreat, more emotionally than physically. She wanted Caleb, but she hated that she never knew where she stood with him.

"If you want me to finish cooking, then I'm going to need space," she snapped at him, but he didn't back off. The tiny dimple in his cheek peeked out when he smiled, his body trapping her against the table.

"Caleb—"

"I'm really not hungry anymore—at least not for food."

Desire ignited inside her, but she tamped it down and glared at him. "This is a game to you. You push me away and then pull me in." She pointed the spoon at him. "I just don't have the energ—"

She'd fantasized about his kissing her from the moment she'd met him. She imagined his lips would be sweet, languorous, gentle.

They were none of those things. He crushed his mouth to hers, capturing her lips in a possessive kiss that made her head spin.

She forgot all about the pancake mix as she clung to him, her arms encircling his shoulders, pulling him closer. He pressed his tongue inside her mouth, tasting her, and she sighed against his lips, her entire body going up in flames.

Her nipples pebbled against the silky fabric of her bra, the slight friction causing her pussy to clench with need.

She wanted Caleb—not just a kiss, or the caress of his roughened hands across her body. She wanted him inside her, making love to her, stroking her to the blinding climax she'd fantasized about every time she thought of him.

She ripped her mouth from his, her chest heaving, echoing the choppy rhythm of his own breathing.

"I want you, Caleb," she said quietly.

He lifted one brow, his face as open and honest as she imagined her own to be. "If we do this, then no games, Celeste. I'm serious."

She knew what he was demanding. He wanted intimacy, not artifice or guile but the real her.

She shook her head. "Why am I the one who's always giving? Always bending?" Caleb was asking way too much of her, and far too soon.

His expression was earnest. "You're not alone here." He slid his hand to the nape of her neck, pulling her close. "Believe me. I'm giving too," he whispered against her brow before dipping his head.

How? She wanted to ask, but he planted his mouth against hers, and she parted her lips, eager for the taste and feel of his tongue stroking hers. Nothing else mattered in that moment as her hands tunneled through his hair, and she deepened the kiss, drawing him into her.

He settled her atop the table, sending dishes and utensils crashing to the ground. They ignored them, and she clasped her legs around his hips, holding him against her. His hands inched along her legs, under her skirt, tracing a path up her thighs. He grasped the firm globes of her ass in his strong hands, and a low moan tore past her lips, a helpless, needy sound.

He released her lips to nip lightly at her earlobe, making her shudder. Wetness pooled between her thighs, and she dug her nails into Caleb's shoulders, her body writhing against his.

He drew back slightly, unbidden lust swirling in the cerulean depths of his eyes. Their gazes locked, and her breath hitched in her chest as he lightly skimmed his fingers to the center of her moist sex.

She called his name, her eyes sliding shut as her head fell back on her shoulders.

"Look at me," he demanded, his voice raspy and hoarse. Her gaze snapped to his face, boring into him when he slipped a long, hard finger inside her.

She shivered, her pussy clenching tight around his thrusting digit. They groaned in unison. She held his intense stare as he pumped his finger in and out of her dripping heat, her entire body crackling with energy. He worked his thumb against her clit, and she dug her nails deeper into his shoulders, every muscle in her body tensing.

"Oh God," she moaned, the first wave of her orgasm building inside her. He nestled his face against the crook of her neck. His breathing was choppy and erratic, his warm breath tickling her heated skin.

She clenched her eyes shut, trying to beat back her climax. She didn't want to come this way. She wanted him inside her, his hard flesh stretching her, filling her.

"Caleb—"

"It's okay, baby. Just go with it," he said, as if reading her mind and giving her permission to let go.

He strummed her clit faster, the stroking of his fingers driving harder. She spread her thighs, taking him deeper inside her, helplessly grinding her pussy against his hand until her orgasm began to rip through her entire body.

"I'm comiiiiing," she cried out in a broken sob. Her body jerked wildly, and she splintered into pieces. Caleb continued to thrust inside her until the tremors subsided and she slumped against him.

She whimpered when he pulled his fingers out of her.

"Oh, don't worry. We're far from done," he said soothingly, his other hand gently stroking her cheek.

She sighed, a weak smile on her face as she watched him suck her juices from his fingers. She shivered at the erotic sight.

When she imagined all the decadent things Caleb had in store for her next, her body hummed to life yet again.

She could hardly wait.

Chapter Nineteen

"I love you, Justin," The words came out unbidden in a jumbled rush. It was hard to love him, with the myriad of uncertainties that hung between them, but she couldn't deny it. She couldn't lie. "I always have."

"Then prove it."

She blinked, not sure she'd heard him correctly. "What?"

He sauntered toward the bed, his gaze burning a hole right through her. "Prove it," he said again.

"How?"

The wicked gleam in his eyes made her heart skip a beat. What was he up to?

"Truth or Dare."

Truth or Dare? "What about it?"

"We're going to play. We started this with a game...."

Scrabble. This had all begun with Scrabble, and now her future with him hinged on what? A game of Truth or Dare? This was insane, but the challenge in his voice was unmistakable. If she loved him, then she was going to have to be completely honest with him.

"Fine, but I won't make this easy for you."

He lifted a brow. "You can make this as hard as you want. I have nothing to hide."

"And what? You think I do?"

"We'll see," he said with a shrug.

She bit her tongue to keep from slinging a sharp retort at him. The game hadn't even begun, and already the gloves were off.

"All right, Justin. It's your call. Truth or dare."

"I go first," he said, crossing his arms.

"Why?"

"My game, my rules." She wanted to wipe that smug look off his face. He thought she would refuse to play because he was calling the shots. *Wrong.* He'd underestimated her yet again. Hadn't he learned anything from their game of Scrabble?

"Truth or dare, Isabella?"

She thought for a beat. He wanted truth, but she would best him at his own game. "Dare."

"You sure?" His deep voice plunged even lower to a husky bass, and she had to fight the urge to shiver. The predatory look in his eyes made her wish she hadn't picked dare, but there was no way she was choosing truth. Dare it was.

"Yep."

"I dare you to tell me when you first discovered you were in love with me."

"You can't dare me to tell you that!"

He arched a brow. "Why not?"

"Because a dare has to be an action. You know the rules. Stop cheating."

His lips furled into a crooked smile. "I think you're just afraid to answer the question."

Her heart skipped a beat. She wasn't afraid to answer the question. That was easy. She'd been in love with him since she was fourteen, although she hadn't known it then.

"I'm not afraid to answer the question. When I pick truth, then you can ask me that again, but since I picked dare, you have to *dare* me to *do* something."

A tiny muscle in his jaw twitched before he let out a shallow breath.

"Fine. I dare you to call my name while you make yourself come."

Her cheeks heated. "Now? Here?"

"That's my dare for you."

"But Celeste and Caleb could come back at any moment."

"I have a feeling Caleb and Celeste won't be back until morning—at the earliest." His eyes darkened a fraction, desire igniting in his gaze. "Stop stalling."

His open desire fed hers, and she drowned in his hooded eyes, her hands skimming down her body.

"Inside your jeans," he croaked out when she rubbed her hand against her denim crotch.

Her movements were slow, achingly so. She delighted in the arousal that emanated from Justin. This was his game, his dare, but she took a small measure of pleasure from the fact that he wouldn't walk away from this any more undaunted than she.

She undid the button on her jeans, and her fingers grasped the zipper and tugged it down slowly. She took her time, and the rasp of metal joined the sound of their uneven breathing. Leaning back against the brick wall, she parted her thighs and slipped her fingers inside her pants, beneath the elastic of her underwear.

She closed her eyes, listening to Justin's low groans. Her skin was hot and damp; she inched her hands deeper inside, through the nest of curls at the apex of her thighs.

Her clit throbbed, and she encircled it with her thumb and forefinger, sending tendrils of pleasure whipping across her entire body. She stroked the hardened nub, rubbing it back and forth until she felt her climax building inside her. Closing her eyes, she leaned back against the wall, her entire body trembling.

"Look at me."

His command came out hoarse and tight, and her eyelids snapped open. She focused her blurry gaze on Justin, whose features were drawn, his attention fixated on the steady movement of her fingers.

Desire burned in his gaze, and he moved toward her, stopping just at the edge of the bed between her parted thighs.

"What are you doing?" she asked when he brushed her hands aside and tugged her jeans off her body.

Mischief danced in his eyes as he lowered himself before her and grasped her legs with his hands. "I'm taking over."

She sucked in a sharp breath. She wanted to ask what had happened to Truth or Dare, but never got the words out when he leaned forward to bury his face between her thighs.

He claimed her with his mouth, his sensual lips latching on to her clit, sucking gently.

"Justin," she cried out, arching into him.

He groaned against her pussy, the hot, wet press of his lips driving her wild with need. She called his name again when he swiped his tongue through the lips of her sex before driving inside her, tasting her cream.

Her eyes were clenched shut, her free hand twisting his hair between her fingers as she held him close. A spark of heat burst inside her belly, spreading throughout her entire body until warmth flooded the area between her legs.

She began to tremble in his arms, his fingers digging into the soft flesh of her bare thighs, holding her legs spread wide as he devoured her. A bolt of fire lanced through her, and she quivered in earnest, her entire world spiraling out of control.

"Justin." His name came out as a needy rasp, and she dug her fingers into his dark locks, just as heat swept across her body, and she shattered all around him.

Her juices gushed from inside her, and he drank deeply from the well between her thighs, even as convulsions racked her. It was a long while before the storm inside her quieted and she relaxed completely against the wall, her entire body satiated.

Justin released her thighs to crawl up the length of her body. The desire in his eyes was only matched by the tenderness there, and she smiled, reaching out with her free hand to cup the back of his head. He dipped down to kiss her briefly before standing to his full height and pulling away. She watched him lean against the bars and cross his arms over his chest, his eyes still glued to her.

The raw emotion shining in his gaze made her heart stutter, and she sighed, realizing that the defenses she'd erected around her heart were starting to crumble. No—correction—they'd crumbled a long time ago. She'd only just now accepted that.

"This Christmas," Isabella said, unprompted.

"What?" Justin questioned.

"The first time I realized I was in love with you was Christmas Day," she said softly, finally answering the question he'd asked earlier. "We were downtown, and I looked over at you standing next to Monica. I wanted to rip her extensions out—that's when I knew I was nuts *and* that I was in love with you."

His lips twitched, and she knew he wanted to laugh. "And it took a game of Truth or Dare to get you to admit that?"

She shrugged. "Well, it took us getting locked in here for you to admit that you even loved me. The way I see it—I'm the lesser extreme."

Their amused gazes clashed, and the anger that had charged their emotions earlier was gone. In its place was the glaring reality that they now had an important decision on their hands, and it was apparent neither of them knew where to begin.

"So, what now?" he asked.

She thought hard before she finally spoke. "I want us to try. I want us to see where this goes. I don't know if it's going to work, but I am ready to give it my all if you are."

He nodded. "Fair enough. I would never ask more of you than I'm willing to give myself."

The meaning of his words hung between them. She was giving her all, and he was giving his. She couldn't argue with that, and she certainly couldn't ask for more.

He walked toward her, his eyes twinkling with mischief as he reached for her. "This isn't on the list, but I am adding to it."

"And what's that?" she asked.

He winked. "Sex in a jail cell."

D esire flared in Isabella's gaze, and Justin's body hardened instantly. He smiled inwardly, hardly able to believe that twelve nights ago they'd been just friends and now they were here. It had certainly been a wild adventure, but then he'd expected nothing less from Isabella. She was nothing if not unpredictable and full of excitement—qualities that had always drawn him to her.

He reached for her, pulling her flush against his body. His hand cupped her cheek, tilting her head back just a fraction. An arrow of heat shot straight to his groin as he settled his mouth against her full lips. The taste was silky and warm, and he deepened the pressure, stroking his tongue inside her.

She twisted her arms behind his neck, holding him close as he backed her up against the bars. The forceful movement elicited a breathy gasp from her lips, and he absorbed it, never once breaking the kiss.

They moved with a heated urgency that pumped through his blood. Still bare from the waist down, she gyrated her hips against his lower body, and he groaned deep into her mouth as his cock grew harder. The scratchy fabric of his jeans was tight across his bulging erection. He held her cheek in his hand while his other hand snaked down the length of her body to slide between her thighs.

She moaned against his lips, her hips jerking. The moist, wet heat of her pussy warmed his fingers, and he gently thrust two of his digits inside her clenching sheath, dragging hoarse sobs from both of them.

He plundered her mouth, his tongue claiming her as his fingers mimicked the action between her silky, soft thighs.

She tore her lips from his, her chest heaving, her cheeks flushed red.

"I need you," she rasped out.

He shook his head, not once breaking the thrusting rhythm of his fingers. "Not yet."

She whimpered, and he thrust harder. More juice trickled from her pussy onto his hand, and she joined in the rhythm, her hips matching the pace of his stroking fingers.

He rubbed his thumb against the aching bud of her clit, and her pussy tightened around his fingers. He leaned into her, his face buried into her neck.

"That's it, Isabella. Ride my fingers," he whispered against her dewy skin. She shivered, her hips moving faster, and he quickened the pace of his thrusting digits, driving harder and harder inside her until she released a loud sob and convulsed around him.

With his fingers still buried inside her spasming cunt, he undid his pants and pulled the hard shaft of his cock from its restrictive confines.

Positioning the tip of his dick at her opening, he entered her in one smooth, slick thrust, pushing past her clenching muscles.

She gripped him tight, and he closed his eyes, taking deep breaths to try to stave off his imminent climax. His first thrusts were gentle and shallow, giving himself a few more moments to gather his control. But his efforts were futile—she wound her legs around his hips, sending him sinking deeper.

"Isabella," he growled out in warning. He tried to still her hips but ended up digging his fingers into her soft flesh, using her body as an anchor as he surged deeper into her. She clung to him, her cries of pleasure mingling with his own, while he fucked her deep and hard against the bars of the jail cell.

Sweat dotted his forehead, the scent mingling with the heavy musk of sex that wafted all around them. He rocked his hips, thrusting harder, and she lifted her own, sending him tunneling deeper, the tip of his cock brushing against the back of her sex.

"That's it," he hissed against her ear, his control beginning to seep from his body.

Like a purring cat, she rubbed her body against him, and all of a sudden he wished they were naked, their bodies flesh to flesh. *Next time,* he thought. Before they left the cell, he would make love to her in every position imaginable, with not a single stitch of clothing separating them.

"Justin." The soft hitch in her voice told him she was on the edge of climax again, and he drove into her harder, gyrating his hips in lazy circles, to brush against her clit. She blew out a sharp breath through clenched teeth, her hands wringing his hair tighter. He ignored the slight twinge of pain. The blinding pleasure of both his nearing orgasm and her own were the only things on his mind.

His climax gathered inside him, and he stroked into her harder, faster, savoring the juicy wetness of her tight sheath. And when she screamed out his name in a high-pitched squeal, her pussy fisting tight around his cock, he allowed himself to let go, bathing her inner channel with his seed as she drowned him in her own essence.

"Shit. Isabella," he growled out against her throat, his breathing short and uneven. He gripped the soft flesh of her hips tighter to keep from collapsing at her feet.

Slowly she unwound her legs from around his waist, and he steadied her with a hand, pressing her into the bars.

When their breathing was finally normal, he glanced down into her satiated face, a smile tugging at the edges of his lips.

"What are you thinking?" he asked, curious.

"That we should do this again—" Her eyes sparkled. "With me cuffed to the bars."

The image that flashed inside his head made his body harden instantly. Isabella, with her hands above her head, cuffed to the bars, her breasts jutting forth, her legs wrapped around his hips as he rode her lush curves to climax.

"Only one condition."

She arched a brow.

"This time we're completely naked."

Heat leapt into her eyes as she smiled, her head nodding. "Now you're talking."

Chapter Twenty

The sun peeked through the clouds the next morning, bright and radiant, as if it knew it was a new day, a new year. It shouldn't have been such a beautiful day, Isabella thought. It should have been dreary and gloomy, the perfect match to her sour mood.

"What are you thinking?"

Isabella glanced over at Justin, who was scrunched up with her on the lumpy cot in the cell.

"We haven't talked about the fact that you're leaving today."

"And let's not," Justin said, pressing his finger against her lips. "I don't need to be back on base until tonight. We have all day together. Let's not spend it thinking about things we can't change."

She sighed as she snuggled deeper into his embrace. He was right.

The front door creaked open, and she lifted her head from Justin's chest just as Caleb strolled into the room. They'd both managed to drag on their clothes early that morning, so she stumbled to her feet, followed by Justin.

"What took you so long? You know I leave today." Justin glanced down at his watch. "And it's almost ten."

Caleb's face darkened with color, and Isabella narrowed her eyes at him. He almost seemed embarrassed. She also noticed that his clothes were rumpled.

"Where's Celeste?" she asked.

His hand faltered with the lock before he finally turned the key and slid the cell door open.

"I think she's at your house."

Something didn't ring true about his statement, and she didn't miss the way he kept avoiding eye contact.

"You *think*? That's odd. You were the last person to see her. Where did you drop her off after you left us here?"

Caleb's face grew even redder, if that was possible, and she knew then that something was definitely up. Oooh, when she got her hands on Celeste, her friend was going to have some explaining to do.

"Come on, Isabella. Leave Caleb alone. You can catch up with Cruella later."

There was no doubt in her mind that she would. She shot Caleb a sharp look that said he wasn't fooling anyone, but she let Justin usher her out of the sheriff's office.

As soon as they were outside she turned to face him.

"I think they hooked up."

Justin arched a brow, but he didn't break his stride. "Good for them if they did."

Isabella wasn't so sure. Ordinarily, she wouldn't bat an eye at Celeste's conquests, but this time things were different. She could tell Celeste liked Caleb more than she was letting on. But those two were like oil and water—they just didn't mix. She just hoped Celeste knew what she was doing and didn't wind up getting hurt.

"Hey, where are we going?"

She'd been so absorbed in Celeste and Caleb's Greek drama that she didn't realize Justin wasn't walking them toward the high school, where their cars were still parked.

"To Angelo's."

She glanced at her family bakery, just a few feet away. "Why?"

A wolfish grin spread across his face. "Because I have fantasized about this for almost two weeks now, and before I leave here, we're having sex in that bakery—the right way. I want to take my time making love to you. I want to cover you in icing and whatever else I can get my hands on." His eyes twinkled. "And then lick every inch of you until there's not a single drop left."

I sabella unlocked the door and slipped inside, followed by Justin, who locked it behind them. Like all the small businesses in Jacksonville, Angelo's was closed for the holiday, so the blinds were closed, blocking out the sunlight. She reached for the light switch, but Justin covered her hand with his.

"Keep it off."

Enough light peeked through the crooks and crevices in the blinds for Isabella to see the muted light accentuating the chiseled planes of his handsome face.

Excitement hummed through her body, and she shivered with anticipation of what was to come. Grasping his hand in hers, she led him toward the back of the shop, where they kept all their cake decorating supplies.

She went straight to the pantry, where jars and tubes of icing sat on a shelf, and pulled out a small tub.

Buttercream icing.

She looked at Justin from over her shoulder.

He gave her a curious look, and she winked at him. He'd talked about his fantasy; well, she had some fantasies of her own—one particularly vivid fantasy she'd had ever since their phone sex adventure. She'd imagined herself on her knees before him, sucking every dollop of the sugary confection from his body.

"Take off your clothes," she said with an impish grin.

One brow shot up, but there was nothing in his expression that seemed resistant.

"All of them?"

She smiled. "Every last one."

He still wore the same clothes from last night; his dress shirt was rumpled and his jeans wrinkled. He resembled a rough-around-the-edges biker stranded on the side of a country road, and Isabella thought he'd never looked sexier.

Her breath stilled in her lungs as he slowly unbuttoned his shirt, revealing his hard, tanned muscles. When his shirt fell from his body, she released the breath she hadn't realized she'd been holding.

His eyes bore into her as she watched him, her heart beating faster, the steady throb of desire and lust pulsing through her body. He undid his boots and kicked them off, casting them aside along with his socks. His hands returned to his pants, and he unsnapped the button, his fingers tugging at the zipper. The harsh rasp of metal separating was the only sound she could hear over the steady pounding of blood in her ears.

He shoved his jeans down his legs, and her entire body leapt to life, heat crawling around inside her. There was neither shame nor modesty as he pushed down his boxers and shucked them aside, standing there wearing nothing but a heart-stopping grin and an impressive erection.

She crossed the small space that separated them. When she was within inches of him, she tugged off the lid of the icing and dipped her finger inside to gather up a heavy dollop. She watched him intently as she sucked on her fingers, soft moaning sounds coming from her lips as the sweet cream melted in her mouth. His eyes narrowed, darkening to forest green pools.

He reached for her, but she took a step back and shook her head.

"You can't touch me until I say so."

He groaned but let his hands fall to his side, balling them into tight fists to keep from disobeying her command.

Just out of reach, she devoured her fingers, imagining it was his cock between her lips, and from the look in his eyes, she was certain he too wished it was his cock she was sucking.

With slow, deliberate movements, she pulled her finger from her lips, her tongue encircling the tip before she shoved it once again into the icing. This time, when she pulled out a blob of icing, she ran it across Justin's chest, paying special attention to his nipples as she swirled the white icing around them.

His breath stuttered, and she looked up at him to see his gaze focused intently on her. She leaned forward, her tongue licking across his chest, his nipples. She laved him with her mouth, leaving a trail of wet kisses across his torso. His heartbeat quickened beneath her searching mouth and questing fingers as she smeared and licked icing off his chest.

When his hand grasped the back of her head, she pulled away.

"No touching til I say so."

"Isabella—"

"*No* touching."

He frowned. "But this is *my* fantasy."

She was sure he didn't realize it, but the tiny pout on his lips was sexy as hell. Sexy or not, his fantasy or hers, he was still going to have to follow the rules. This was her game now.

"No touching or I stop." The expression on his face told her he was doubtful she would hold him to that. He was right. There was no way she would stop, but he didn't need to know that.

He dropped his hand back down to his side with a small nod. She curled her fingers around his cock, rewarding his obedience. His head fell back on his shoulders with a low groan as she pumped him with her fist. With one hand still on him and the other holding the container of icing, she dropped to her knees before him. Setting the tub on the floor, she swiped more frosting onto her finger.

She stopped jerking him off to place a dollop of the icing on the tip of his cock. The muscles in his abdomen flexed, and she glanced up at him to see that he was watching her, waiting in anticipation for her next move.

She dipped her head and ran her tongue over the crown of his dick, licking up the icing in a single stroke. She moaned around his cock, taking him deeper into her mouth, the combination of buttercream and hard flesh bursting on her tongue.

Opening her mouth wider, Isabella took him to the back of her throat, wrenching a deep groan from Justin. She fucked him with her mouth, her head bobbing on his dick as she fisted his cock with one hand and massaged his balls in the other.

She trained her eyes on him as she worked her lips up and down his shaft. His head was thrown back, the purplish veins in his neck standing out against his ruddy skin. From the way he clenched and unclenched his fists, Isabella could tell it was taking a great deal of effort for him to keep his hands off her.

He was close; his body trembled around her, and she took him deeper inside her mouth, sucking harder, her tongue whirling around his hard length.

"I'm coming," he croaked out, just as he tensed above her, his cock swelling.

She took him fully inside her mouth, the head of his dick grazing the back of her throat. He let out a hoarse shout as he came, the warmth of his essence flooding her mouth. She drank from him deeply, swallowing every drop until he was spent.

When he grew soft, she settled back on her heels, letting him slip from her mouth. She stood to her feet, and he enveloped her in his arms, kissing her deeply. So much for her "no touching" policy.

She wrapped her arms around him, returning his kiss until she finally drew back to take in a breath of air.

"Now it's your turn," he declared, his eyes twinkling as he took a step back. "Take off your clothes."

Isabella bit down on her cheek to keep from grinning. So he wanted to turn the tables? She could handle that.

It took her mere seconds to strip off her clothes, and she stood there before him, naked and humming with anticipation.

She gasped when, without warning, he grasped her by the waist and lifted her atop the work counter. The cool metal chilled her bare skin, and she shivered.

He scooted her toward the center so that she could plant her feet against the counter's edge.

"Lean back," he said, his deep voice hoarse with need as his eyes fixated on the nest of curls at the juncture between her thighs.

She did as commanded, ignoring the slight chill when her back touched the cold metal. In seconds it was replaced by nothing but heat when Justin settled his mouth on her pussy.

Lightning shocks of heat whipped across her body, and she stiffened when he sucked her hardened bud between his lips.

"Oh God," she moaned as she arched into his mouth, crying out when he shoved a long finger deep into her dripping cunt.

She moved her hips back and forth on his finger, the juices of her pussy drenching it.

"More," she demanded, and he obliged, thrusting two fingers inside her greedy sex as he continued to suck on her clit.

His hot mouth and tongue probed and pulled at her, and he shoved his fingers deep inside her, ramming and thrusting against her G-spot. Tiny explosions went off inside her as she writhed against the counter, panting his name. He devoured her pussy with hungry strokes of his tongue, and she arched deeper into his face, grinding her sex against his mouth until she was powerless to stop the cresting wave building inside her.

"Justin!" Her voice was raspy and raw as she cried out his name, clinging to the edge of the counter, her back arched as she gyrated against him. Hot, wet juice poured from her pussy, and he licked it up, his tongue dragging through her swollen folds, drinking down her cream.

She collapsed against the unyielding counter, a boneless mass of jelly. Justin's hands lovingly stroked her thighs until she found the strength to sit up.

His sweat-dampened hair clung to his forehead, and she reached up to push back a lock. Tenderness swelled inside her. She had never felt this way for any man in her entire life.

She gazed into his handsome face. She was happy that it was Justin she'd developed these intense feelings for. Despite their stubborn personalities and heated fights, there was no one who knew her better. They just fit together—they always had.

She gasped when he lifted her into his arms.

"What are you doing?"

He crooked his lips into a dashing smile. "That much should be obvious."

Justin bent her over the counter and spread her thighs. Her mouth curved into a small O.

It was definitely clear *now*.

Her entire upper body rested over the counter, her ass high in the air. He rubbed his hands over the round globes of her ass, massaging the soft mounds.

"Mmmm," she groaned when he slid a finger inside her pussy, still wet with the cream from her climax, and then moved to press the same finger against the pucker of her anus.

He stroked his finger in and out of her rectum, and she experienced a wave of pleasure she'd never felt before as the ring of muscle clamped down on his finger even as her pussy clenched. He leaned over her, his lips pressed against her ear.

"One day I plan to take you there too, but not today." Her pussy gushed with more wetness at the image of Justin's cock buried deep within the tight tunnel of her ass, but then all thought ceased as he slid inside her pussy, inch by torturous inch, until he filled her, claimed her, completed her.

Her sighs of pleasure blended harmoniously with his deep groans as he moved within her, working his hardened shaft in and out of her pussy. His deep strokes grew intense, and she whipped her head around, her hands clutching the edge.

"You feel so good wrapped around my dick," Justin murmured against her sweat-soaked skin, and she trembled against him, his hot words sending a gush of wet heat flooding her pussy.

They groaned in unison, her juices coating his thrusting dick, the sound of him pumping in and out of her sticky cunt echoing off the walls.

Their bodies dripped with sweat, and they slipped and slid against each other, the friction driving her closer and closer to climax. She dragged in deep breaths, fighting against it. She didn't want it to come to an end so soon. She wanted to savor every moment, make it last for as long as possible.

"Don't fight it, Isabella," Justin growled, reading her effortlessly.

She shook her head, ignoring his command, still fighting the building heat inside her. He twisted her hair around his palm, gently tugging her head back.

"Don't fight it, Isabella," he commanded again, his words and actions more forceful this time.

She couldn't deny him even if she wanted to. He plunged into her, his deep thrusts out of control, sending her tumbling over the edge.

Her orgasm started at the center of her core before erupting like a volcano and spreading throughout her entire body.

"Yes. Oh God, yes," she screamed into the darkened room, nearly blacking out as sharp arrows of light flashed behind her clenched eyelids.

In the distance she thought she heard Justin call her name, but she couldn't be certain. Her orgasm went on forever until she had nothing left, and she slipped into a deep, hazy, languorous fog, where only pleasure existed.

Chapter Twenty-one

"Feel better now?"

Isabella's eyelids fluttered open, revealing the wide hazel eyes that always made him think of Hershey's Kisses.

"What happened?"

"You passed out," he said as he helped her sit up.

"No, I didn't. I've never fainted in my life."

She sat atop the counter, and he stepped within the crook of her parted legs to rest his hands against her hips.

"What can I say? I'm potent."

She swatted at his shoulder. "You're incorrigible. What am I going to do with you?"

"You could marry me." He said the words playfully, but as soon as they were out he knew they'd been the wrong ones. He didn't regret saying them; he'd been toying with the idea since last night. He just wasn't certain how Isabella would react. She sat frozen in his embrace, withdrawing from him both emotionally and physically. Well, at least he now had his answer.

"Are you serious?"

"Would I joke about something like this?"

She shoved a hand through her hair, clearly upset. What was so wrong about them getting married? They'd known each other all their lives, they were in love, and he was leaving the country tomorrow. He didn't see what the issue was. And that's exactly what he told her.

She pushed at his chest and hopped down from the counter, her expression incredulous.

"Just hours ago you accused me of being confused and fickle because I was engaged to Harry, whom I didn't love, but now all of a sudden you think my judgment is sound enough for me to marry *you*?"

He stilled. "Isn't it?"

Her eyes grew wider. "I don't know! This is all so . . . so fast."

"You claim you love me—"

"I *do* love you."

"Then what's the matter? We don't have to get married *now*. I'm simply asking you to marry me."

She narrowed her eyes at him, her piercing stare boring into him. He hated it when she looked at him like that, as if she could see straight to his soul.

"What is this really about, Justin?"

He decided not to pretend that he didn't understand her question. She was too smart for that, and he had too much respect for her to insult her intelligence.

"I need to know that you're going to be here when I get back," he said finally, after several heartbeats.

Seconds ticked by in silence before comprehension dawned in her gaze, and her eyes softened. "You don't have to marry me to know that. I'm not going anywhere, Justin."

Like everyone else. These were the words left unspoken—the words that hung between them. Like his parents, his brothers. He hated the look of pity in her eyes. He didn't want her to feel sorry for him. He wanted to know that when he returned, she wouldn't be off enjoying some new adventure with Celeste—or worse, with some new guy because she'd grown bored of the idea of a dull life with him.

She folded her arms across her chest, a wry chuckle bubbling out of her. "Marriage? You're serious?"

He nodded. He was. He was sure of *his* feelings; he was just looking for some sign from *her*. One that proved she was interested in a more permanent commitment. Thus far, he didn't have it.

"Fine, I'll marry you—"

He glowered at her as he reached down for his clothes. "Don't do me any favors, Isabella."

"On one condition," she said, plowing ahead as if he hadn't spoken. "You go back to practicing law."

The words were barely out of her mouth before he started shaking his head. "No."

"Your dad wanted you to take over his practice—"

"Isabella—"

"But instead you sold it."

He was prepared for the knife that twisted in his gut, but that didn't make it hurt less. Yes, he'd sold his dad's law practice and left JAG. At the time he'd wanted nothing to do with law. Before Isabella had started picking at old wounds, he would have said he *still* didn't want to have anything to do with law. But now—now he didn't feel quite as strongly as he used to. When she brought it up this time, the waves of guilt didn't hit him as hard as they had before.

"Drop it, Isabella."

"Why are you being so stubborn about this? You back me into a corner with this whole marriage thing, but I don't get to bring up the 'off limits' topic." He shoved on his pants, shooting her a baleful look when she used air quotes for "off limits."

"So, let me get this straight. You're issuing ultimatums now?"

She stopped in the middle of dragging on her own clothing. "Isn't that what *you* just did?"

He stared at her like she was crazy. She had to be. "So asking someone to be your wife is considered an ultimatum these days? Interesting. I thought a proposal showed one's long-term commitment to the person they love. But what do I know?"

She stopped in the middle of shoving her leg into her jeans, and although he was still mad at her, he couldn't help but think how sexy she looked, all wild and disheveled.

"You want me to marry you so that you know I won't leave you. A little screwed up, but I get it. What about me, though? I want to know that you will be here for me too—that you will be *alive*. I'm not marrying a Navy SEAL—point blank."

She stood there staring him down, her hands on her hips. He shook his head. They were getting nowhere. They both had two very different versions of what long-term commitment meant.

"Where are you going?" she asked when he moved toward the door.

"Home. We both need to cool down before we say things we don't mean."

"I meant every word I said. I love you, Justin, and if marrying you today, tomorrow, or six months from now is what you need to be certain that I am here for the long haul, then I'll do it, *but* not if you're still a SEAL."

"You're serious about this ultimatum?" He couldn't believe it. She had to know how unreasonable she was being.

"I am," she said solemnly, which now left him with a lot to think about.

"I need to head home to finish packing. I'll call you later," he said. Isabella nodded as he slipped out, but the expression on her face told him that on this one point, Isabella was not prepared to budge.

———

sabella felt like she'd been pacing back and forth in her bedroom for hours when Celeste finally burst in.

"Where the hell have you been?" Isabella asked, rolling her eyes when a secretive smile spread across her friend's face. Didn't need Einstein to figure out what she'd been doing all night. She swept her gaze over her friend. Rumpled clothing, bed hair, swollen lips. Either she'd gotten into a dangerous pillow fight, or she and Caleb had ushered in the New Year with some serious fireworks.

"You know what? On second thought, I don't think I really want to know," Isabella said, holding up her hand.

Celeste flopped down on her bed. "Good, because I'm too exhausted to tell you everything right now."

Isabella bet she was.

"So, what's up with you? And what was with that crazy message you left on my voice mail?" Celeste asked. "I thought you and Justin made up last night."

"We did, but then we got into another fight—"

"Another one?" Her eyes rounded. "What is it with you two—fuck and fight, fuck and fight—"

"And now he won't answer his phone," Isabella said, cutting her off.

"But he's due back to base in three hours."

Isabella stopped pacing to flop down on the edge of the bed. "I know, and after today I won't be able to talk to him because he has military stuff to do before he leaves tomorrow. I just feel so horrible about how we left things."

Celeste sighed. "I'm probably going to regret asking this, but what did you argue about this time?"

Isabella gave her the CliffsNotes version. She hardly felt like rehashing it. Time was of the essence, and besides, she felt bad about issuing Justin such a harsh ultimatum. Love wasn't based on ultimatums; it was based on trust and acceptance. He accepted her, flaws and all. It was time for her to do the same.

"Did you stop by his house?"

Isabella shook her head. "He seemed so mad when he left. And since he's not answering his phone, I really don't expect him to answer his door."

"All right; then how long does it take you to get to Justin's base?"

Isabella thought about it for a second. "About an hour. Why?"

Celeste shot to her feet. "Because I know you don't want your last words to Justin to be fighting words," she said, grabbing Isabella's hand and pulling her toward the door before she could get another word out.

Justin swore under his breath and flipped his cell closed. Isabella still had her phone off. "What's wrong?"

Justin glanced at Caleb. "She's still not answering her phone."

Caleb rummaged inside his pocket and punched in a few numbers. Two seconds didn't even tick by before he was ending the call. He punched in a set of numbers again, and ended it just as abruptly.

"I called Isabella and Celeste, and *both* went straight to voice mail. Maybe she's not mad at you. I heard all over the news that another storm is supposed to be rolling into town tonight. Maybe it's messed with the cell phone towers."

Justin sat up straighter. Caleb's suggestion wasn't that far-fetched; it had happened to his cell before. And if he was right, then that meant Isabella wasn't purposely ignoring his calls.

Justin punched another number into his phone: this time it was Maggie's cell. He hung up with a scowl when it too went straight to her voice mail.

"I'm an idiot."

"I told you not to leave without talking to her."

Justin sent Caleb a sidelong glare. "How was I supposed to know that the phone lines could actually be to blame? That Isabella wasn't just having one of her fits?"

"First, because I've never known Isabella to have fits. And second, because even if she was pissed, is this how you really wanted to say good-bye?"

Justin felt as if Caleb had just punched him in the gut. Of course this wasn't how he wanted to leave things, but when he couldn't get through to Isabella, he assumed she didn't want to talk to him. He was just trying to give her space. He'd planned to call her again tomorrow before he shipped out.

He glanced at the clock in the waiting area at Norfolk Air Force Base. They had an hour and a half before his entire team would be there, and as soon as everyone arrived, they would begin briefing for their trip. He couldn't leave. It was too late. He would never make it back in time before the briefing began.

He shot out of his seat.

"Where are you going?" Caleb asked, standing with him.

"Since there are no phones here, I'm going to see if I can get on a land line over at the commissary."

Caleb's expression was skeptical, but all he said was, "All right. I'll go with you."

They walked outside. The sun was already setting over the base, and they followed the street lights along the sidewalk toward the base exchange and commissary.

Justin had just stepped off the curb when a siren blared in the distance, and he glanced up as a pair of flashing blue and red lights danced before his eyes. The car rushed past him in a flurry, but he didn't think anything of it until Caleb let out a string of curses from beside him.

"What is it?"

Even in the dim light he could see Caleb's face twisted in anger, his cheeks mottled red.

Caleb turned to him. "I don't think we're going to need to call Isabella after all."

Justin stopped in his tracks. "Why not?"

"Because if I'm not mistaken, Celeste just drove by in my squad car, and I'm pretty sure Isabella was with her."

"Are you insane?" Isabella gripped the car door and braced herself against the passenger seat. "If we get caught, we're both going to jail."

"Relax. We're almost there anyway."

Relax? Isabella glared at Celeste. They had broken every speeding law in existence to get there, and had run just as many red lights in a squad car they'd not only stolen but *hot-wired*—and Celeste wanted her to *relax*?

"The least you could do is slow down now that we're on base." How they'd gotten on base was still a mystery to Isabella. They weren't on any list. They should have been stopped and forced to get visitor passes, but all Celeste had to do was turn on her infamous charm, and flash her driver's license along with one of Caleb's *stolen* badges, and all of a sudden they were through the gates.

Celeste slowed down the car and cut the lights and siren. "Didn't you say Justin's team was meeting somewhere near the air strip? Do you know where the runway is, then?" she asked as she peered through the window.

"No, but pull in over there. We'll ask someone."

Celeste drove into a parking lot with a few cars scattered about and cut the engine. They piled out of the car, and she looked around. At this time of night, the base was mostly deserted.

"We should have asked for directions back at the gate. How am I going to find him at this late hour with no one around?"

Celeste abruptly stopped. "Um, I don't think we're going to have to worry about finding Justin."

Isabella's gaze snapped to Celeste. "Why not?"

Her friend gave a sheepish grin. "Because, if I'm not mistaken, Justin is headed straight for us."

She turned in the direction of Celeste's pointed finger and frowned. Oh, they were both going to jail now. Justin marched toward them in his dark fatigues, with Caleb beside him. Both wore matching scowls, leaving her uncertain which one was angrier.

"What the hell is wrong with you two?" Caleb bellowed as soon as he stood before them. His gaze was focused solely on Celeste, so Isabella didn't feel the need to interject. Besides, this *had* been Celeste's idea in the first place.

Celeste shrugged, nonplussed by Caleb's hard glare. "Isabella needed to get here before Justin's briefing began."

"So you thought you would just *steal* my squad car—"

"Borrow—"

"Steal. I'm throwing you back in jail as soon as we get back to town."

"But—" Caleb seized Celeste by the arm and pulled her away, although Isabella could still hear their hushed angry voices as they bickered down the sidewalk.

"Please tell me this wasn't your idea," Justin said, gesturing toward the car.

"Not my idea, but I didn't exactly discourage Celeste, either."

He arched one brow. "I see that." He closed the distance between them, his hand reaching out to cup her cheek. "But for once, I'm not mad at you for putting yourself in harm's way."

Her eyes widened. She couldn't be hearing correctly. "You're not mad?"

"I'm sure somewhere deep down I am, and I'm also sure that I'll be furious later, but right now I'm just glad you're here."

She released the breath she hadn't realized she'd been holding. "I didn't know if you'd be happy to see me or not. You didn't pick up your phone when I called."

"Not on purpose. I tried calling you but couldn't get through. I thought you were ignoring my calls too, until I realized Caleb's cell was doing the same thing. The storm coming in tonight must have messed with the phone lines."

The phone lines were out? Relief flooded her, but with it came a tinge of embarrassment. "I'm such an idiot. I thought you were angry with me. I thought you didn't want to talk to me after that whole ultimatum fiasco. I—"

Justin silenced her with a single finger pressed against her lips. "I know," he said softly. "But I'm not angry with you; I'm angry with myself." He took a deep breath, and she found herself doing the same. The intense look in his eyes made her heart pound with nervousness.

"I had a lot to think about on the drive out here, and I realized you were right—"

She shook her head. "No, I was very wrong, Justin. Love isn't about ultimatums—"

He clamped his fingers over her lips. "No, but it *is* about compromise. You were right all along—about me running from the past, the memories of my parents, my law career. I just didn't want to face any of it."

Her heart ached when she saw the look in his eyes. She could tell that the time he'd taken for self-reflection, and what he'd discovered, had not been easy for him.

"So what are you saying? Do you really plan to leave the Navy?"

"To be honest, I don't know yet." He shrugged. "The only thing I do know is that I love you and I plan to do whatever I have to do to make this work."

His words made her heart stutter, and she lifted on her tiptoes to wrap her arms around him.

He was as committed to making this work as she was. Until he'd said the words, she hadn't known for sure.

She captured his lips with hers, pouring her entire heart into the kiss. No other words were necessary. She had Justin's love and his whole-hearted commitment to their future together. She was confident the rest would sort itself out in time.

Chapter Twenty-two

First, Isabella quit her job, much to the horror and dismay of everyone, including Harry, who wailed for days about how the firm was losing one of its best junior partners. Celeste still hadn't quite forgiven her, but Isabella was working on her. She had yet to tell Justin, though. At best, their conversations were infrequent and short. She didn't want to waste the few precious minutes that they were able to talk and have him pump her with questions on the soundness of her decision—like everyone else.

Why did she quit? She was so good at her job. Her decision was always met with questions and statements along these lines. She snorted. They just didn't understand. She was good at a lot of stuff; that didn't mean she was necessarily happy doing any of it. The thought of waking up and returning to the firm had left her feeling restless and on edge. She hadn't found her job fulfilling for a long time. She just hadn't decided to do anything about it until now.

A dollop of paint splattered across her cheek. She grimaced. Unlike law, painting was one of those things she *wasn't* so good at.

"Is this what love does to a person? Makes them up and quit their job, convinces them they can start their own business, and they can paint to boot?" Celeste stepped through the doorway but stopped right there. "If that's love, then I want no part of it."

Isabella rolled her eyes and set her paintbrush aside. "Says the woman who has spent every weekend of the past four months with Jacksonville's resident sheriff."

"That's just lust."

Whatever it was, she'd never seen her friend happier. "Sure it is. What are you doing here so early? I thought you were driving down after you finished up at work."

Celeste shrugged. "Decided to leave early. Wanted to check in on my best friend to make sure she doesn't slip any further into insanity."

"And as you can see, I'm completely sane."

Celeste sniffed, her eyes darting around. "That's debatable. You think you can spare a few minutes to grab an early dinner?"

"Sure, just give me a second to clean up and I'll walk over to Joe's with you."

Fifteen minutes later they were seated across from each other in a dimly lit booth.

"So, you're serious about not telling Justin about your decision?" Celeste said between bites of her salad. "Have you thought about how he might react to the news?"

That was all she thought about. Either Justin was going to love her idea or he was going to absolutely hate it, but she had no way of knowing which until he returned home and weighed in. She both anticipated and dreaded that day.

"To be honest, every day I second-guess my decision, but in my heart, I know it was the right one. I want this for both of us. In the end, I hope he's supportive, but I need to remember that I'm also doing this for myself. This has always been a dream of mine."

"I know it has." Celeste reached across the table to cup her hand. "I'm happy for you, and I'm sure Justin will feel the same way."

Isabella gave Celeste a small smile. "I hope you're right." And she sincerely did, but every day a tiny voice of doubt nagged at her, and she often wondered if she was making a huge mistake.

Justin returned home a month earlier than expected. His team managed to complete the mission ahead of schedule. They'd subdued most of the cartels by taking down their leaders, and the Colombian government had been able to regain control while the groups scrambled to find new leadership. The outskirts of Bogota were quiet—at least for now.

Instead of renting a car and driving straight to Jacksonville, he decided to head to DC to surprise Isabella. The East Coast was beautiful in the spring, with cherry blossom trees and wildflowers bursting with color along the interstate.

It was late afternoon when he arrived in DC, and he called Isabella on the way to her condo. But she didn't answer. He left a message; and when the front desk agent at her building told him that she no longer lived there, he left several more.

"What do you mean she doesn't live here anymore?" he barked at the young employee.

The poor boy's eyes widened. He didn't look a day more than twenty-one. Justin immediately felt bad, and tempered his voice.

"Can you at least tell me when and where she moved?"

It took a few minutes for the clerk to search his books. "I can't give out forwarding addresses, but I can tell you she sold her condo in March."

Justin started to press the guy but decided against it. There was no way he was getting Isabella's new address out of him.

He hopped back into his rental and called Isabella again. When he still didn't get a response, a chill of unease settled over him.

Isabella. His wild and impulsive Isabella. Where the hell had she gone? It had been a week since they'd last spoken. She'd sold her place more than a month ago, but never thought to mention it?

He flipped open his phone and dialed another number. It rang three times before someone picked up.

"Justin?"

"Yeah, it's me. Where the hell is Isabella?"

"What do you mean, where the hell is Isabella?"

"I'm sitting outside her condo, or what *used* to be her condo, but they just told me she moved."

There was a pregnant silence on the other end, which made his entire body grow cold. "Where is she, Celeste?"

"Ummm, stay put. I will be there in fifteen minutes."

He said her name again, but the phone was already dead. He banged the steering wheel with his palm. "Damn it. What the hell are you up to, Isabella?"

When Celeste arrived *thirty* minutes later and told him to follow her in his car, he expected to take a quick trip around town. What he didn't expect was to end up on the two-lane highway to Jacksonville.

He called Celeste a dozen times and, for good measure, Isabella, too. Neither one of them answered. He had half a nerve to pull over and force Celeste to tell him what was going on, but decided he preferred to wait until he could confront Isabella himself. It was better to just go straight to the source.

They arrived in Jacksonville an hour later, the sun setting in the horizon. All of a sudden he was exhausted. He'd spent a full day on a plane, and half of another driving up and down the East Coast chasing after one elusive woman. All he wanted to do was find Isabella and then find a bed to crawl into.

He followed behind Celeste until she came to a stop on Main Street. He cut the engine and piled out of his car.

"What are we doing here?" He'd expected to end up at Maggie's.

"Just look around," she said as she folded her arms across her chest and leaned against her car.

Look around? He'd grown up in this small town. Not much had changed in the last thirty—

The moment he saw the renovated office building, he froze.

"Where's Isabella?"

"I'm guessing inside. She's not picking up her phone, and Maggie says she hasn't seen her all day. When I was here two weeks ago, this was where I found her. This is the only place she could be."

Whatever Celeste said after that, he didn't hear. He was already marching inside.

"Isabella?" He made his way into the building. It used to be a dry cleaner's, but the space had been boarded up for at least two years.

"Justin?"

He faltered when he saw her. She'd cut her hair in soft shoulder-length layers that framed her face and accentuated her hazel eyes. Dressed in loose-fitting gray slacks and a black sweater, she was breathtaking.

"What are you doing here? You weren't supposed to arrive for another month." She launched herself into his arms and he held her close, kissing her soundly. He'd missed her so much, and he almost forgot that he was angry with her—almost.

"Why didn't you answer your phone?" he asked when they finally parted for air.

"I accidentally left it at home this morning."

Her statement jarred his memory.

"Home? And where is that these days?"

She regarded him warily and pulled out of his arms. "You found out that I moved."

"Yes. Would have been nice to know *before* I drove all the way to DC. I wonder what else you've neglected to tell me these past months."

He swept his gaze around the open space. Two desks were set up just outside two private offices.

"When were you going to tell me?" he questioned when he finally settled his gaze on her once again.

"I wanted it to be a surprise when you arrived." She seemed so uncertain, so unsure of herself, which was completely unlike her.

He drew in a deep breath, searching for the right words. He realized then that he wasn't angry. It had all just taken him by—well, *surprise.*

"Okay, so this is what I've been able to piece together so far. You quit your job, moved to Jacksonville, and opened your own law practice?" He ran a hand across his face. "Am I forgetting something?"

She nodded, pointing to the golden marquee on the wall. "Not my practice—*ours.*"

She nibbled on her bottom lip, and her nervous action didn't go unnoticed. She was waiting for him to say something, to react.

He sighed. "You're pushy; you know that?" He reached for her, dragging her into his arms. "You're also unpredictable—"

"You're mad. I knew you would be mad—"

He kissed one cheek and then the other. "You also have this uncanny and very annoying ability to read my mind."

She looked confused. "What are you talking about?"

He grinned down at her. She wasn't the only one with a surprise. "I put in for retirement. I was going to start looking for a job in a couple of weeks." He glanced around the room. "But I see now that won't be necessary."

Her smile was tentative. "So you're really not upset?"

He thought about it for a second before shaking his head. "I'm not." And he wasn't. He'd spent the past several months thinking about his plans for the future. He'd finally made peace with his past. It was time to move forward with a new career and the woman he'd loved practically all his life.

He gazed down into her beautiful heart-shaped face. After he'd made the decision to retire, he'd decided to begin practicing law again—Isabella had just made things easier for him. That was one of the million reasons why he loved her. She got him, in ways no one else ever had.

"So, which one of these offices is yours?" he said, backing them toward the wall.

"I didn't pick one. I wanted to wait until you got back to do that."

He looked between the two rooms. "Well, which one do you want?"

"I don't care. Why?"

A wicked grin spread across his face. "Because every morning when you sit down at your desk to work, I want you to remember just how hot the sex we had on top of it was."

Two red splotches darkened her cheeks, an impish glint lighting up her eyes.

"Breaking in the new desk. I like it."

He did, too. He just hoped they didn't end up *breaking* the desks by the time they were done.

sabella yawned as she stretched out across Justin. "We better get up before we stay here all night."

Justin grumbled beneath her, but he stood before helping her to her feet. "I'm too old to be having sex on desks and floors." He massaged the back of his neck and rotated his shoulders.

She rolled her eyes and dragged on her clothes. "Sex on the desk was *your* idea."

"But the floor was all yours."

She bit back a tiny smile. That it was, and she had the carpet burn to prove it, but it was well worth it.

Isabella slipped on her shoes and turned back around to face Justin, but drew up short just before she nearly tumbled over him.

"What are you doing?"

He looked up at her as if she were stupid. As if to say, what did she think he was doing down there on bended knee?

She smiled, ignoring the tiny butterflies that fluttered in her belly. "Yes."

He scowled at her. "I didn't even say anything. You didn't even let me open the box."

She waved her hand. "I'm sorry." She cleared her throat. "Go ahead."

She didn't hear a word, but it was perfect. The ring, his declaration of love, his proposal. She wasn't sure if she said yes again, and she had no idea how the ring ended up on her finger.

The only thing she remembered vividly about that moment was how Justin looked up at her while perched on one knee. As if she was the most beautiful woman in the world, the only woman in the world. Her heart burst with love when he finally stood to his feet and claimed her lips in a sweet kiss.

Whatever thoughts they had of getting home were long forgotten. They stayed there, locked in each other's arms, long after the sun set outside.

Epilogue

The wedding was beautiful. No frills—just a simple, quiet ceremony on an ethereal spring afternoon. With only a few guests in attendance, the couple exchanged their vows in Maggie's backyard.

"I certainly didn't see this one coming," Celeste whispered beside her.

Isabella followed Celeste's gaze across the lawn. Maggie stood next to Reginald, their hands clasped together as they posed for pictures.

Isabella turned her serene smile on Celeste. "You keep saying that."

"It's because I'm stunned speechless—"

Isabella's eyes twinkled. "If you were stunned speechless, you'd actually have to be *speechless*, you think?"

Celeste glowered at her. "I'm just saying. I never thought Maggie would remarry."

Isabella hadn't either, but her mother was happy with Reginald. Their seemingly whirlwind courtship and rushed nuptials had taken her a bit by surprise. She glanced over at Justin, who was handsomely dressed in a custom-tailored charcoal suit. But then again, she couldn't exactly talk, either. Apparently, whirlwind courtships and rushed nuptials ran in the family.

Besides, Maggie had made a very good point when she announced her engagement to a shocked Isabella. "Life is too short to wonder and wait for things to happen. If you want something, you have to go after it. Simple as that."

Isabella couldn't agree more.

"So . . . you and Caleb?" Isabella let the words hang between them as she sent her friend a sly glance.

"Me and Caleb nothing. We're dating, and we're both fine with that. So get it out of your pretty little head that there will be any more white dresses and wedding bells in the near future."

Isabella quirked a brow. "*Near* future? So that means there is still the possibility for *a* future."

Celeste rolled her eyes. "This conversation is over. I'm sending your husband over here so you can badger him instead of me."

"Did I hear you call my name?"

"I don't think anyone called for Captain Save-a-Ho, *but* since you're here—"

"Celeste! We had a deal." She'd promised to lay off on the insults.

"It's okay, sweetheart," Justin said, wrapping his arms around Isabella to stare at Celeste from over her shoulder. "Some dogs are just impossible to train."

"Oh, he's a real charmer, Isabella. Definitely a keeper," Celeste said dryly before walking off to join Caleb, who stood on the other side of the lawn.

Isabella hung her head and sighed. She'd talked to both of them and had gotten assurances from both that they would be civil. God knows she'd tried, but she guessed some things never changed.

She glanced up at Justin from over her shoulder, a radiant smile on her face.

"She's right, you know."

Justin's face twisted in skepticism. "About what, exactly?"

"That you're a keeper."

His gaze was tender as he leaned down to place a brief kiss against her lips.

"Have I told you today that I love you?" he said when he finally lifted his head.

"No, but I always love hearing you say it."

"I love you, Mrs. Isabella Andreu-Rourke."

Her smile grew wider. She loved hearing her name on his lips. A month after he'd proposed, they'd decided to skip all the pomp and circumstance of a big wedding, and elope. Isabella couldn't have been happier. Maggie had been disappointed, but Isabella was convinced that this surprise wedding of her mother's was Maggie's way of getting back at her.

"I love you too, Mr. Rourke."

He kissed her again, and everyone else around them seemed to melt away. Life didn't get much better than this. She'd married the man of her dreams—a man she'd always loved—and now had a career she was proud of. One that fulfilled her in ways her last job never had.

She couldn't believe how much her life had changed in the past year. It seemed like just yesterday she and Justin were making dares and stripping off clothes across a Scrabble board, and from there it had evolved into so much more.

Twelve steamy, sexy, unforgivably naughty nights—that was how this had all begun. And now—now they had a lifetime together, full of love, laughter, and no doubt many more wicked fantasies.

ABOUT THE AUTHOR

Nadia Aidan lives in the Southwest. Under her real name, she holds a PhD in political science and public policy, and by day she works as an assistant professor at a public university. She writes multicultural erotic romance across all genres. Visit her Web site at www.nadiaaidan.com.